MW01128663

Dancing in the Wind

Dancing in the Wind

The Escape Series Book 3

Sandra J. Jackson

Copyright (C) 2020 Sandra J. Jackson
Layout design and Copyright (C) 2020 by Next Chapter
Published 2020 by Beyond Time – A Next Chapter Imprint
Cover art by Cover Mint
This book is a work of fiction. Names, characters, places, and
incidents are the product of the author's imagination or are used
fictitiously. Any resemblance to actual events, locales, or persons,
living or dead, is purely coincidental.
All rights reserved. No part of this book may be reproduced or
transmitted in any form or by any means, electronic or mechanical, including photocopying, recording, or by any information
storage and retrieval system, without the author's permission.

Dedication

In loving memory of my father

Acknowledgments

Once again, a big thank you to my family, particularly my husband, for putting up with my absence when I was still physically in the room. And for helping me to figure out if certain positions were physically possible.

Thank you to my beta reader, Leslie Brown, whose opinions and suggestions are always appreciated.

To my Creative Editor, Ron Bagliere, whose 30 plus years of writing and editing experience gives me the confidence that I'm putting out the best book I can. I thank you for all your support and encouragement.

A big thank you to my readers who have waited patiently for this final installment of the trilogy. I'm sorry it took me so long to get this finished.

And finally, thank you to Next Chapter Publishing, for your effort in getting Next Chapter Authors and their books noticed. I continue to look forward to this and other published works.

One

Back

There were no curtains or blinds decorating the rectangular window in my room. A piece of duct tape secured the nylon string of a crystal suncatcher to the frame. It hung in the middle of the glass and refracted the afternoon sun. The double-paned, fixed-glass centered on the back wall allowed light and nothing more. Positioned below it was my single bed covered in a green, queen-size blanket which draped to the floor.

I kneeled on the end of the bed, leaned forward, and touched my cheek to the smooth glass. The action sparked the memory of gazing out another window. For weeks that window was the only link to the outside for my sister, Beth, and me. Behind it, we'd planned our escape and dreamed of freedom. But we also wondered about the condition of the world and what lay beyond the forest surrounding our prison. Fuzzy recollections of the last five years filled my head interspersed with the odd detailed memory, but it was different for my sister. Beth remembered little, and I feared she would not regain what she lost.

A wave of tiny bumps rose on my bare arms and travelled up to the top of my head. I shivered and replaced my cheek with my hand. The window from my memories faded as I returned to the present.

A single snowflake drifted toward the ground in a graceful dance against the blurred backdrop of dim reds, burnt oranges, and pale yellows of the distant trees. My gaze broke from the intricate ice crystal and concentrated on the outlying forest edge. Random flakes fell and melted the moment they touched the ground. *If you don't like the weather, just wait five minutes and it will change*, my father's voice repeated inside my head.

Within seconds, the grey sky morphed into blue. Treetops brightened as sunbeams stretched out from behind the fading clouds and kissed the leaves, turning the dim to vibrant, burnt to fiery, and pale to bright. The forest edge erupted into blazing colour as if someone set it on fire, reminding me of campfires from both years and only weeks ago. The snowflakes disappeared with the clouds. It was mid-October, and while the temperature had dropped, it would be another month before the snow fell and stayed.

A large raptor soared on chilled air currents, searching the ground below for its next meal. A V-shaped formation of southbound geese moved in perfect synchronicity across the ever-brightening sky. The corner of my mouth tugged into a half-smile as two stragglers hurried to catch up to the flock.

Oh, I wish I were a bird. As free as a bird, my father liked to say.

A flash of light caught my attention. I focused on the rows of photovoltaic power stations in the large clearing outside my window as sunlight reflected off the black panels. Months ago, someone had disconnected all but one from the grid. Marigold, one of the engineers who maintained them, explained the single station had its own meter and combiner boxes. This system provided localized power to the facility until the engineers reconnected the breakers and battery bank. Now the entire solar panel system worked to provide power to the entire building.

I closed my eyes. "This is real," I whispered and swallowed the pain rising in my throat. This wasn't the only world catastrophe I lived through, though it was the worst. Ten years ago, the first pandemic to attack the earth in a hundred years, brought about fear and change. I had just turned ten, and life twisted upside-down. There was no school, we quarantined, stayed away from others. wore masks, and did what we could to stay healthy. Despite the losses, the world survived and normality eventually returned. But from that moment, anxiety took up residence in my head.

My no-longer-forgetful mind had returned as hyper-thymesia made it possible to recall events in my life as though it just took place. The smallest memory always triggered an unstoppable need to reflect on the past and remember everything with precision. I gave up trying to fight it and allowed my thoughts to wander back to the last few weeks of summer.

Noah, a young man who seemed immune to the Butterfly Flu and whom my parents happened upon after escaping the fire at the compound, had helped to save us. It was his drone that had located my siblings, Marcus, and me wandering in the forest. We hiked the trails aimlessly; held there by mind-control games and the subliminal messages they'd subjected us to when we lived at the Contagion Eradication Centre for Intelligent Life. It was no coincidence the acronym C.E.C.I.L., used to refer to the compound, spelled out the name of its narcissistic creator, Cecil. And while the subliminal message compelled Beth, Caleb, and others to wander through the forest, it did not have the same effect on me. My reason to stay was because of them, and I could not leave, though I tried.

Our rescue and subsequent reunion with our parents answered many of the questions we'd had regarding Cecil, the compound, and the virus. When Beth produced the manifesto she'd found, we learned so much more. Four days later, living in a strange house in a virtual ghost town with personnel who'd escaped the fire, I was ready to search for the lost. August was nearing its end, and time was not on our side.

"I'm going with you." I grab my backpack from the closet and toss it on the bed. The brown teddy bear with the purple bow sits on my pillow, indifferent to the commotion.

"But April..." Mom places her hand on my shoulder.

I shrug it off and turn to face her. "No! I'm going."

"What's going on?" Dad says from the doorway to my room, a room I'd occupied for less than a week and once belonged to someone else, a child—a stranger.

Mom folds her arms. "April wants to go on the search."

Dad nods, slow and contemplating. "Av," he uses my nickname, short for Avril the French word for April, "don't you think it's too soon? The others–"

I glare at my father. "No, I am not like the others." I sound childish, but I don't care. "Yes, I agree Beth, Caleb, and Marcus are still drawn to those trails and must stay here, but I'm fine. The subliminal messages didn't work on me. I'm helping you find the other... Butterflies."

We called those still wandering in the woods, Butterflies, as Cecil had in his manifesto. Like Beth, my brother, Caleb, and me, they too had a small tattoo of a butterfly on the nape of their necks just at the hairline. The tattoos marked us as special. It was a complicated mess. But in summary, Cecil planned for years to gather gifted and intelligent children, wipe out civilization with a virus he created, and start anew.

I stopped ruminating. It was crazy. Cecil was crazy. And now I feared I was too. My stomach turned at the thought of him, and I vowed at that moment not to speak his name again. Another memory came to mind, and the fine grip I held on the present slipped, returning me to the past.

We were a rescue group of eight, my parents, four other former employees from the Contagion Eradication Centre for Intelligent Life, Noah, and me. Noah, having not been a resident at C.E.C.I.L., hadn't known what transpired there, nor had he experienced the effects of the hypno-drug. The drug Cecil used to keep us under his control. But he suffered as much. He'd seen everyone he loved die from the pathogen Cecil created. Noah was the sole survivor of his community. Like Marcus, who had happened upon C.E.C.I.L. a year before our escape, Noah was immune to the virus nicknamed the Butterfly Flu because of its constant mutating. Though it was no flu. While the eight of us set out on a mission to search for the lost, Beth, Caleb, and Marcus had stayed behind in Kearney. For three months the small town housed the staff who'd escaped the compound after the fire, and it was now our home too.

Our search led us on kilometers of trails I'd hiked before and a few new ones. The smell of death, brought to our noses on the wind, followed wherever we went. Animals, birds—people, remains in varying stages of decay scattered the trail and the bush. The unfortunate critters appeared to be victims of the virus that still infected the living, but many survived. Like Marcus and Noah, they had a natural immunity. For everyone else, the vaccine my parents created while at C.E.C.I.L., continued to ward off illness.

"Come on, it's this way," I say, stepping over the skeletal remains of a squirrel in the middle of the trail. An hour earlier, Noah's drone sent back live video to the controller,

5

and we saw a group of three headed in our direction. The plan was to reach the small clearing in their path first and leave food. Then we would watch them for a time before approaching.

The drone hovers overhead and Noah lands it safely on the ground. "April, hang on a sec." Noah picks up the drone.

"We have to get there first," I say, walking ahead.

"Yes, I know that, but we don't have the food."

I sigh and train my gaze beyond Noah as my parents and the others round a bend and come into view.

Dad wipes his brow with his forearm. "April, can you do us a small favour and slow down a bit?"

Red and sweaty faces turn in my direction. "Sure, sorry."

Dad touches my shoulder. "It's okay, we just don't know these hiking paths like you do, and we can't become sepa-rated. How's the power holding up?" Dad says to Noah.

"About half."

"If we can convince this bunch to come with us, we'll head back today and recharge the battery. This will be a slow process," Dad says.

Sometimes we spent a few days in the bush looking for the lost, other times we got lucky and returned to Kearny within hours, the newly rescued in tow. There were periods when we encountered groups from five to more than a dozen cognizant hikers. But others weren't so fortunate and they lived inside their heads, roaming on auto-pilot by themselves or as stragglers among the consciously aware. Most of these larger groups formed when smaller clusters merged, and the cognizant hikers took longer to convince they needed to leave the trails and the forest. But after gaining their trust, they told us their stories and what they remembered. They told us about those who perished, not from the flu but for other reasons, according to the ones who witnessed their deaths. Their companions dragged their remains into the trees and covered them with whatever they could find. The dead included the lucid and the catatonic—death did not discriminate.

I left my ruminations and thought of poor Shaun and Caia, once a part of my group when I wandered the trails. But now they were dead, their bodies buried beneath rocks and branches. And then I thought of The Collector, a psycho who stalked us while we roamed the forest. When he caught up with us, he shot Caia as Shaun, who had just come out of his drug induced stupor, launched himself at our attacker. The two of them fell over a cliff to their deaths. Beth had grown fond of Shaun, taken care of him, and it was she who searched for his body. When she found him, she covered his remains with broken branches and rocks. And she did it on her own, not wanting my help. As for The Collector, Beth glimpsed him too, but rocks and underbrush blocked most of his body from view. We left him to the elements and wild creatures; he deserved nothing more.

I rubbed my hand over the back of my neck as images of Shaun and The Collector falling over the cliff played like a movie. "Enough," I said, recalling the final day of our search and rescue.

"That's it then?" I say to my mother as we climb into the rear seat of the old pickup truck. It is the middle of September, and we haven't found signs of anyone in several days.

Mom reaches up and plucks a twig caught in my father's hair as he sits ahead of her in the driver's seat and starts the engine. "Yes, I think so. According to the manifesto, process of elimination, etcetera, we found all those who escaped and survived."

We'd rescued thirty-one survivors ranging in age from twelve to twenty-two and confirmed their identities from photographs and statistics discovered in the manifesto.

The pickup rumbled and as we pulled away from the side of the road, the wheels stirred up dust. There was a knock on the rear window. I turned to see Noah sitting in the truck's bed with three others, neither of whom started with us at the outset of the rescue mission. The first three, engineers at C.E.C.I.L. when it operated as a research facility, abandoned the mission after four days. They had more urgent affairs. At the time, I didn't know what that was, but learned later about their vital tasks.

In three weeks, the population of Kearney grew. While the town had enough housing for everyone, those in charge, my parents among them, announced we would soon be under one roof. With winter coming, they decided it was essential we be together. Those who had undergone months of brainwashing and subjection to the hypno-drug were unfit to be on their own—even me. When the new location became inhabitable again, we'd packed up the few vehicles and over several days, moved everyone into the renovated home.

The glass made a dull thump as I rested my forehead against the window at the thought of a day I wanted to knock from my brain. My search for home did not end the way I'd planned. *Home is where the heart is*, my father had said. And though we were together, my parents' decision to return to this place angered me.

I slapped my palm against the window while my other hand curled into a tight fist. Blood warmed my cheeks, and I clenched my jaw.

"Are you ready, April?"

Noah's voice startled me, and I spun around; my heart thudded as my blue eyes melted at the sight of his chocolate ones. His week-old haircut suited him. But I missed the soft waves of longer light brown hair at his neck though there was still some length at the front to remind me. Dressed in blue jeans and a black fitted t-shirt that showed off his toned physique, he looked as though he stepped from the pages of an online catalogue.

"Sorry, I knocked." He smiled and jutted his thumb over his shoulder to the door behind him that had opened and closed without me noticing, "But I guess you didn't hear."

Probably because I was rapping my skull off the window, my cheeks flushed with my thought. "That's okay."

Noah raised his eyebrows. "So, are you?"

My stomach rolled, and I nodded, forcing a smile.

"Sure about that? Cause your eyes contradict your grin and not-so-convincing nod."

I plunked onto my bed. "That obvious?"

Noah held out his hand, and I groaned with apprehension as I stood and crossed over to him. Strong fingers entwined with mine and he kissed my cheek; the blush returned.

He tucked a piece of my brown hair behind my ear. "A lot has changed," he said and squeezed my hand.

"How would you know? You didn't live in this place."

Noah shrugged. He opened the closet, took out a red jacket, and handed it to me. "So, I've been told. Why don't we check it out, and you can see for yourself?"

"Do we really have to?" The coat was a little too big as I poked my arms through the sleeves. I straightened out my purple t-shirt and zipped up the jacket.

He winked, took my hand, and led me toward the door. It slid open, quiet and effortless. The silence unnerved me. In my head, it always made a whooshing sound and that was what I expected.

No matter how much they cleaned the compound, I could still detect the faint odour of smoke from the deliberate fire set almost six months earlier. The fire had granted us our freedom from C.E.C.I.L. but it also caused other forms of captivity. For Beth and I it was another imprisonment and for the others who'd fled, the forest enslaved them. The smell made my nose wrinkle. *It's all in your head*, my father told me, and he was right. It was ALL in my head. Every. Single. Bit.

We stepped out into the hallway. The beginnings of colourful murals now adorned the once-white walls.

I was back—returned to the one property I vowed never to see again. And no matter what they did to change its appearance, underneath the façade it was still C.E.C.I.L., and once again I felt trapped.

Two

Real

Small paintings dotted the white corridor that stretched out in front of me. While the colourful murals softened the stark walls, they didn't conceal where we were. Behind the mask, this was still C.E.C.I.L.

I tried to keep my focus straight ahead, but as usual my gaze wandered to the drop-tile ceiling. Not yet removed from its mount, one of a few remaining security cameras aimed down the hallway. Although inactive, I worried the device would suddenly power-up and follow my movements with its red eye and mechanical whine. For so long, the intrusive objects had monitored my activities, and it was hard to shake the paranoia that someone still watched.

I shook my head at the absurd notion. The motion detecting cameras no longer operated, and when they had, they made no noise. I had imagined it all as the hypno-drug wore off and changed my perception, affecting every sense. Distortion was the worst effect I'd suffered. The sliding pocket doors never whooshed as loud as I'd thought. There was only a faint airy sound heard in the quietest of moments.

Thinking about the distortion reminded me of Jasper, my caretaker. Jasper had reduced the hypno-drug that led to the return of my conscious awareness. And it was Jasper who set the fire that ultimately freed everyone.

As Noah and I continued along the hallway in silence, the recollection of altered realities transported me to the past.

I push the button on the bathroom wall and pull the door open. The warning alarm buzzes as the five-second countdown begins. I step over the threshold into my room, and the door closes behind me. An audible hissing sound travels through the door, and I know scalding hot steam is filling the small room on the other side.

The vision faded, and bitterness replaced it. The exaggerated hissing of steam heard behind closed bathroom doors was a figment of my imagination. My fingernails dug into my palms as I clenched my fists.

As I regained control of myself, I struggled with the accuracy of my memory. Although hyperthymesia allowed me to remember everything, I'd recently learned some memories were false, and Beth suspected it first. She'd suggested a while back the possibility that someone planted the memories in our heads. Her suspicions had been right. Not all our recollections, or at least how I remembered them, were correct. The drug changed them or Cecil did.

For instance, the first meeting with him in our home and later encounters weren't exact. By confirmation from our parents, we never called him Uncle like he said we had, rather we addressed him as Mr. Banks. It relieved me to know he'd never been Uncle to us and concerned me that outside influences could so easily alter my infallible recall. *What else within my psyche had changed?*

"Ready?" Noah's voice interrupted my thoughts.

We stood at the end of the corridor. Sheets of plywood replaced the glass walls damaged from the blaze that ravaged this part of the building five months ago. In the centre of the solid wall was a wood door. Behind it, a stairwell led down to the first-floor rooms.

With his hand on the handle and the other gripping mine, Noah gave a small tug as he turned the knob.

"Noah, wait!" I cried, stopping him. "Give me a moment." The knot in my stomach rose into my chest.

"April, you've had days to prepare. This is not a surprise."

"Yes, I know, it's just..."

He cocked his head to the side.

My shoulders slumped. "Fine," I said, stepping forward and allowing Noah to lead me through the exit.

We walked down the stairs; our footfalls resonated in the stairwell. At the bottom we had two choices, continue down another flight of stairs to the basement or pass through one of three doors. The exits to the left and right led to the first-floor hallways, and the exit straight ahead, to what remained of the forest simulation room. For years residents used the room for daily exercises all the while undergoing thought control. Subliminal messages whispered through speakers, veiled by the sounds of nature. As inhabitants conditioned their bodies, he conditioned their brains. The directives to stay on the trails in the nearby woods were fail-safes. Should someone ever escape, he'd be able to locate them.

I stared at the entrance in front of me. Bile rose in my throat as the grisly image of a gnarled and charred hand sticking up from the ashes forced its way out from my memories. The unfortunate soul burned along with the contents of the simulation area, and it had been my misfortune to run across the remains several weeks afterward.

Noah's thumb brushed over the back of my hand. "Okay?"

I bit my lower lip and nodded.

Noah reached out for the doorknob of the steel entry and pulled. Bright sunlight made me blink as a cold breeze fluttered my hair. I zipped my jacket all the way up, tucked my chin inside, and stepped outdoors.

Noah was right. The simulation room looked nothing like before, not when fake trees, winding trails, and recorded bird songs filled the space. And not when it was a blackened mass of molten plastic and ash.

The renovations began just after Beth and I had left the compound we'd rediscovered after our escape from the old house. Had we stayed for another day, the reunion with our parents would have taken place sooner.

Marigold and her team of engineers worked many long hours to make this facility inhabitable again. Two backhoes and a loader had pulled down a section of the far end wall and the pitted steel door and replaced it with a wide metal gate. The longer side walls survived, and the rubble was long gone. While not finished, the objective was to turn the large outdoor space into a courtyard.

I turned a slow circle and examined the area. Blistered paint was all that remained of the forest mural that once covered the now blackened concrete walls. They'd removed the concrete slab from the centre, leaving the rest around the perimeter to form a walkway. A wood bench rested against the rear wall with a view of the clearing and the rows of solar panels beyond the gate.

I stepped toward it; Noah trailed. When I approached the seat, I shivered.

"The bench is a memorial," Noah said.

I bent forward and read the names engraved into a metal placard attached to the backrest. My finger traced over the etchings, and my eyes stung as I read Jasper, Shaun, and Caia. The plaque, while not big enough to list everybody, mentioned the other eighty-four residents who'd lost their lives. Twenty-nine test subjects exposed to the virus during multiple vaccination trials, and the fifty-five who perished or disappeared without a trace on the trails. There was no engraving of Cecil's name. No recognition to those who helped him, had approved of his plan, and died or escaped and never returned.

I sat and stared out toward the field and the distant multi-coloured trees. "What did they do with the rock?"

Noah wrinkled his brow. "Rock?"

"The huge boulder. It was..." I scanned the area, "over there." I pointed.

Noah shrugged. "Probably melted like the plastic trees and they scooped it up with the rest."

"No, it was real."

"Are you sure?" he said. "I thought everything in this room was a fake." Noah swept his hand through the air before wrapping his arm around my shoulder. We had grown close over the weeks since my rescue.

As he pulled me near, I sighed, breathing out all the stress and tension I held in my body. "No, it was real," I whispered and rested my head on Noah's shoulder.

The rock had to have been real. But then I wasn't so sure what real was anymore.

Three

Noah

Noah had saved us. Without his drone we would still be on the trails, walking endless circles. He had saved me. Without him, I would have lost my mind.

Seated on my bed, I stared at the black leather cover of Jasper's journal resting in my lap. Inside it, he had penned his experiences at C.E.C.I.L., how he'd come to learn of the plan, and what he personally suffered. On his deathbed, Jasper told me where I would find it and that it held answers to my questions. Apart from my memories, the journal was all there was left of Jasper's existence. His employer, the man whose name I wouldn't say or think upon, had destroyed any other personal belongings he'd had at the compound. But there was more than just Jasper's words written inside, I had added my own thoughts. The idea seemed absurd now. My brain was my personal journal, and I could flip back to any moment and recall the events. Yet I contemplated reading my scribbles as I thought of that particular day.

When my parents had announced the plans to spend the colder months at the compound, I lost control. I was like an inconsolable two-year-old throwing a tantrum. No one else reacted the same way. Then again, no one had my memories—real, imagined, or altered. My arguments claiming the building was uninhabitable were futile as the structure underwent weeks of renovations. C.E.C.I.L.'s reunited inhabitants boarded over broken windows, washed walls, and cleaned out debris. They'd fixed what was necessary to make it safe for the winter, and they collected supplies and furnishings from homes and shops in Kearney. A few rooms suffered minimal damage, and their restoration was quick. Like a phoenix, C.E.C.I.L. rose from the ashes, repaired, sustainable, self-sufficient, and inhabitable. I refused to believe and refused to go.

For two days, I stayed in the purple bedroom of the house we inhabited in Kearney and wouldn't speak to anyone, leaving my room only to use the bathroom. Confinement would be on my terms. For two days, Noah brought food and spoke through the closed door even though I wouldn't respond. And on the third day he sat outside my room, played his guitar and sang.

I opened the journal and flipped to the last quarter where I had scrawled my thoughts on the blank pages.

Noah has a beautiful voice. I didn't know he could sing or play the guitar. He sang a song called Butterfly by an artist I'd never heard of before but it was beautiful. It made me wish I was a real butterfly.

Inside my head I heard Noah's voice singing, and I closed my eyes.

"Is that yours?" The bedroom door squeaks as I open it.

Noah stops playing and looks at me. For the first time, I notice the depth of his brown eyes. "The guitar?" He holds it up and nods.

"And the song?"

"No."

17

"Who sings it? Sang," I correct, not knowing if the artist is from years ago or more recent and whether they had survived given the world's latest history.

"Lisa Loeb," he says.

"Never heard of her." I confess.

"Lisa was one of my mother's favourites, and she loved that song."

"The lyrics, tune, are pretty." I sit on the floor, and he starts again. I touch the back of my neck, imagining a butterfly flying away. At that moment, it's what I want.

I closed the journal and stuffed it between the mattress and box spring, too tired to read anymore, too unfocused to write. A jumble of memories, imaginings, and lies played in my mind. I needed air and an escape from the constant racing thoughts. The door slid open, and I took a deep breath before stepping into the corridor. My footsteps echoed in the hallway. A weak smile crossed my face as I greeted others.

Noah's room was halfway up the long hall. He stayed in one of the windowless accommodations, the same kind Beth and I shared when we'd lived here under the control of the hypno-drug. A muffled reply answered my knock, and I stepped closer, activating the door.

Once inside, I focused on the far corner of the room. The bracket was all that remained of the surveillance system. Below the bracket, and above the head of the bed, was a poster of a lynx taped to the white wall. Noah lay curled on his side on top of his poorly made bed with his head propped on his hand. A tuft of synthetic filler stuck out from a slight tear in the rumpled blue comforter beneath him. A wayward piece of brown hair hung in his eyes, and he swept it aside as he turned the page of an old book.

"Can we go for a walk?"

Noah looked up from the novel and smiled; his cheek dimpled. "Sure." He closed the book with a slap and tossed it on a small table beside his bed. He pointed at me. "Maybe it's warmer than this morning, but not warm enough for short sleeves."

I thought of our visit to the courtyard earlier that day and glanced at my purple tee. "Yes, I guess you're right." The weather had been so erratic, one day called for a sweater and the next a t-shirt.

"Here, put this on." Noah tossed me the red hoodie lying on the end of his bed.

The sleeves were soft and warm as I stuck my arms through them. "What about you?" The hoodie smelled of a blend of sweet and spice, and I breathed in the light and fresh scent.

"No worries." He smiled and took a black sweatshirt from a dresser across from the foot of his bed. A framed picture of his parents sat on the top. He rolled down his blue shirt-sleeves, covering his toned biceps and the compass tattoo on his right arm, and pulled the sweatshirt over his head. "Anyway, you look good in red."

My cheeks flushed like they always did when he paid me a compliment.

"Let's go then." Noah led the way out of his room and down the hall toward the front entrance.

Inside the compound's vestibule, hidden from peering eyes, Noah grabbed my hand and led me out the door and along the side of the building. We crossed the lawn and stepped into the woods.

"Same?" Noah said.

Tears threatened to escape if I opened my mouth, so I nodded instead and squeezed Noah's hand.

We walked in silence on a trail we had carved out over the past few weeks. Leaves fluttered to the ground from the fiery canopy overhead like the snowflakes had earlier that day. When we reached the wall, we followed its length until we arrived at a ladder. Noah had constructed it on our second outing to the wall using two small trees he'd cut as the rails and scrap wood for the rungs. Although we were free to roam, it was only within the ground's boundaries. We were not to venture outside of the enclosure. The ladder was my salvation from the trapped sensation that accompanied me everywhere. Once over the cement fence, I collected colourful leaves as early fall flowers were much harder to find.

Tucked in among the trees, a small shed came into view. Caleb had hidden inside the rickety building for twenty-four hours when he first escaped the old house. My grip tightened on Noah as we neared. The house had not only been Caleb's prison, but served as one for Beth and me. Jasper had thought we would be safe, bringing us to shelter there the night of the fire. But he was wrong, and our haven turned into a house of horrors.

We stopped by the weathered tool shed for a moment. A fly buzzed, caught in a web woven inside a hole in the wood cladding. The insect struggled. I poked my finger through the silk trap, freeing it.

"Ready?" Noah said.

I nodded. My focus trained on a window at the rear of the house across the overgrown lawn. It looked ominous, and I almost expected to see Jasper's ghost waiting for us to emerge from the bush. I squeezed my eyelids and replaced my imaginings with the memory of sticking my head out that window. Sunshine warmed the top of my head as I inhaled my first breath of outside air in a long time. The orange and yellow scrap of cloth used to cover my nose from the putrid odour of death hung from my neck.

As we stepped out from the woods and into the neglected yard, I shifted my gaze to the clearing among the stand of pines.

Goosebumps covered my arms as we approached; wooden crosses grew larger the closer we got. I shuddered, and Noah clutched my hand. No matter how many times I walked the same path, I would never get over imagining Cecil's white-haired phantom watching me from the kitchen door with dead grey eyes. A sneer pasted to his face.

We stopped at the edge of the small cemetery. "Okay?" Noah said.

"Ahem, yes." My voice cracked, but I stayed strong.

At each wooden cross I placed a colourful bunch of leaves and a few wilted blooms, saying a prayer as I did. When I reached the last one, I allowed my tears to fall. The grave was Jasper's resting place. I set the remaining bundle of autumn foliage next to an older bouquet of dead and faded flowers and whispered one last prayer.

"Are you ready?"

I wiped my tear-stained cheek and smiled. "Yes."

"So, where to now?"

A sudden breeze fluttered my hair. "You know where."

Noah draped an arm over my shoulder and we walked through the pines to our special place. The late afternoon sun stretched its rays through the trees like long golden fingers. Leaves crunched, and twigs snapped beneath our steps. The slow climb was easy until we reached an out-cropping of large rocks. Here, we had to be careful as we hiked to the top.

The view was spectacular. The sunlight bathed us in its warmth as we rested on a flattened rocky area and stared out at the landscape.

Noah gathered me into his arms, and we sat still and quiet. I leaned into him, enjoying his body heat. "I wish we could stay here," I whispered.

"You say that every time."

I straightened and turned to him. "But it's true. I don't want to go back." My vision blurred, and my throat ached. The thought of returning to the compound caused my anxiety to heighten.

Noah held my face between his warm hands, and he rested his forehead against mine. "Av, it's only temporary," he said. He had taken to calling me by the nickname only my family used.

"But I..." Noah's lips cut off the rest of my words. My body melted into him, and he held me close.

He eased me down onto the rock, keeping one hand behind my head and protecting it from the hard surface. I wrapped my arms around him and pulled him to me. In his arms I was safe, I was happy—I was free.

Four

Beth, Marcus, & Murals

The room was spacious. LED lights hung from the ceiling and cast a sterile glow over the entire area. Partial murals adorned the once-white walls, much like the hallways of the first and second floors. Four rows of five rectangular tables, each seating up to a dozen people, filled the space. Neat stacks of black plastic chairs with shiny metal legs rested against part of the back wall.

The cafeteria wasn't just for dining, but supplied a spot for group and private meetings. It was where the aware discussed the next plan. Where the cognizant helped those still in semi and complete unresponsive states. And where the brainwashed came for psychotherapy and reprogramming. It was a safe place where we examined problems with our memories and fears. Since returning, I made my discontent with the living arrangements known and argued with my parents often, hoping to convince them to allow me to spend the winter in Kearney. The small town was about a forty-five-minute drive south of the compound and centred between two small lakes. I would have threatened to leave, but I learned they would reinstall the cameras, so I yielded and kept my hope of escaping to myself.

From inside the entrance, my gaze swept over the people scattered in the room. When I spotted my target, I crossed the floor.

Beth occupied a table at the far end of the lunchroom. The multi-coloured sweater she wore blended with the mural on the wall behind her, making her almost invisible.

"Hi," I said to my younger sister as I pulled out the chair across from her. The felt-covered feet slid silently over the pale grey tile.

"Hey," she responded without even a glance in my direction. Her focus was on a large text. An awkward silence descended like a thick fog hanging in the air.

"What are you reading?" My voice parted the white haze. We'd spoken few words to each other since returning to the compound.

Beth picked up the volume and showed me the cover. I nodded, not surprised by the grip the medical tome had on her.

"What do you want?" Beth said. The move back to C.E.C.I.L. hadn't halted the progress she'd made regaining her identity. Her to-the-point, say-what-you-mean, feisty-self was still intact. Even the stutter that appeared as the hypno-drug wore off faded, but for the occasional relapse.

The argument I had with Beth weeks earlier filled my head. "To apologize." I closed my eyes for a moment, struggling to keep my composure, which crumbled with my words.

Beth broke away from reading. Her gaze softened, and she reached out and touched my hand. "No worries," she said.

My eyes burned, and I wiped the tears before they trailed down my cheeks. "Thing is... " I stopped as I struggled to explain. "I thought I was over it." Marcus' face flashed in front of me and with it, the memory of my jealousy over his relationship with Caia.

"It's good to see you, Caia," Marcus says, picking up the rocks from around our fire pit.

"You know each other," I say out loud, confirming what I'd suspected.

Beth gapes. "Do you?" she says.

"She was in my group before." Marcus lifts another rock and adds it to the two he cradles in his arms. His biceps flex under the load.

"We got separated," Caia adds.

"Have you been alone all this time? What have you been doing?" Marcus says to Caia. His question softens her tough-girl act and Caia nods; her eyes brim with tears. Marcus smiles, leans forward, and kisses her tenderly on the cheek. For a split second, I wish it is my cheek he's kissed.

The memory faded as quickly as it had started, and I finished my apology. "Not that we ever had anything. What I felt was one-sided. He didn't have a clue about my growing feelings for him. Then Caia showed up, and it was obvious they had something. And then later you and Marcus were... anyway, you grew close and I... well, I'm sorry. The entire situation was my fault, and my reaction was childish."

"Really, it's okay, I understand. Marcus helped me deal with Shaun's death. We've supported each other. And anyhow, he's got five years on me."

"Closer to four and a half." I shrugged, Marcus was the same age as Noah, two years older than me. "Anyway, I wouldn't care if you and... "

"Friends, April. And Mom and Dad probably would care." Beth smiled, and she returned her attention to the book. After a few moments, she flipped the page of the text.

"Why did you use your hand?" I questioned. Beth had a telekinetic talent that she'd rediscovered while we wandered the forest. Though not perfected, she showed it to me one day by flipping through the pages of a nature book she'd found.

Beth closed the volume, ending my recollection. "I've given that up."

"But I thought you were strengthening your skills so you could move bigger and heavier things. Don't give up!"

Beth shook her head. "That's not what I want anymore. I want this." She tapped the book. "I wish to help people and save them from illness or injury. Telekinesis will not do that. And developing some silly ability was what... Cecil wanted." She hesitated on the name that made me cringe. "This is what I choose," she reiterated and tapped the book again. "Anyway, my talent was one reason for this mess."

I nodded. If only I could give up my memory recall as easily.

"Everything okay?" Marcus appeared behind Beth. His muscles flexed as he folded his arms.

"Sit," Beth commanded, and he peered at her with one eyebrow raised. Beth sighed, "Please."

Marcus smiled and sat next to her. "I'm trying to teach your sister manners, you know."

"Good luck with that." My mouth contorted into a half-smile.

Beth turned her glare onto me, then laughed. "Ya well, what can I say." She shrugged.

Marcus' his hand rested on the table beside Beth's, her white skin looking even more pale in contrast to his brown. I smiled, happy that my blue eyes were no longer tinged with green.

"So, everything's okay?" Marcus repeated.

Beth grinned. "Av just came to apologize."

Marcus pointed a finger back and forth between us. "So, we're good?" he said.

"Yes," I chuckled. "We're good."

We chatted and laughed for a while as we enlightened each other on what we'd been doing since the move. The mood was light. The awkward fog lifted.

"So," Beth said, her voice rising. "Are you ever going to finish any?"

My brow creased, but I rubbed the tension away with my fingertips as my blank gaze drifted between Beth and Marcus. The vast beginnings of what would be seascapes, landscapes, and cityscapes on the walls that surrounded us caught my attention, and I understood what my sister meant. "How did..."

"Everyone knows it's you, Av," Beth said.

"I'm not the only one painting."

"True, there are some smaller paintings and drawings from others, but yours are the only ones that are unfinished."

The painting started the first night of our return to the compound. Visions of stark-white corridors had invaded my dreams. Unable to sleep, I'd confiscated paint and brushes we'd brought from Kearney and placed in a room we used as storage. Every night, I covered walls until I could no longer see, and exhaustion replaced the restless thoughts that prevented me from sleep.

"I don't think I can," I admitted.

"Why not?" Marcus said.

"Because of all the things trapped inside my head, these are the ones I can't remember, don't know. I'm not sure what the world looks like anymore."

Five

Butterfly

"NO!" Beth screams and runs to the place where Shaun fell. She drops to her hands and knees and peers over the edge, screaming his name between gasping cries. I rush forward to help Caleb and glance at Marcus kneeling by Caia. His hands cover her chest. But when I see the blood gushing between his fingers and a puddle growing beneath her, I know nothing can save her.

The mattress amplified my pounding heart giving it somewhat of a twangy sound as it echoed in my ear. I rolled over onto my back and stared at the darkened ceiling. Light from the almost full moon filtered in through the window. The nightmare receded.

I sat up, brushed aside the damp pieces of hair stuck to my forehead, and flipped back the blankets, swinging my legs over the side of the bed. The plush area rug caressed my skin, but did little to lessen the cold emanating from the tile floor underneath. I shivered and grabbed the pair of socks lying on the nightstand and Jasper's ID card hidden inside the top drawer.

With a loud sigh, I rose and made my way toward the door. A press of the button on the wall released the lock, and I exited my room. The soft whisper of the door more audible in the quiet of night as it slid closed behind me.

Small, dim lights bathed the hallway in a warm glow. The eerie stillness unsettled me until the loud snore of my neighbour, a woman named Lydia, shattered the silence and made me jump. A chuckle escaped my lips at my reaction, and I was thankful I couldn't hear her through the walls of my room, else I would never sleep. I continued my walk toward a room a few doors down that served for storage, careful not to slip on the floor with my socks.

The unlocked door slid open and the overhead light switched on as I crossed the threshold. There were boxes with clothing of all sizes along one end wall and bins filled with household items from dishtowels to small appliances along the other. Four mattresses stood against the longer rear wall, with various furnishings leaning against them to keep them from toppling. Two bunches of plastic chairs stacked ten high rested in the far corner. Lined along the wall across from the mattresses were three, four-drawer dressers and a small armoire. On top of one dresser sat the large knapsack of supplies I'd left the night before. I snatched the bag and turned toward the door. Visions from my nightmare haunted me again, and I shut my eyes against the memory, willing it away. When it faded, I left the supply room.

Faint snores behind locked doors followed me up the long corridor. As I passed Noah's apartment, I envisioned him sleeping in his bed, and I was envious.

With cautious steps, I walked to the end of the hall and out of the north wing into the east passageway that stretched along the front of the compound. Once through the exit, I turned right, only pausing for a split second as I glanced at the door belonging to my parents' small suite to my left.

I stopped in the middle of the hallway, resisting the urge to look at the next doorway. The suite behind it was Cecil's, and it stood as empty as his heart and dead eyes. I adjusted the pack on my shoulder and faced the entrance to the centre corridor, placing Jasper's ID on the screen of the scanner. I'd found the identification card months ago tucked inside Jasper's journal. Other than Beth, no one knew about it, and I wanted to keep it that way. The light flashed green on the scanner, and the door opened.

The short hallway was silent and cold. No lights lined the walls, the doors to each empty room stood wide open. A hint of smoke hung in the stale air. No one lived here—no one visited.

My body tensed as the inky darkness enveloped me, and it was as if I'd stepped into a void. For a moment I wondered if this quiet space was as the minds of those able to forget and turn off their memories.

A click echoed and blue-white light erupted from the large flashlight in my hand. I shuddered, but it wouldn't be long before my activity took my mind off the cold. I set the heavy pack down and removed several tubes of acrylic and small cans of latex paint, three paintbrushes, and a jar of murky water for cleaning. Then I pulled out a stained t-shirt and tossed it on the floor.

"Are you ever going to finish any?" Beth's voice whispered in my head.

The flashlight beam illuminated the mural I'd started a few days ago. The new painting wasn't like any of the others. Those renderings were of various panoramas that revealed themselves to me one area at a time. While I recalled the world of trees and lakes, it was difficult envisioning other landscapes. In one mural, I painted tall buildings stretching toward a darkening sky with distant stars dotting the heavens; remnants of the sun tinted the horizon in shades of red and glowing-orange. But I could not fathom what lay at their foundations. And so, the painting went unfinished; the skyscrapers floated on the white background with no foreground to set them in place.

I shook my head, clearing away the image of the incomplete city-scape along with other thoughts of murals I'd started and never finished. Tonight, would be different, and I would not waste any more time reflecting on failure. I busied myself preparing the paint and brushes before settling in to work.

I fell into a peaceful rhythm, loading brushes, applying paint to the wall, and cleaning the brush before I applied the next colour and detail. Each stroke brought the mural closer to completion. The activity eased my mind and calmed my nerves. While my other pictures left me wondering how to finish them, or trying to visualize the landscape, this one gave me clarity. It was important that I complete this tribute. Every few minutes I picked up the flashlight, stepped back, and shined it on my painting.

Seconds turned into minutes, minutes into hours. My arm ached, and my eyelids grew heavy, but I was too close to finishing and would not stop. The blending and shaping of paint was the only thing that kept memories of any kind from invading my head, nightmares forgotten.

I detected motion in my peripheral vision and shined the light down the hall. A mouse squeaked and ran out from the shadows and into the room behind me. The creature startled me, and my heart skipped. The little boost of adrenaline kept me going.

Dirty brushes soaked in muddied water. Tubes and cans of paint scattered the floor. Paint smeared the balled-up t-shirt. I wiped the back of my hand across my forehead, sure that as I did, it left behind a streak of paint. My hands kneaded my lower back, then I stretched upward and a ripple of pops travelled along my spine. The flashlight blinked, grew dim, and then brightened again. I bent forward and picked it up off the floor and illuminated my first completed mural.

I traced the shape with the beam of light and smiled. If it weren't so big, I would think it was real. The detail in which I'd painted was the best yet and looked as though it could fly off the wall. I rubbed the nape of my neck. The image was fitting. What better than a larger-than-life swallowtail butterfly. Black and yellow wings spread wide as it perched on lilac blossoms.

The walk to my apartment was long and cold. Every step closer wasn't close enough, and it became increasingly difficult to keep my eyelids from closing. My feet carried me past Noah's room and past the storage area, and they did not stop until I reached my door and stepped inside my room.

I dropped the backpack of painting supplies at the entrance, tromped toward my bed, and climbed in. A shiver travelled up from my feet as I snuggled under the blankets. My aching body gave in to exhaustion with each exhale, and within seconds I drifted into a dreamless sleep.

Six

Communication

"Com'in." My speech slurred like I was drunk. In the time Noah took to enter and cross the room, I had drifted back to sleep.

"Av!" My name whispered in my ear, and my eyelids opened wide enough to see Noah standing by my bed.

I grunted and rolled away from him, pulling the blankets over me in one fluid motion. My body not yet prepared to start the day.

"Av!" A weight settled on my arm, but I allowed sleep to drag me down and ignored Noah's call. "April!" he said louder.

"Hmm," I groaned and curled into a tighter ball; annoyed by the interruption.

Noah's hand shook my shoulder, preventing me from drifting further. "There's a big meeting and we've got to be there."

"Go by yourself and tell me about it later."

"Av, your mom and dad want you to be there; it's important."

"Aargh!" I threw the blankets off and sat up facing the wall. Noah rubbed my back, and I sighed.

"Wait, what are you wearing?" The rubbing stopped.

I gazed down at my paint-stained, cut-off grey sweat pants and blue t-shirt and remembered my late night. "Forgot to change." I propped my elbows on my knees and rested my chin in my hands.

"So, you were painting?"

"Uhuh," I nodded.

"Thought you were done with that."

I turned around and swung my legs out over the edge of the bed. Noah sat, and I leaned against him. "No, it's the only thing that helps me fall asleep."

"But every night?"

I didn't answer.

"Come on, we should go," Noah said after my lengthy silence.

"Like this?" There was more than a splattering of paint on the shirt as a multitude of colours spread over it like a rainbow.

"No, you're right, better change. Actually... " Noah brushed his fingertips over my brow, and his soft touch made my skin tingle, "maybe shower first. It's not just your clothing covered in paint."

I grumbled in protest, but made my way to the small bathroom, peeled out of my stained clothes, and stepped into the shower stall. Water flowed over the top of my head and spilled down my face. The warmth and the soothing sound made me want to curl up and sleep. I shut my eyelids and lost myself in the sensation.

A pounding on the door startled me. "Hurry, April, or we'll be late," Noah called from the other side.

Groaning, I grabbed the body wash and squeezed a dollop of the vanilla-scented soap into my hand. I wiped the gel over my forehead and the nape of my neck. A quick glance in the mirror before my shower had shown me the streaks of black on my face. As the lather rinsed away, the black tinged suds slipped down the drain. Though it was just paint, I wished it was the ink from my butterfly tattoo. Minutes later, I dressed and headed out the door with Noah.

The walk to the basement was quiet. But it wasn't for a lack of trying on Noah's part, I was far too tired for conversation.

The cafeteria was full when we arrived. Everyone who lived at the compound was there. Fifty-nine people stood, sat in chairs, or huddled around tables pulled together in the back corner of the spacious room. I scanned the space looking for Beth or Caleb when my gaze settled on the face of a boy close to Caleb's age. He sat at a table and stared up at the ceiling with vacant eyes while the two adults with him chatted to each other. Apart from his red hair, he reminded me of Shaun, and I wondered if he would ever wake from his trance.

A hubbub of voices filled the room as people talked while waiting for the meeting to begin. I remained quiet, listening to those speaking around me, and when addressed I nodded and smiled through a sleepy haze. Finally spying Beth at a table with Marcus and Caleb at the back of the room, Noah and I made our way through the crowd. When my father spoke, the conversations died.

"As you all are aware," he began, "we've been working on the communication systems. Everything is functioning and the transceiver radio is manned twenty-four-seven."

My heavy eyes inspected the group standing with my parents. There was Drew, the youngest of the medical staff who also helped counsel a lot of the younger residents. He was someone people were comfortable talking to, and he always had a smile on his handsome face. Next to him was Dr. Reese, a woman I and many others respected. When she spoke, you listened. She was close in age to my mother, but her almost white hair made her appear older. Beside

Dr. Reese was my father and next to him was a shorter, portly man named Archie, neatly dressed in a blue and beige plaid shirt. The sleeves pushed to his elbows exposed a tattoo of a snake coiled around his right forearm from his elbow to his wrist. Grey streaked through his short brown hair, and he pressed his thin lips into a hard smile. His pinched nose, which was too small for his round face, wrinkled as he glanced at the other scientists and employees that had worked at C.E.C.I.L. Most of these people had not been aware of the founder's greater plan. I swallowed as Cecil's face loomed in front of me, and I blinked his image away.

As my father talked, his listeners elicited several reactions. Some nodded, others stared at him with what appeared as admiration, while a few had an expression of indifference as their attention wandered. Their gazes fixed on the floor or elsewhere. I too was a part of that latter group.

"A little after five thirty this morning..." My attention reverted to my father. "Archie here," Dad clapped him on the shoulder, "picked up chatter."

Archie nodded and crossed his arms.

The surprised and elated voices of everybody, including me, drowned out my father's voice. "Hold on!" Dad called out above the group. "Don't get too excited just yet. Arch, do you want to explain?"

Archie stepped forward. "Thanks, Ian. Okay, so while I heard a definite voice, I can't tell you where it came from, or even what language. It was broken and garbled. We will work on trying to get a stronger signal. Remember, we don't know what kind of devastation the virus had on the rest of the world. If there was a lot, we're starting over. There will be few people running radio or cellular tower equipment, if any at all. Patrols of nearby towns have yet to locate any other survivors. With that bit of information, we can assume the disease had an overwhelming effect. But don't give up hope. People like Marcus and Noah were immune. There are likely more. We just have to find them."

I glanced at Marcus with Beth standing by his side and then at Noah. He'd moved and stood across from me. I stared at his back, wishing I felt comfortable letting everyone see our friendship had grown into something more.

"And. . . " my mother's voice returned my focus, "we know that there were other facilities such as this one around the world. While tests have shown the virus is still a threat, we hope that the other facilities have also found a vaccine or treatment by now." Once again, the room filled with the sound of optimism and bobbing heads.

"Okay, folks, that's all the news we have for you today, but we will most definitely keep you informed." My father looked at me, and he smiled. I returned the expression, though it wasn't easy with a yawn about to interrupt.

The cafeteria erupted into conversation again. I pulled a chair out from the table and plunked down, pillowing my head on my folded arms.

"Are you okay, sweetheart?" My mother said.

I lifted my head. "Fine, just tired."

Mom nodded and gave me a weak smile, a look of worry in her eyes.

Since returning to the compound, conversations with my family members, especially my parents, had been awkward and forced, and I had withdrawn into my world of unstoppable memories.

"Can we talk?" Mom sat.

"Aren't we?"

"You know what I mean. Like we used to."

I shrugged.

My mother sighed. "I understand coming back here has been hard on you, but under the circumstances, we had no choice."

My cheeks warmed, and I breathed a loud sigh. The sudden build-up of tension drained from my body. "You could have allowed me to stay in Kearney. I would have been fine." My voice was steady.

"Could we? When the snow comes and stays, and the roads become impassible, could we really have left you there alone? Or even with someone else?"

Once again, I rested my head and closed my eyes. More stress melted away as I gave in to accepting my parents had been right to bring us here. My mother's warm hand settled on my arm. "Are we good now?"

"Yes." My voice bounced off the surface of the table just below my lips and echoed in the dim space between my face and folded arms.

"Why don't you go get more rest? I think you can skip your therapy session this morning. Noah! Would you walk Av back to her room?"

A sense of relief washed over me. While the therapy only amounted to a half hour discussion with Drew about my feelings, I did not wish to discuss anything today. And I did not worry Drew's day would be empty without our meeting. All of us recovering from the hypno-drug had sessions, and someone else would take my place.

I raised my head. Dad and Noah stood off to the side, and both looked in my direction. Everyone else had left the cafeteria to get on with their daily routines and work schedules.

"Sure!" Noah walked over with my father beside him.

"Av will skip her therapy, and I'll tell Drew." Mom smiled at me and squeezed my arm. "Anyway, I don't think she'll need too many more," she said and turned to my dad. Her pale eyes glinted with more happiness than I'd seen since she'd found us.

Dad's eyebrows rose. "Feeling better, Av?"

"Let's say I have accepted our current situation." I had resigned to the fact we were in the best place for the upcoming season. As for better, that was not possible. I wouldn't be better until I was free. Trapped by memories and confined in this facility, the approaching winter was another imprisonment I would have to endure.

Seven

A Glimpse Outside

Mom and Dad finally allowed me to go on a supply trip, now that no one feared I'd run away. As much as a part of me wanted to take off, I understood why I had to stay, but I didn't have to like it.

My footsteps resounded in the stairwell as I headed down the stairs to the basement. The concrete walls closed in around me. I sucked in a deep breath and shook off my claustrophobic thoughts as I stepped through the open door.

There was a lot of activity and no one noticed as I strode past laboratories and offices. On the night of the fire, my parents saved as much equipment as possible. Despite a few setbacks and minor inconveniences, research on the virus continued should the current vaccine fail.

I peeked through the open door, finally seeing my father. He huddled with Archie around a desk, engrossed in whatever they were doing. I knocked.

"Sh!" Dad turned and hushed, his eyes bright and wide. A smile brimmed at the corners of his lips.

"What's going on?" I whispered.

Dad stepped out of the way. Marcus wore a brilliant pair of red headphones. His hands tinkered with the old transceiver radio sitting in front of him, an array of parts strewn all over the desktop.

"Marcus is trying to get a stronger signal." My father explained.

The memory of Beth and I exploring the same office months before our rescue came to mind. The room itself remained intact, but most of the paraphernalia was in various states of disrepair. Someone had destroyed the equipment. "Did you fix everything?" I said.

Dad shook his head. "No, the damage was too extensive. We salvaged what we could. Marcus and Archie have been fixing an older transceiver we found in Kearney."

"Have you heard anything more?"

"Not yet. The signal was weak and what we heard the other day was brief, but it was someone, somewhere, and we will hear it again." He smiled; his blue eyes sparkled with optimism.

"Have you seen mom? I have to get going," I whispered.

Dad looked up from the radio. "I imagine she's up in our apartment getting rest. She has a headache." He put his arm around my shoulder and walked me from the communications room. "So big day, today?"

"Yes."

"Nervous?"

I shrugged. "Nervous, excited, scared of what we'll find." I reigned in my imagination before it took over my head.

"You don't have to go."

The walls of the hallway seemed to move closer to us. "No, but I want to. I need a change of scenery, to see something besides the outside of this place or the forest beyond. Even if it's only for a little while."

Dad nodded. "Do you feel like this place is closing in on you?"

"Sometimes."

Dad kissed my forehead. "See you later, Av and be careful."

"Don't worry, I will. Bye." My father stepped inside the communications room, and I headed to the cafeteria.

Nine of us gathered in the meeting area for last-minute instructions before we went out. I clenched my fists against the mounting excitement at the thought of driving through the gates and leaving the vicinity of the compound. I wasn't planning on escaping, not with winter looming, but it wouldn't hurt to know the best route outside my confines should I need it.

The supply team divided into three groups, and we took three of the four solar cars; their batteries charged the night before using stored solar energy. The gas-powered vehicles in the fleet were useless. Gasoline syphoned from pumps in nearby towns and from other vehicles degraded with time, and it didn't take long for that to happen. Solar powered cars were now our prime source of transportation.

I sat in the back while Noah rode in the front passenger seat. Hester, a woman I didn't know much about, drove. While I had limited contact with her, she wasn't entirely unknown to me. Her height and deep red hair made her conspicuous. She also had a thin but noticeable white scar that traced her jawline on the right side of her face.

Sunlight flickered through the window as we passed under the trees lining the drive. Noah's and Hester's voices faded into the background; tires crunched over the dirt road. I leaned my head against the car door and closed my eyes. Shadow and light flashed behind my lids.

With each supply run, the teams travelled further from the compound. But today we planned to return to a place visited on two other occasions. A little over an hour away, the tourist community spread out over an extensive area. Teams on earlier visits had marked the houses, motels, and stores they'd searched with a blue ribbon tied around the doorknobs. A week had passed since the last supply trip, and the focus was on medical supplies, though no one ever overlooked food. Unfortunately, no past missions had resulted in encounters with survivors. Every town and village the teams searched was as desolate as the last.

Hester pulled up in front of a rustic resort aptly named Pine Lodge. The two-story, log cabin style construction with a green steel roof rose above the parking lot. A wood 'No Vacancy' placard hung from a chain in the front door's window. Attached to the outside wall beside the entrance were two other wooden signs with the words restaurant and office carved into them. Set back from the main building, a one-level motel cladded in what appeared to be wood siding, stretched along the edge of a pine forest.

I climbed out of the silver vehicle. Crows cawed in the trees overhead. A sudden and brisk wind made me tremble, and I pulled the zipper of my red jacket up to my chin. The sunshine and blue sky deceived, and it wouldn't surprise me if snow fell. The black SUV and the other silver one in our fleet drove past us on their way to search another part of the widespread township.

"Do you think this motel will have any medical supplies?" I said, eyeing up the resort. Hester and Noah took up positions on either side of me, and we stared at the eerie building. The entire place seemed a veritable ghost town.

"Hard to say, but I imagine first aid kits anyway," Noah said; his hand brushed against mine.

"Bodies?" I said when my eyes landed on a car parked by the side of the building.

"Maybe." Hester walked forward. Loose red curls bounced on the top of her shoulders. "Let's go. And be careful."

The odour hit me the moment we opened the door. I faced the open door and inhaled a gulp of fresh air, swallowing the bile that rose in my throat.

"Are you okay?" Noah's hand rested on my shoulder.

I nodded, pulled my mask from my pocket, and placed the elastics over my ears. Noah and Hester did the same. "All good," I half-smiled behind the mask. The putrid smell was not as pungent but still detectable.

"Keep that door open," Hester said as she lifted blinds at the front of the restaurant. Sunlight shone through the windows; dust danced in the beams.

There was no sign of whatever caused the scent of decay in the open area of the restaurant. Noah walked around the bar and pulled bottles of alcohol from underneath and set them on the counter.

Hester unscrewed the cap from a bottle of whisky, lowered her mask, and took a big whiff. "Whoa, that's strong." She replaced the lid.

"Looks like there's a lot here we can use." Noah set a large first aid kit beside the bottles.

Hester smiled. "Let's go get the bins," she said to me.

By the time we returned with the empty bins and a cart, Noah had covered the varnished wood counter. He'd found more bottles of alcohol and another first aid kit. Two un-opened cartons of tissue, an open box of adhesive bandages, and a bottle of acetaminophen sat next to it. A small fire extinguisher, three pairs of scissors, and an unopen jar of olives crowded the top of a bar stool.

Hester flicked her head toward the kitchen door. "What about in there?"

"Not yet." Noah walked over and opened the door a crack. A pungent odour poured out from the kitchen. He heaved and coughed. My hand pressed the mask closer to my face.

44

Hester swore. "Think I found the source of the stench." Noah coughed again.

Hester pinched her nose through her mask. "Boy, you sure did. Still have to check it though."

Noah wiped the sweat from his forehead. "We'll need flashlights."

Hester went over to the cart, taking the lid off from the top bin, she pulled out three flashlights. "Way ahead of you. Now where's that whiskey?" She scanned the bar covered in everything Noah had hauled out from behind it.

"Little early for a drink," Noah said.

Hester sorted through the bottles. "Not to drink." Her hazel eyes brightened, and she grabbed the whiskey she'd opened earlier. "To help kill the smell." She took off her mask and placed it over the mouth of the bottle and tipped it, allowing the alcohol to dribble onto the material. Noah and I braved the odour and held out ours for her to do the same.

"Ready!" Noah said as Hester and I stood behind him waiting for him to shove open the kitchen door.

I inhaled; the whiskey burned my nose, and my eyes watered. "Yes," I coughed.

He pushed on the door, and we clicked on our flashlights.

The stench enveloped us as we stepped over the threshold. My foot crunched on something and I pointed my light at the floor. An open, and now squashed, box of crackers spilled out under my shoe. I shined the flashlight around the floor. Rotten bread, crushed crackers, what looked like flour, a box of pancake mix, and several undetermined dry foods covered the floor. And all topped with a sprinkling of mouse poop. "Gross," I whispered.

"It doesn't look like there's any salvageable food here." Noah kicked a broken pickle jar out of his way and reached for the handle of the refrigerator.

"Stop!" I yelled.

He turned; his eyes wide. "What? Why?"

"You won't find anything edible in that fridge, and it's bad enough in here, don't make it worse."

Hester shined her light on a shelving unit. "Looks like canned stuff only" She pulled a can of tomatoes from the top shelf then grabbed an empty, plastic dish bin and filled it with canned goods.

"Jeez, that's gross!" Noah called out.

"What?"

He stepped back from the area he explored. "Bloated raccoon. Really bloated, like it could burst at any second."

My stomach rolled. "And I was hoping the stink was just from the rotted food."

"Let's get out of here." Hester grabbed the bin of cans and carried it toward the door.

"Right behind you." Noah followed.

I trailed my flashlight over the walls; the beam landed on a first aid kit mounted above a sink. I walked over to it and took it down, before following the others out of the kitchen.

We packed up the bins with everything we found, including two blenders, and loaded the vehicle before exploring the rest of the lodge.

Outdated bags of chips sat in a basket at the front desk. "Remind me to grab those before we leave," Hester said, moving the basket to the middle of the counter.

With our bins filled and no other container in sight, I grabbed an empty wastebasket from behind the counter. I yelped when a mouse scurried out from under a box on the floor. My heart raced.

"Everything okay?" Noah smiled.

"Just a mouse." I opened the box on the floor and found it empty. "Here, you can use this," I said handing it to him. I glanced at the wall beside the desk. Forty hooks with forty numbered keys hung from a board. We were lucky the quaint lodge still had old-fashioned keyed entrances. I pulled a key from every hook and tossed them into the wastebasket in my hand.

"Are you two coming?" Hester called from the staircase at the far end of the main level.

I looked at Noah and held up the last key. "Guess she was planning on busting open the doors."

Noah snickered. "Better follow her before she does."

Flies buzzed and crawled on a window to the right of the landing, others bounced off the glass, their bodies making a pinging sound as they hit. A beam of sunlight streamed in and lit up the long, wide hallway.

There were ten rooms, each door numbered with a black metal digit in its centre. The number one marked the door at the top of the stairs. We'd decided on our way up we'd search three rooms apiece with Noah taking the extra one. Hester had the first three, Noah the next four, and I took the last rooms.

With my three keys in hand, I headed down to the end of the corridor to start with room number ten. The lock clicked as I turned the key. I held my breath and opened the door. The room was clean, though dusty, and cobwebs decorated all corners. Espresso coloured furnishings, taupe walls, grey oak plank flooring, it was more modern than I expected. I stripped the two double beds of their white linens, folded them and placed the bundles, along with white bathroom towels, inside a recycling bin I found under the desk. The ice bucket was large enough for the toiletries and the packets of coffee and tea bags. I slid the full bin out into the hallway.

Feeling more at ease, I entered the next room and did the same, noticing the decor was like that of the other room.

When I finished, I had another recycling bin filled with more useful items.

A fly buzzed my ear, and I shooed it away as I placed my key in the lock of room eight and turned it.

"Hey!" Noah called from beside me. "Last one," he said as he tapped on the number seven with his finger.

"Did you skip one?"

"No, I stripped the other three already," he said, pointing to the recycling bins lining the hallway. Wadded sheets, balled-up towels, and other objects piled high inside them.

I glanced past Noah's full containers and saw Hester entering her last room, then fixed my gaze on Noah and shook my head. "You didn't even try to fold anything, did you?"

"Nope." He turned the doorknob and entered the room.

I laughed and pushed open my door.

Flies buzzed and swarmed. Bile burned my throat. The bloated body of a fully clothed male lay face up on top of the bed. Greenish fluids leaking from the corpse stained the white duvet. I slammed the door shut and fell to my knees, heaving. Visions of Jasper, Cecil, and the bodies we found at the compound before its renovations filled my head. I gagged and gasped for air. The whiskey coated mask sucked into my open mouth. The vapours from the alcohol warmed my tongue.

Noah kneeled in front of me. "What happened?"

"In there... a... a body. And by the looks, he hasn't been dead more than a week or two."

Hester walked out from her room and called down the hall. "What's going on?"

Noah glanced over his shoulder. "Dead body."

Hester and Noah helped me to my feet, and I wiped my eyes. "Can we just go? Another team can search the other thirty rooms of the motel later."

Hester nodded. "Yup, I was about to suggest we leave. It'll be a tight fit putting the rest of this stuff in the car. And we'll have to repack Noah's haul." She looked toward the bins in the centre of the hallway.

Noah followed her gaze. "What's wrong with that?"

"Not compact enough. April, why don't you take the bins down. Noah and I will bring the rest over to the landing and then we'll see if there's anything useful in number eight."

I grabbed one of my containers while Noah and Hester carried the other two, and I hurried down the stairs. When I reached the front entrance, I threw open the door and rushed to the car.

The sunlight warmed the top of my head, and I ripped the mask from my face, inhaling the fresh air. I placed the bin inside the cargo area of the SUV, noting there was enough room for two or three more. The others would have to ride on one rear seat and on the floor.

By the time I headed back to help with another load, Hester and Noah came out with their hands full. It took us five more trips before all the supplies we'd found were down the stairs.

When we finished, I placed the trash can of keys on the front desk and grabbed the basket of expired chips. Noah pulled a note from his pocket and placed it on the desk beside the keys. It was a message for anyone who wanted help. It was too late for the guy upstairs, but maybe someone else would find it and then find us.

With the vehicle stacked to the roof, a bin on my lap, and one on Noah's, we left the resort. Hester drove to a pre-arranged site where we were to meet with the other two teams.

"You were right about the body," Hester said. She glanced at me through the rear-view mirror as we drove down a desolate road.

49

"About what?"

"It hadn't been there too long. I mean, my guess is he died about a week or two ago."

I saw the corpse in my head and squeezed my eyes shut.

"Hester thinks she knew him," Noah said from the passenger seat.

"What? Really?"

Hester nodded. "Think he was one of Cecil's men."

Several minutes passed before I spoke. "Wouldn't he have been vaccinated?"

"Probably, but then again, Jasper wasn't," she said.

Cecil had refused Jasper the final vaccine. *But if it mutated again,* I pushed my fingers into my forehead, suppressing the thought. I rejected the notion he died from the virus. *But what if he did?* The thought came back. "Could you tell what killed him?"

"There didn't appear to be any obvious mortal wound like a stabbing or gunshot, not that I got a good look. And if it wasn't the virus, it could have been anything. Infection, ruptured appendix, poisoning, heart attack."

We were lucky. Our facility had medical doctors, and they could help sick or injured residents. But lone individuals, people like Marcus and Noah who survived the virus, might not survive other medical crises. For the diabetic who ran out of insulin, or the cardiac patient whose blood pressure meds dwindled, survival would be difficult without the regular production of drugs. Only healthy individuals had a chance in this new world. From our observations, we could only assume many places were in a similar state. Humanity was starting over and until we established new factories, hospitals, and other necessary manufacturing, the butterfly virus was only one concern.

"You're quiet," Noah said as we rode in the rear seat of the black SUV on the way to the compound. We'd reorganized cars at the rendezvous and shifted contents and people. We were now five in the vehicle we rode in while the remaining members in the team split up between the other two SUVs.

I shrugged. "Just tired." I dreaded going back to the compound—my prison.

"You can rest your head on my shoulder," Noah whispered.

I glanced at the passenger sitting on my other side. His name was Khelden, one of the first residents we'd rescued from the forest months ago and a member of another recon team. Tall, with a somewhat athletic build, his knees touched the back of the seat ahead of him. He combed long fingers through a cowlick, but it did nothing to settle the wayward chunk of brown hair. Settling in his spot, he immersed himself into an old physics book he'd found.

"Everyone will eventually find out." Noah said and stretched his arm over my shoulder, pulling me close. I gave in and rested my head, closing my eyes. My muscles twitched and jumped as the ebb and flow of the road rocked me to sleep.

I knew for certain now that life would be difficult. Humanity, or what remained, would have to come together if we were to survive.

Eight

Behind Closed Doors

Above the handle of the steel door, a deep scratch zigzagged through the black paint and ended at the hasp where a rusted padlock hung. The entry at the end of the central corridor in the basement was almost invisible in the dim light. Many residents were aware of its existence, but most couldn't care less.

I stared up at the exit as it beckoned and dared me to pass through and follow the long, dark tunnel on the other side. I stepped closer and rested my ear against the cold steel. The tunnel led to the old house. It was through that passageway that Jasper pushed a laundry cart carrying my and Beth's unconscious bodies to safety the night of the fire. Kept locked, only a few of Cecil's accomplices knew what was behind it.

"What are you doing?"

I startled and spun, leaning back against the door. The cold from the steel seeped into my body, and I shivered. The flutter in my chest settled as I stared into Caleb's eyes.

Recovering from the abrupt intrusion, I walked past him and over to a stack of boxes, bins, and other containers sitting in the hallway. I bent forward and shoved one of the larger cartons into the storage room. The cardboard box emitted a loud hush as it scraped along the concrete.

"Did Mom or Dad send you down here to look in on me?" I said, pulling at the flaps and opening the box.

"No, to help." Caleb's hands came into my field of vision as he reached into the package and pulled out two cans of food.

I straightened up and stared at him. "Please check the dates first before putting them on the racks."

"Ah, I'm not new at this." Caleb turned the can around and looked for the stamp on the bottom. Then he placed it at the front of one of the nearly full shelves. Canned goods that had just passed their expiry date, or was close, filled the shelf. "This has been one of my chores since moving here." He pulled another can from the box and inspected it.

It wasn't news, but as my relationship with Beth had been awkward, the same was true with Caleb. Since our return, I had treated him with little respect and hadn't even celebrated his thirteenth birthday a few weeks ago with everyone else. But unlike Beth, I had yet to apologize to him. Caleb had tried to keep interacting with me but had given up. The worst part was he had done nothing wrong. It was all me, my childish behaviour and unwillingness to accept the situation. But now that I had, my brother deserved an apology.

"Caleb, I'm sorry," I blurted. My eyes welled, but I contained any further emotion.

Caleb smiled. "Don't worry about it." He engulfed me in a brotherly hug. In the time since finding each other, he had grown and though the youngest in the family, now towered over me.

"How are you so big?" I pulled out of our embrace and studied him.

He shrugged. "You and Beth got the smart genes, and I got the giant ones."

Images of our family flipped through my head. "Giant genes? From who? And you are smart," I said, settling on a particular recollection.

"Grandpa Linden, that's who," Caleb said.

I nodded. Caleb not only shared our grandfather's stature but also his easygoing manner. "Well, giant," I quipped, "let's get these supplies unloaded. Noah is meeting me here in a little while."

Caleb and I worked with efficiency as we unpacked boxes and stocked shelves. Our conversation eased into a comfortable rapport, recognizable of one between brother and sister, complete with sarcastic remarks and teasing banter.

"So, what's up with you and Noah?" Caleb said after a rather lengthy laughing session. The question surprised me, and my ability to concentrate on work stalled for a moment.

After the brief pause, I found the rhythm of stocking shelves again. "What do you mean?"

"What I mean is when are you going to stop hiding how much you like each other."

I dropped a tin on the metal shelf, and it clanged and echoed in the concrete room. "How do you—?"

Caleb's chuckle cut me off. "Everybody knows, Av. What no one can figure out is why you need to keep it a secret."

The tips of my ears burned, and my cheeks warmed. "Everyone?"

Caleb nodded.

"How?" In the same instant, I thought of Khelden, perhaps he hadn't been as immersed into his physics book as I'd assumed. "Never mind." I stopped Caleb before he could say anything and rushed to unpack my last box. Noah would arrive soon.

"Finished?" Noah said as I arranged the last can on the shelf. He stood in the doorway.

"Almost, Caleb has a few more." I reached toward Caleb's bin.

"Nope, all done." My brother placed the last of his cans on the rack and pushed the bin aside. "Go, I'll lock up."

"Sure?"

"Yup."

Noah stepped out into the hall, and I followed. The black steel door and rusted padlock caught my attention again.

"Come on." Noah said, pulling my focus to him.

"See you later, Caleb," I called to my brother as Noah and I walked up the corridor.

"Remember, you can hold hands now, everybody knows." Caleb's laughing voice followed behind us.

Noah grabbed my hand, and I relaxed in his grip. Inside, I both rejoiced and scolded myself for acting ridiculous. At nineteen, I was hardly a child. Even Caleb behaved more mature. I pulled my shoulders back, deciding I needed to grow up. And as we approached the end of the hallway and my parent's office, it would have to start now.

"Well, glad to see the cat's out of the bag. . . " Dad said as he stepped out from his office and smiled at us.

I rolled my eyes as heat moved into my cheeks. "Dad." Noah clutched my hand and gave it a gentle squeeze when part of me wanted to pull free.

Dad held up his hands in acquiescence. "Sorry, I promise not to mention it again," he said and winked.

Mom came out from the small lab next door. Her eyes swept over our clasped hands. "Honestly, it's about time," she said as she wiped her palms on the front of her white coat. She had piled her long, dark locks with silver threads on the top of her head. A few wisps strayed from the bun and framed her face.

"Maggie," Dad said.

"What?" My mother's eyes darted between us.

"See you two later." Dad turned and linked his arm through my mother's. "Why don't you show me what you've been working on," he said as he towed Mom back into the lab.

Noah and I made our get away; Mother's questioning voice seeped out the door and faded the further we got. We walked until we were outside Noah's room. He placed an ID card over the screen, and the door unlocked.

I stood in the hallway as he stepped over the threshold. Footsteps and voices floated to my ears. "Okay, see you later," I said a little louder than necessary.

Noah turned and stared at me with raised eyebrows. "Aren't you coming in?"

The owners of the voices drew closer. "No, I have work to do."

"Get in here." Before I could react, Noah reached across the threshold and pulled me into the room; the door closed behind me.

"Wow, your face is red." Noah tilted his head to the side as though to get a better look at my embarrassment.

"Is it?" I turned away and fanned my face with my hand. "Why?"

I shrugged, my back still to him.

Muscular arms wrapped around me, and Noah pulled me close. He kissed the top of my head.

"Because everybody knows about us now. I don't want people to think we're doing... stuff. Things would be different if we weren't all living under the same roof."

Noah's hands rested on my shoulders, and he turned me to face him. "Av, you've been in my room plenty of times before, and me in yours. How come you didn't worry about people thinking we were doing 'stuff' then."

"That was before everyone found out about us." I rubbed the creases in my forehead.

Noah laughed. "Av, they've always known, or at least suspected."

"Yes, but that was when I didn't know they knew. Now I know they know, and now it's weird." I pushed down the little voice in my head telling me I was an adult.

Noah leaned forward and rested his forehead against mine. "Stop over thinking so much."

"But thinking is what I do." I squeezed my eyes shut on a bunch of random memories that suddenly wanted to make themselves known. "Anyway, maybe this is moving too fast, maybe–"

Noah's mouth stopped what I was about to say as he sealed his lips over mine. Words turned to thoughts; thoughts turned to garbled nonsense in my head. My body melted into him as he led me toward his bed, and our tongues and bodies entangled. His warm hands wandered under my t-shirt, and I allowed him to pull it up and over my head. Then I helped him remove his. He unhooked my bra, slid the straps from my arms, and tossed it on the floor. I wrapped my arms around Noah and pressed my naked chest to his. I no longer worried, or cared, or thought about anyone on the other side of the door. We had stuff to do.

Nine

Secrets in the Snow

Tiny, perfect ice crystals floated to the ground, each one as unique as a fingerprint. The gentle fall of snow was mesmerizing. The dull landscape of withered browns and faded greens transformed into a pristine white canvas, crisp and cool–exhilarating. It was the first real snowfall of the season, and I would step outside and revel at the moment before snow and winter became more trouble than beauty.

I walked out through the front entrance of the compound, shut the door on the world within the walls, and stepped into magic.

My hands pushed deep inside my pockets, I moved out from under the cover of the portico, and tilted my face toward the pale grey sky. I closed my eyes and enjoyed the tiny snowflakes as they landed with a gentle touch and melted on my skin. I inhaled the cooled air, clean and odourless. My ears filled with the sound of nothing. The quiet snowfall was peaceful, and I stuck out my tongue and tasted winter.

Fluffy white powder dusted the ground and sprayed off the tips of my boots with my steps. I imagined walking on a cloud as each step took me further from the confines of the building. Memories of past winter days occupied my head.

"Hey, wait up!" Noah's voice came from behind and disrupted the silence.

I stopped and turned. Noah jogged toward me; his blue jacket was vibrant in the almost colourless realm of the outdoors. A smile spread across my face as he approached.

"What are you doing?" Noah took my hand, warming my icy fingers, and we strolled toward the forest edge.

I brought a finger to my lips. "Sh! Listen!"

"What am I listening for?" he whispered.

"Nothing."

"Nothing?" He pulled my hand into his pocket and held it.

"Yes." After a few more seconds of stillness I said, "Isn't this nice?"

"The snow?"

"The snow, the air, the quiet. It's peaceful. There's a poem that describes this..." I pulled my hand from Noah's pocket and waved it around.

"Winter? There are probably a lot of poems about the season."

Several fitting poems came to mind. When I remembered the words of the one I searched for, I recited them.

"Standing in a field of snow,
Wintery breezes start to blow.
Tiny snowflakes flutter down,
Gently falling to the ground.
Pure and white, each flake precise,
Transforming water into ice.
Blanketing ground, leaves, and trees,
Snowflakes cover all it sees.
While growth, and warmth, and colours cease,
There's nothing quite like winter's peace."

I took Noah's hand, and we walked again.

"Does that poem have a title? Who's it by?" he said.

"The title is Winter's Peace, and I have no idea."

"You don't remember?"

"No, it's not that, I never knew who wrote it."

Larger snowflakes fell, coating our uncovered heads, and as we crossed the threshold into the forest, the trees provided protection. Dead leaves crunched, and twigs snapped under our feet. A chickadee called out its name as it flitted from tree to tree, branch to branch. When we reached the concrete barrier, we followed it until we came to the ladder.

"After you," Noah bowed.

"No, not today," I said and smiled.

"What?"

"Let's keep walking. I don't feel like climbing over to the other side."

We kept a steady pace, and while we strolled away from the barrier, it was still within view as we walked its length on unfamiliar ground.

After several minutes, Noah pulled our hands from his pocket, and he released mine. He stepped over a small fallen tree, his steps quickened as he moved further from me and closer to the wall.

"What are you doing?" I called. Though the surrounding trees provided shelter, it didn't keep out the weather. Without warning, a blast of wind blew through the forest, and I tilted my head. Leafless branches swayed and rattled in the breeze. I tugged on the zipper at my neck and tucked my chin into the warmth of my jacket. In the half hour since we'd left the compound, the light snowfall was intensifying.

"Come over here and look at this."

What I wanted to do was to go back, but I made my way over to Noah instead. Another gust of wind took my breath; the temperature dropped.

When I reached him, Noah knelt by a mound of branches piled against the wall.

"What's so fascinating about that?" I said, looking at the tangled mess.

"It's not the branches but what's underneath." Noah lifted the brush. Beneath it and next to the wall was a neat stack of logs. "Someone stacked these here."

"So..." While I thought the pile was strange, I wanted to hear Noah's theory.

"So... it wasn't that long ago." Noah pulled out one log. Both of its ends were the pale yellow of freshly cut wood and not the grey of old, weathered logs.

"Let's head back." A strong gust whipped through the trees causing them to squeak and groan as they rubbed against each other. The eerie sound made my skin crawl, and the tranquil mood turned foreboding.

Noah rose to his feet, the log still in his grasp. "I'm bringing this with us. But first..." Noah wrapped his free arm around my waist and pulled me in for a kiss. When we parted, I was breathless once again, but it wasn't the wind this time.

The weather spurred us forward, and I dug my hands into my fleecy pockets, tucked my chin inside my jacket, and hunched my shoulders. Despite keeping my focus in front of me, I caught my toe on a tree root buried under light snow and dead leaves. I regained my balance before I found myself face down on the ground. The return trip was quick and wordless. The wind swallowed any conversation we attempted, and we gave up trying. I spent the journey back concentrating on my footsteps and on the questions that formed in my head.

"How did you notice it?" I said, touching Noah's arm as we stood under the portico at the front entrance to the compound.

Noah looked down at the log he carried in his hands. "It wasn't the pile of wood that caught my attention."

My gaze narrowed. "What do you mean?"

Noah turned a little and held up his arm. "Reach into my pocket."

I unzipped the pocket of his jacket and dipped my hand inside. My fingers searched until something soft fell between them. I pulled out my hand and uncurled my fingers. Lying in my palm was a small tattered piece of faded orange cloth with tiny yellow flowers. The fabric transported me to the moment Beth had spied my old orange pyjamas hanging in the wardrobe in the room where Cecil held us captive. On the day we'd escaped, we'd cut strips from the sleepwear to cover our mouths and noses from the stink of death.

My thumb rubbed over the worn piece of material I dug from Noah's pocket, and my stomach churned.

Ten

Hide and Seek

"Sure it's yours?" Noah said, taking the small bit of cloth from my hand. He inspected it, turning over the faded scrap and rubbing it between his fingers before tossing it onto the cafeteria table. Beth, Marcus, and Caleb sat across from us with their eyes fixed on the piece of material. Beside it, the log rested like a Christmas centrepiece minus the greenery, berries, and fake snow.

"No doubt about it," Beth spoke before I had a chance. "Hated April's pyjamas when we were little, hated them more having to make masks out them to block out the stench in that house."

The memory of the fabric tied over our noses to decrease the sickening stink of decay caused me to rub my hand across my mouth. Even the oblivious would never forget the reek of death.

"Could it have fallen from your backpack when you were on the trails? Wind or animals might have eventually carried it to where we found it." Noah stared at me, waiting for my answer.

I shook my head. "No, we left them at the house on the day we escaped. And what about the log?"

Marcus picked it up and examined the cut ends. "Chainsaw, and it's not that old," A section of bark fell on the table as he set down the log. Holes riddled the wood underneath.

"Have you told anybody about this?" Caleb reached for the scrap of cloth.

"No, just you," I said.

"Don't tell anyone, at least not now." Caleb tossed the strip of material onto the chunk of wood.

Noah picked at imaginary grit on the table. "Maybe we should speak to someone," he said, not looking at anyone, especially me. We were on opposite sides of this conversation, having discussed it before meeting with the others.

"That'd be fine with me." Marcus sat back in his chair and folded his arms.

"No!" Everyone's attention fell on me. "Not yet. We don't even know what this means. If it means anything at all. Everybody's busy with other things, why get them worried? The five of us can monitor the situation. If we feel there's trouble, then we say something." Unnecessarily worrying someone was a legitimate reason, but I had another bigger concern. If anyone else came out to the wall, they'd find the ladder, and I couldn't risk losing it. It was the only escape I had.

"Looks like I'm siding with April and Caleb. No offense, boys, it's a sibling thing," Beth said.

"Fine," Noah's voice echoed, "But there has to be a reason for this." He waved his hand over the centrepiece.

The skin on my arms prickled as each hair stood at attention. While a part of me believed our discovery meant nothing, I couldn't shake the feeling there was something more sinister about the findings.

Beth perked up and straightened her slouch. "Hold on, Mom and Dad said they and a few others had been at the house several times after locating it. Maybe that old hunk of material was accidentally dragged out by someone when they removed the bodies and cleaned the place."

Jasper's blanket-covered body and Cecil's putrid, fixed glare flashed in my head. I squeezed my eyes shut to erase the memory. "That sounds plausible." Beth's suggestion eased my sense of dread.

Plenty of ideas about the log went around the table. The only two thoughts we agreed upon was the freshness of the hewn chunk of wood and that we should keep its existence hidden, at least until we investigated further.

"I'll stash it in my room for now." Noah reached toward the log.

"No, I've got a better place." Caleb grabbed it first and stood; a smirk on his face.

Noah and Marcus rose to their feet. Marcus focused his attention on Beth. "Later?" His dark brown eyes softened as he looked at my sister.

Beth waved him away. "Sure," she laughed. "But don't forget your promise."

A sly grin spread across Marcus' face. "Oh, I won't."

The exchange was rife with innuendos, and I planned to ask Beth about their cryptic conversation but changed my mind, deciding it wasn't my business. Though I couldn't help but wonder if their friendship had turned into something else.

The boys left, leaving Beth and me with an uncomfortable silence. While we'd spoken often since my apology, we had yet to be alone for any length of time. The situation struck me as odd, as we'd spent weeks with each other. The two of us confined in a room, our constant companionship the only thing that held us together—kept us alive. And now not even alone for a minute, in an area four times the size, and the awkwardness that hung in the air was thicker than...

"Pea soup," I mumbled.

"What's that?" Beth said as she focused her gaze on me.

"Nothing. Have you ever noticed how often dad uses strange and old expressions?"

Beth nodded. "Yes, and it's rubbed off on you."

"Oh! I don't use expressions too much; I think of them a lot, but..."

"No, you say them. Come on, let's walk." Beth got up from her chair, and I followed. "The last time we toured this place together it was a mess and empty," she said as we tramped up the stairs from the basement to the second-floor corridor.

"I still find it weird to see people in the halls." My voice resounded in the stairwell.

We stepped through the doorway and walked down the short hallway. I glanced at a bracket up on the wall, the inactive surveillance camera no longer attached to it. We passed the door to my room and turned the corner to follow the north wing. Our limited conversation occasionally interrupted by the pleasantries of others. At the end of the corridor, we entered the stairwell next to our parent's apartment. Our footsteps echoed as we tromped down the stairs.

"Have you been down there?" Beth said as we reached the bottom of the staircase and crossed into the east corridor on the first-floor. Her long, slender finger pointed down the hall toward the entrance to the south corridor that led to the room we shared for a brief time. The room where I had spent two years in a drug induced, hypnotic state, that stole my memory bit by bit. Beth still didn't remember her first room before they moved her in with me, though she learned where it was because Mom and Dad had shown her. As for our parents, they lived in a suite in the basement near the labs. Cecil forced them to work on finding a vaccine for the virus he had set upon the world. Their only contacts with us were minimal as Cecil's ludicrous plan to rebuild humanity with a more intelligent and special race revealed itself.

I shook my head. "No."

"Let's go then." Beth took my hand and pulled, but my feet remained in place. "Come on," she said, "time to face your demons." She smiled. "That's one of Dad's." She tugged again, and my feet released their hold.

"Are you sure no one lives in here?" My finger brushed over the slight mark on the door. The scratch proved the room once mine—ours.

"Absolutely." Beth swiped a card through the reader, and the door slid open.

We walked over the threshold. The lights turned on the moment we stepped inside. The space was empty and very white.

"I used to think all the doors made a whooshing sound when they opened." I ran my hand over the door of the dumbwaiter.

"And the cameras whirred," Beth said from behind me.

I turned to look at her. "You too?"

She nodded. "Mom explained it was the effects of the drugs wearing off."

I returned my attention to the dumbwaiter and inspected the wall. My fingertips searched for something my eyes couldn't find.

"What are you looking for?" Beth said.

"I don't know. I remember being shocked whenever I didn't follow procedure. And I remember realizing not following protocol was a mistake the second I heard a buzzing sound."

I hesitate before reaching in and pulling the small tray from the compartment. My thoughts drift to earlier events, and for a moment, I forget all procedure. I place the tray on the table and pull the lid free.

The moment the buzzing reaches my ears, my stomach drops. I have made a mistake. It is all I have time to think before the flash of blue light.

I pick myself up off the floor; my legs shake under my weight. I climb back into my chair, fold my arms on the top of the table, and I rest my head. The smell of singed hair is in my nose. I inhale and fill my lungs several times before rising on shaky legs and making my way over to the washroom.

"Are you sure about that?"

The memory faded with Beth's voice. "What do you mean?"

She shrugged. "You imagined the whooshing doors, the whirring cameras, you could have imagined the electric sh-shock too. Remember, not all are memories happened the way we think they did. Cecil made certain of that." The slight stutter in Beth's speech was the first I'd noticed in a long time.

I tugged on a piece of my hair. "And the burnt hair scent?"

Beth crouched low, inspecting the floor and running her fingers over the wall. "Maybe that too. There's nothing here," she said, looking up at me.

The image returned complete with sounds and odour. But Beth was right. There was nothing anywhere to suggest a device had delivered any electric shock. Cecil had put that false memory into my head along with the others. *What did he do?* I shook the thought away and continued around the perimeter.

In the corner and close to the ceiling, the camera still mounted to its bracket. A chill crept up my arms.

"This was where my bed was." Beth stood at the end wall. "The desk was in that corner." She pointed to the spot across from me. "Your bed was there, the dresser in that far corner, and that's the bathroom at the other end. Am I right?"

"Yes," I said and crossed the floor, stopping at the bathroom. My fingers wrapped around the clear glass knob, and I pushed the door into the room. "That solves that mystery," I muttered.

"What?" Beth stood behind me.

"The door. Sometimes I thought it pulled out, other times pushed in and all within the same wonky, distorted memory. And it also doesn't close on its own."

"That hypno-drug fucked us up, can't trust your memory from those first few months coming off of it," Beth said.

In a clockwise direction, my eyes scanned over the vanity to my left, the vacuum tube hanging from the ceiling that sucked away garbage, and the toilet. Then moving across was the shower stall.

Stepping over the threshold, I caught my reflection in the mirror above the sink. Many times, I had looked into that mirror and not known who I was. This time it was different. I leaned closer and stared into my blue eyes. Within a six-month time-frame, we'd been freed from one place and imprisoned in another. We'd escaped our confines and certain death, fought our way out from a forest that wanted to keep us lost, only to find ourselves back where we'd started.

The memory of my old history book came to mind. I saw its black cover and the word history printed in silver. And inside, on one of its pages, a yellow highlighted word floated in front of my eyes. *Escape.* Yes, I still needed to escape, not just from the compound and the winter that would keep me trapped, but I needed to escape from inside my head.

Eleven

Jasmy

The brush swirled and stroked with the guidance of my
hand as it deposited a load of paint. My thoughts focused
and the image I had in my mind came alive, and I fell into
a simple rhythm, lost in the tranquility of early morning.
In this moment, I was at peace.

Every once in a while, I stepped back and stared at my
work, searching for imperfections, missing pieces, and forgotten elements. I envisioned my light source and noted
where to place highlights and shadows. I mixed and re-
mixed the paint, achieving the perfect hues. When I was
ready, I continued laying down paint until it was time to
critique again.

"Pretty!"

An unexpected, quiet voice with a subtle but indistin-
guishable accent, surprised me, and my heart skipped. I
stepped back from the mural and stood beside the adoles-
cent girl who'd offered her opinion.

The wall in the cafeteria was awash with ocean blues and
sea greens of varying shades. Waves curled onto the sandy
shore; a small blue crab emerged from the tide as sea birds
soared high above in search of an easy meal. I folded my

arms and considered my work. *What other creatures lurked under that water?*

I stared with longing at the horizon. The thin line created by the meeting between water and air, sea and sky—heaven and earth. It captured my attention and stirred my imagination, pulling me into the painting.

"That is the ocean, right?" The girl's voice sucked me back to reality.

The girl seemed only a few years younger than Beth. Her vibrant red shirt was the perfect background for her sleek, black hair that hung below each shoulder and ended at her elbows. The depth of her dark brown eyes framed with long black lashes almost swallowed my gaze as we stood face to face. The corners of her light plum-coloured lips twitched into a shy smile; her flawless brown skin glowed.

I nodded. "Yes."

She turned away and gazed at the mural again. "Yes, I thought so." The room returned to the quiet of early morning. "Is it finished?"

"Almost," I said, resolute to finish one of my murals now that my artistry was no longer a secret.

"What else will you paint?"

The question made me contemplate my work a little longer. There was something missing. Until I figured out what, it would not be complete. "Something, I'm just not sure yet. So..." I turned my back to the wall and my attention on my admirer, "have you remembered your name?"

The girl closed her eyes. "Jasmy—spelled with a J, pronounced like a Y. At least that is what I am told." She paused, as though considering what she said. "Anyway, it feels right."

"I remember when my name first came back to me."

Jasmy's brown eyes widened, the ceiling light reflected in her black pupils. "Do you!"

"A dream revealed it." It was the first time I heard myself called something other than A2, the first two characters of the alphanumeric identification given to me at C.E.C.I.L.

"And you knew for certain that was your name?"

"Well, I had to ask someone, but even then, I knew. Deep inside, like you said, it felt right."

Jasmy nodded. "Someday I will dream of my name."

"Maybe you will. Do you remember much of anything else?"

Jasmy's dark eyes narrowed. "Sometimes, when I think everything has returned, a new memory comes, and then I realize I am missing pieces of my life," she said; her voice was small, and her chin quivered.

Does she remember the day we discovered her? Like the other Butterflies, she'd been fluttering around the forest on an aimless and unending hike. She had been as blank as Shaun, her mind lost to the hypno-drug, her body lost to the trails. One of the other teams found her, along with two others who were more lucid. When I first saw her, she had a familiarity about her I could not place. Even now there was something.

"Don't worry, it'll come. Look at how much progress you've made already." I encouraged, remembering her in her stupor.

She twisted a piece of her black hair around a finger. "Yes, while much is still missing, a lot has returned. Each day I wake up feeling more whole, more... connected," she whispered her last word. While what she'd said was optimistic, there was a hint of sorrow tainting her words as though she didn't quite believe what she said.

I pointed to the mess of paint and brushes strewn across a table. "I should clean up my stuff." Soon the cafeteria would be full of people eating their breakfast.

Jasmy swept the lock of hair she twisted back over her shoulder. "Will you not finish it today?"

"No, not now. Painting with an audience makes me uncomfortable." I tightened the lid on a pot of blue paint.

Jasmy lowered her eyes. "Oh."

I placed my hand on her shoulder. "Not you, though. You can come and watch whenever."

A broad smile parted Jasmy's lips, showing off her perfect teeth. "May I stay and watch you clean up? I would help, but I don't know where to start." She looked around the table at the various containers of paint and brushes, some soaking in water, others lying on the table clean and dry.

"If you'd like," I said, cleaning up the mess. It took a few minutes to put the jars and tubes of paint back in the old green canvas bag along with the clean brushes. I swished the dirty brushes in a jar of water and dried the bristles on an old rag. Then I rolled them up in another cloth and sealed the paint-brush-washing-jar with its lid. Both the jar and brushes would get a better cleaning later. The job was complete as the first few inhabitants arrived for their morning meal.

Noah and the others showed up minutes later, and I introduced Jasmy to the bunch. Our small group grew by one as she joined us for breakfast.

Twelve

Oh, Brother!

I bolted upright. Unsure of my whereabouts, my eyes darted around in the dark searching for something familiar. Air expelled and filled my lungs in quick bursts, and my heart thudded. Sweat trickled from my temples. I swept my hair from the back of my neck and shuddered. As the whisper in my ears faded, so too did my confusion and the dream.

12:31 AM glowed in red from the clock on the nightstand. Moonlight poured in through the window. The crystal suncatcher caught a moonbeam and glinted. As my heart returned to a normal rhythm I crawled from under my covers and gazed out the window.

Two weeks earlier, snow had arrived and stayed, and the full moon reflected off the snowy landscape. Apart from the night sky, it appeared as almost daylight. Solar panels flashed in the moonlight, and beyond, the shadowy forest edge encircled the field.

A yawn stretched across my face, and I glanced at my bed. The soft pillow and warm blankets invited, but I would not sleep and chance returning to the nightmare. I refused to recall whatever fragments of the dream lingered, and if I couldn't relax, I would make use of the time instead.

Dressed in sweats and a grey t-shirt, I snatched up the canvas bag with the paint pots, tubes, and brushes set by the door and walked out of my room. Another mural was near completion, and I headed to the cafeteria.

With every stroke of the brush, my mind and body eased despite the restless pace in which I worked. The rhythm spurred me on and within an hour the painting materialized. A desert scene with mountains in the distance and flowering cacti in the foreground stretched across the end wall under a bright blue sky. A small grey quail with a black head plume stood in the shade of a tall cactus while a roadrunner weaved between long tufts of desert grass.

I yawned and stepped back, satisfied. Exhaustion gripped my body, and my eyes watered. The thought of my bed hurried the packing up of paints and wrapping of brushes in plastic to keep them from drying out. The wish for sleep was stronger than cleaning them, and they would wait until morning.

With half-closed eyelids, I stepped out from the quiet cafeteria and flicked off the light switch. Small yellow lights lit up portions of the hall. The dim glow made me sleepier, and I rested against the cafeteria door. Never had my bed seemed so far away.

In an instant, the overwhelming need for sleep disappeared as two voices travelled to my ears. I tiptoed toward the sound, picking out the odd word, but most were incomprehensible.

The door to the communications room was open a crack, and I peeked through the opening. Someone sat at the desk with his back to the door. He tipped his head forward. "Say again," he uttered. The radio crackled.

I pushed open the door, and the hinges squeaked. The man spun around in his chair.

Archie resembled a child caught doing something he shouldn't be doing. His brown eyes widened with the sudden intrusion, and I could almost see the list of explanations rolling behind them as he glared at me. *Hands in the cookie jar*, I heard my father say. Archie griped the armrest of the chair. The tension in his forearm seemed to animate the snake tattoo as he leaned forward. The radio crackled again.

My eyes darted around the room. "Sorry, Archie. I heard voices and thought Marcus was here."

The look of surprise disappeared from Archie's face, and he turned to the transceiver, but not before I noticed a brief expression of anger replacing the shock. He twisted the knob on the old radio, changing the channel. Loud crackles of static exploded from the speaker, then settled into a steady hum. "No, just me," he said, not hiding the annoyance in his voice. He spun around in the chair and faced me. "What are you doing up in the middle of the night?" He pursed his thin lips as he changed the subject.

I took a step back toward the door. "Insomnia. Wasn't Marcus supposed to be working nights this week?"

"Yes, but I told him to take another day and start tomorrow." Archie smiled, but it ended at the corners of his thin-lipped mouth and did not engage the rest of his round face.

"Is that what it was then, the voices? Someone talking over the radio?"

"No! I mean, it might've sounded like that, but it was just static." He reached back and flipped a switch on the transceiver. The green power light faded, and the hum disappeared.

I nodded, outwardly agreeing with Archie, but I believed my ears. A wide yawn took over my face and caused my eyes to water. "Sorry to have disturbed you. Night, Archie." I stepped from the office before he said anything else; my heart raced.

The conversation replayed in my head as I hurried to my room. Archie hid something, and I planned to find out what that was.

3:17 glowed from the clock as I climbed into bed and my body sunk into the mattress. I shivered a little under the cold bedding tucked under my chin. My muscles twitched, and my breathing slowed. As my awareness faded, the whispers that had woken me hours earlier returned, but despite them, I fell into unconsciousness.

The rest of the night was undisturbed by nightmares or dreams, and when I woke it was as though I'd slept for days. I rolled onto my left side and stared at the door. The warm bed was cozy, and I was reluctant to leave its comfort. But breakfast waited, and my stomach reminded me with a loud rumble. There was also the encounter with Archie. The entire situation seemed dubious, and I wanted to share the experience with the group. I flung back my blankets and dressed; my news couldn't wait any longer.

"Are you sure?" Noah said for the fourth time.

I rolled my eyes and sighed in exasperation. "Yes. There was another voice."

"Av, maybe it was static," Caleb said.

"Caleb, I can tell the difference between radio static and a voice."

Caleb shrugged. "Just checking."

Beth put down her mug. "Well, I believe you."

"Thanks, Beth. So, we agree to keep this amongst ourselves and watch him like a hawk?" I folded my hands, resting them on top of the table.

"Dad!" Beth stared at me with raised eyebrows.

"Where?" I glanced around before understanding what she meant. Every time I uttered an expression, Beth made a point of mentioning it. I shook my head, and she grinned.

"Agreed?" I said again and waited for everyone at the table to confirm.

Caleb, Noah, Beth, and Jasmy, now a permanent member of the group, all mumbled in agreement.

Marcus pushed his chair back from the table. "Sorry, guys, you'll have to leave me out on this one."

"Marcus?" Beth questioned as he rose to his feet.

"Look, I know Arch better than any of you, and he's given no reason not to trust him. See you later." Marcus headed for the exit.

Beth jumped to her feet and grabbed her tray of dirty dishes. "Wait, I'm coming with you." Sorry, she mouthed and followed Marcus.

"Duty calls." Caleb stood. "Yes, I know, Dad says that too," he said before I commented, and he walked away.

I sat with one elbow resting on the table and cradled my head in my hand. With the other, I traced invisible lines on the smooth surface with a fingertip. I'd wanted to discuss an action plan, but that would not happen. Jasmy, Noah, and I sat without speaking.

"When did you finish that mural?" Jasmy pointed over my shoulder after several moments of silence.

"When I was down here last night." I'd told no one why I'd been in the basement and only said I couldn't sleep and walked the halls.

Jasmy nodded.

I glimpsed my hands and picked the dried paint out from under my fingernails. "But there is more to why I couldn't sleep."

Noah shifted beside me as my words must have piqued his interest and pulled him away from whatever mulled around in his head. "Oh?"

Jasmy stared at me, and once again I saw a familiarity in her eyes. Noah's gaze studied my face.

"A dream woke me. Nightmare, really. I dreamt of... Cecil," I whispered his name, breaking the promise I'd made to myself weeks ago not to speak it. His dead grey gaze flashed in front of me, and I shook my head. Noah's warm hand covered mine. "Anyway," I continued, "I don't remember what he was saying, but he kept whispering in my ear. The same thing over and over." The memory caused me to shudder.

"Don't worry, it was just a bad dream." Noah squeezed my hand. "What you went through, you're bound to have nightmares."

Noah was right. But there was something about the dream that made Cecil's whispered words seem so real. And intuition told me I'd had the dream before but had not remembered it.

"April, you should speak with someone. Talking about stuff has helped me," Jasmy said.

"Can I ask what you talk about?" My question was intrusive, but I was curious. Jasmy didn't share much of what she remembered.

Jasmy shrugged. "Just my dreams and the bits of memory that have returned. My counsellor helps me to put the pieces together."

"What sort of memories?"

"Mostly about what I remember of my family, particularly my brother."

My heart fluttered. "Brother?"

Jasmy nodded. "Yes, he was much older, but I was fond of him. And he was here. At the compound. Before."

"Was?" Noah said; it was his turn to pry.

Jasmy's eyes misted over, but she did nothing to hide her sadness. "They told me he died."

"Maybe it's a mistake." I thought of the graves in the forest clearing near the old house. Had he been one of Cecil's guinea pigs?

Jasmy shook her head. "No, it's true." She focused her attention on her hands resting on the table. "You knew him, April," she mumbled.

My eyebrows drew together. "What do you mean I knew him?"

Jasmy turned her gaze onto my face. "His name was Jasper."

My mouth fell open as her words touched my ears. "Jasper?"

Jasmy's head bobbed in slow motion. Her familiar eyes begged belief and stared into my soul—Jasper's eyes.

Thirteen

Reflection

The stock room felt smaller today, the air heavier to breathe. I grabbed a reusable shopping bag and filled it with items on Lydia's list. She'd woken me early in the morning and given it to me before heading to the kitchen to prepare breakfast. While I stocked the shelves after supply runs, I occasionally delivered supplies for the kitchen staff as well whenever the foodstuffs in their pantry dwindled. It was tedious. Everything was tedious.

I reached toward the back of a shelf and grabbed a tall plastic container of peppercorns. As I brought it forward, the bottom of the bottle knocked over a can which set off a chain reaction. Soup and vegetable tins toppled like dominoes; they clanged against the steel shelving before rolling off and crashing to the floor.

"Damn!" I yelled, kicking one of the cans. I tossed the peppercorns into the bag, slipped the long strap over my shoulder, and slammed the door.

The hallway seemed to lengthen as I stomped toward the kitchen. Once there, I dropped the bag onto a stainless-steel prep table in the centre of the room. Gwen, a plump woman wearing a bright red apron looked up at me from her position near the grill. She flipped over a pancake and smiled, but I hurried out before she engaged me in conversation.

My feet grew heavier with every step toward my room; breaths came in short pants. I was suffocating.

Back in my bedroom, I pulled on my boots and jacket. And then I ran.

The bitter cold burned the inside of my nose as I inhaled the frigid air. A gust of wind sent a spray of gritty snow in my direction; tiny shards of ice stung my face. My jaw tightened as I trembled inside my jacket. The weather was colder than it should be for early December. The brilliant sun and bright blue sky had looked inviting from my bedroom window. But the display had been an illusion. *Looks can be deceiving*, my father's voice whispered in my head.

I thrust my hands deep into fleece-lined pockets and tucked my frozen chin under the zipped-up collar. The snow squeaked with every step as I trudged past the bench in the courtyard covered with several centimetres of snow.

The sun reflected off the white expanse, snowflakes sparkled. A powerful gust blew the snow across the frozen ground. When the wind died, the icy diamonds sparkled once again. Bathed in sunlight, the black glass on the large solar panels glinted. I squinted and focused my attention on the forest edge beyond the confines of the facility. *Will I ever be free?* I wondered.

I looked back at the door and the promise of warmth behind it. My will to stay where freedom surrounded me was strong. But numb toes and fingers, chapped lips, and icy skin begged me to return. I exhaled a frozen breath and trudged toward the compound.

A shiver surged through me as I stepped into the cafeteria, and the remaining chill in my body dissipated. My gaze locked on Jasmy, and her eyes reminded me of her lineage.

Two weeks had passed since she'd told us that Jasper was her brother or half-brother, a detail she recalled a few days later. A product of their father's first marriage fifteen years before Jasmy was born.

"Where's Marcus?" I said to Beth as I sat in the empty chair between Caleb and Noah. Marcus was the only one missing from the group.

Beth shrugged. "How the hell should I know?" Her gaze narrowed.

I shook my head, deciding it was better to dismiss Beth's foul mood than to ask further questions.

Noah's hand settled on my thigh. The heat from his touch caused a sudden shiver. "Jeez, your leg is cold. Where were you?" He wrapped his arm around me and pulled me close. My tense muscles eased as I leaned into him.

"Outside."

"Seriously? The temp has got to be like minus fourteen or something." Noah hugged me tighter.

"Colder," Caleb spoke. "Factor in wind chill and it's closer to minus twenty-one."

"The sun is so bright I thought it would be nice," I said.

Beth raised her eyebrows. "Why would you go out?"

"Because I needed air—space." I confessed.

"Winter can do that," Caleb chimed in again.

"No, it's not just the season, but this place too. Aren't you bothered being stuck here?" I directed my question to Beth.

"Not really. And anyway, where else are we going to go?"

The tips of my ears burned, and my cheeks warmed. While I was warming up, it was everyone's gaze that made me flush.

"Come on, it's not that bad. We've got food, shelter," Caleb said.

"And friends," Jasmy added. I looked over at her, but her focus was on Caleb.

"Okay, Av." Noah squeezed me tighter.

"No, you don't get it. None of you understand." I pulled away from Noah.

"Come on, Av." Noah reached for me, but I moved further away.

"Get what?" Marcus pulled the chair out from the table next to Beth. She glowered at him and folded her arms tightly over her chest. I realized now that Marcus caused Beth's foul mood.

Marcus understood her body language and sat beside her, though he shifted his chair over a little more than usual. He trained his focus on my face as if to wait for my answer, but I glared back instead.

Marcus threw up both hands. "Okay, jeez! Nothing like getting 'the eyes' from both of them."

Caleb laughed, but an intense glare from Jasmy cut it short. That and what appeared as a kick to his shin from under the table. A groan escaped from his lips as he reached down and confirmed my suspicion.

"Where were you?" Beth snapped as she stared at Marcus.

"Helping Arch."

Beth rolled her eyes at him.

"Hey, you'll be glad I was," Marcus said.

Beth shifted in her chair and turned her body toward him. "Oh!"

"I overheard some news... and it's not good," Marcus' voice dropped to just above a whisper.

I folded my arms on the table and leaned closer. For the moment, I let go of the fact I would find no sympathy from this group.

"I had to get something for Arch, so I left the office for a bit. When I came back, I heard voices."

"See, I told you," I said, sure that Marcus had heard the same thing I had weeks earlier.

Marcus shook his head. "No, there were others in the room, specifically your father."

I glanced at Beth, then Caleb. "That's not unusual, Marcus," I said.

"No," he agreed, "but what they were talking about was, or actually kinda scary."

"What?" Noah moved his chair closer to mine and put his arm around my shoulder. This time I didn't shrug him off.

Marcus ran a hand over his thick curls. "Someone's sick."

"Sick! What do you mean, and do you know who?" Beth said.

Marcus nodded. "Neil, and they said flu sick."

There was a collective gasp at the table.

I swallowed. "Maybe it's just stomach-flu sick."

Marcus shook his head. "No. Butterfly Flu sick."

My hand rubbed over the back of my neck. My flesh prickled underneath, and I could almost feel the outline of the butterfly tattoo beneath my fingertips. "No, it can't be true," I whispered.

"How did he get sick?" Noah said. He'd lost everyone he'd ever known to the virus, buried his family in shallow graves in the backyard. The cemeteries filled quickly in the first year. And when there were only a few townspeople left, they buried each other, until Noah was the sole survivor.

"Your dad said they think it was a mosquito. That one got inside."

"What?" Beth's voice rose, and she clamped a hand over her mouth as her eyes darted between our faces. "Mosquito?" she whispered, "Mosquitoes haven't been around in weeks. It's winter, too damn cold for mosquitoes," she whispered.

Marcus shrugged. "Don't shoot the messenger." It seemed my father's use of idioms had rubbed off on him too.

"The wood!" Caleb spoke, and I stared at him.

"What?" Jasmy said.

"The log you brought in. The mosquito must have been hibernating under the bark." Caleb looked at Noah and me.

"Where did you hide the log?" Beth said.

Caleb combed his fingers through his thick brown hair. "Canned food storage. Since only five of us have access to that room, I figured no one would find it."

What Caleb had said was true. Apart from him and myself, only three others had entry to that room and Neil was one of them as he worked in the kitchen with food preparation.

"Now I know why Lydia had me get a few things for her this morning. Neil couldn't."

Noah's hand over my arm. "It'll be okay though, right? I mean, we've got Marcus here and me and we're immune. They've made vaccines from our blood, we've been inoculated."

"Noah," Beth said. "Neil was vaccinated too, and now he's sick."

"What if it's something else then?" Noah said.

"No, it's not. It's confirmed," Marcus spoke.

"But how?" Jasmy's small voice caught everyone's attention.

There was only one explanation. "The virus mutated again," I said. My stomach dropped.

The Butterfly Flu was back, and we brought it inside the compound.

Fourteen

Rumour

Neil died three weeks later, on New Year's Day. His plastic wrapped body taken away and placed somewhere outside, left to the elements until spring when we could bury him. He'd had no family in the compound, all he'd left behind was more illness.

"Someone else is sick," Beth mumbled under a surgical mask as we sat at our usual table in the cafeteria for supper.

Marcus touched Beth's arm for a second before snapping his hand away. "Two more, maybe."

"Two!" My gaze darted between Beth and Marcus. Noah squeezed my leg.

Marcus shrugged. "What I heard."

"What d'you hear?" Caleb and Jasmy placed their dinner trays on the table and pulled out chairs across from each other.

Marcus turned to Caleb on his right. "Two more, you know, sick."

Caleb nodded. "Think it's three that are sick."

I held my finger to my lips. "Sh! Someone might be listening."

"Who?" Caleb looked around the empty room. With the return of the virus, most of the inhabitants became extra cautious. The only moments they spent away from their rooms was to tend to their duties. At meal break, they picked up their food from the cafeteria but did not eat there. Even our gang spent little time together apart from chores, though occasionally Noah came to my room or I went to his.

Every three or four days our group of six gathered to discuss the things we couldn't while we worked. The brief meetings did not allow for regular small talk, such as how monotonous life inside the compound had become, or how much we laboured. We reported on the facts and shared whatever information we'd learned. Tending to our tasks was not our only focus—spying and gathering intel was a priority. With the medical staff not delving into the details, how many more had fallen ill, if they neared a solution, we took it upon ourselves to find out. And my parents were not exempt from our eavesdropping. Whatever information they thought they were protecting us from, we wanted to know.

"Anyway, why should we be quiet? Everyone else is whispering about it when they can, speculating on what's happening." Caleb stuck his fork into a mountain of spaghetti and twirled the noodles. He lifted his mask, pulling it up to the top of his head before taking a bite.

I pushed my food around my plate, tomato sauce oozed out from under the pasta. "Well, that's a problem then. Everyone is wondering, but no one really knows. Why won't they give us more information?"

"Because they don't want anyone to panic." A loud noise from the kitchen distracted Noah, and he looked over his shoulder for a moment. "Anyway, it's understandable," he said.

"Understandable, sure, but speculating and circulating rumour is worse; the facts are what we need." The argument was one we'd deliberated before. All I knew was that our parents worked tirelessly on a new vaccine and treatment.

And that Noah's and Marcus' blood proved useless; they were as immune to the new mutated strain as the rest of us.

"When was the last time you had a good night's sleep?" Beth stared at me with raised eyebrows.

"What does that have to do with anything?" I sniped.

Beth shrugged. "Cause you're awful cranky these days."

"Shut up!" I nudged my plate into the centre of the table and pulled my mask up from around my neck.

Caleb wiped the back of his hand over his sauce-covered lips, streaking some of it across his cheek. "And you say Beth and I squabble all the time." He shoved another fork full into his mouth.

I rolled my eyes, but Beth had the right to call me out. "Fine, it's the nightmares of him... Cecil." Every time I uttered his name, it left an awful taste in my mouth. Weeks had passed since I'd had a restful sleep, since before the nightmares began. And now they were worse. The images in my head and his voice in my ear was so real I woke several times with the scent of Cecil's cologne in my nose. The only detail I could not remember were the words he so often whispered. Words I couldn't grasp, but somehow, I believed held importance. They were a secret—a mystery. But there was one positive that came from dream-disturbed sleep and resulting insomnia. The hours allowed me to complete all the murals I'd begun, but as for starting new murals, I was out of ideas.

Caleb burped loud and long. "'Scuse me," he said when he finished.

"Was that necessary?" Beth glared at our brother.

"Yup!" He glared back then turned his attention to me. "Well, I hope you get sleep tonight. We gotta be in the greenhouses first thing tomorrow morning. Russ won't like it if we're late." Russ, the head gardener, was a stickler for punctuation. With the medical team taking care of the sick and working on finding a new vaccine, the rest of the inhabitants took on more chores. Caleb, Beth, Noah, and I along with a few others were now responsible for maintaining Greenhouses A and B on either side of the central corridor and harvesting their yields. The garden vegetables were a welcome complement to the canned goods and the three freezers stocked with small game, wild turkeys, fish, and one large moose. Homes in Kearney had not only supplied us furnishings and other necessities but also hunting and fishing gear.

"Don't worry about me. Where are you helping tomorrow?" I said to Jasmy as she chewed her last bite.

Jasmy finished eating and wiped her mouth on a cloth napkin. "Laundry in the morning with Marcus."

Marcus dropped his fork on his empty plate. "What? Oh, right, laundry. Woo-hoo," he said, showing little exuberance.

Caleb stacked his plate onto Jasmy's. "Just you two?"

"No, there are four others helping."

"And the afternoon?" I said.

Jasmy scrunched her nose. "Lucky me, gets to gather garbage. But at least it's with Esther."

Beth stretched her arms over her head, "Now that sounds like fun... not."

"Actually, it might be. Esther is hilarious." I thought of the petite woman with long blonde hair. What she lacked in height she made up for in physical strength.

"That is true," Beth said, "and, I hear she and Russ got together."

"Beth!"

"What? It's true."

I shook my head. "What about you?" I said to Marcus.

Marcus folded his hands on the top of the table. "Sleeping. I got the night shift in comms starting tomorrow night."

Bingo! That meant Archie would be in the comms room tomorrow afternoon. With Marcus not wanting to spy on him, it was up to Caleb and me. As we passed by the communications area on the way to food storage, we took every opportunity to listen-in on Archie whenever he monitored the radio alone. Unfortunately, neither of us had discovered anything incriminating nor out of the ordinary over the last few weeks. Nothing like I was sure I'd heard earlier. I covered a yawn, even though my mask hid my mouth. "Sleeping. Yes, I think I better go to bed. See you all in the morning." I stacked several plates onto a tray and carried them away from the table to deposit in the bins near the kitchen door.

Tomorrow would begin another long day, where cold and isolation froze time, and life became a monotonous existence.

Fifteen

Truth and Consequences

Three weeks after the newly mutated virus' first casualty, we'd learned one more inhabitant succumbed to the illness. There were others who were sick, but who and how many was also a mystery. With most people distancing themselves, isolating in their rooms, some even refusing to work, it was easy to lose count of who was well and who wasn't. Winter was proving longer than I could ever have imagined. The world in which I lived grew smaller with each passing day as the Butterfly Flu lurked in the shadows, and I wondered who would be its next victim. I had to escape from behind closed doors and the ramblings in my head. And I had to understand the toll this mutation took on our community. Thanks to Jasmy and the information she'd overheard, I had an idea where to search for the answers.

Hester sat in a chair near the front entrance, an old and tattered book in her hands. There'd never been anyone guarding the door before and seeing her made my stomach knot.

"Hey!" I said, "didn't expect to see you here. Good book?"

Hester looked up and smiled. "Not bad. Beats sitting here with nothing to do. Going somewhere?"

I tugged the zipper on my jacket up to my neck and pulled on the gloves I held in my hand. "Just out to get some air. That's okay, right?"

"Sure. But don't be too long. It's cold out." Hester returned to her reading.

Fresh air filled my lungs as I stepped out the front door, and I held it in for as long as I could, then let it escape through my open mouth with a loud exhale. Breath turned into white vapour in an instant.

I stood inside the portico, acclimating to the cold and stared at the spot above the steel door. Still attached to the grey brick were the silver-toned letters, the acronym for the name of the facility. Easily read by anyone from the walk out front, the name would go undetected from a distance, hidden under the portico roof. Much like Cecil himself, from afar he seemed an ordinary scientist working on a vaccine to save the world. But on closer inspection he was a mad scientist wanting to rule it instead.

A gust of frigid wind disturbed a small piece of blue plastic lying on the step near my feet. Before I could grab it for further scrutiny, the incongruent fragment flew out between the columns, catching in the bare branches of shrubs planted next to the building. Months ago, those same bushes cradled broken glass from the second-floor windows. My gaze shifted upward for a moment and rested on the boarded windows of Cecil's apartment. Another rush of air returned my focus to the plastic in time to see it sail away on the current and further from view.

I stepped onto the packed, snow-covered ground. Frozen, distorted footprints tracked along the front of the building and disappeared around the corner. Snow squeaked under my boots as I followed the well-worn trail. The overcast sky looked as though it was ready to dump more snow at any moment, and it spurred me forward.

They came into view as I rounded the corner. Five bundles wrapped in blue plastic, and I knew at once they were bodies. Each one lay parallel to the side of the building, against the wall. Each resembled a cocoon, only no new life would emerge from them come spring. Snow had almost buried the first two and partly covered two others. The last, brought out earlier this morning, the second death I was sure of, lay untouched by ice crystals. But it wouldn't be that way for long. I glanced up at the sky and blinked as a perfect snowflake landed on my nose.

The plastic was too thick to see through, and though I was curious, I didn't want to know. There had been enough deaths in the last several months, and I wanted no more; it hurt too much. Learning how many had died only solved part of the mystery. Now I wanted to learn how many more were sick and who they were.

Back inside, my footsteps echoed down the eerie and vacant hallway. Apart from Hester at the entrance, the compound now seemed abandoned. I arrived at my room and shed my outer winter clothing. My cheeks burned from the wind and cold. Static electricity snapped as I pulled a black sweatshirt over my head, and I felt my hair rise. But there was no time to worry about my appearance, I was in a hurry to share my discovery with Noah.

He did not come to the door when I knocked, so I rapped harder. I leaned closer, called his name through the door, then pressed my ear against it. After several seconds I moved on, thinking it odd that Noah wasn't in his room. I'd told him earlier of my plan to find out the true number of casualties, as we expected there were more than two. Why he hadn't stuck around to hear the answer seemed strange.

I grunted under my breath in frustration and made my way toward the basement. The cafeteria would be the next place to look, though it had been almost two weeks since our group last gathered.

Disembodied voices rose from the stairwell just before I took my first step down the stairs. My foot hovered in midair, and I pulled it back and placed it on the floor. I stepped aside and made room for a mask-covered Noah limping up the stairs supported by someone dressed in a white hazmat suit.

My mind flashed to the white blobs that injected me with mind-altering hypnotic drugs, and test vaccinations as Cecil and his team worked on the virus. Back then, I'd had no idea what he'd planned. I squeezed my eyes shut to erase the memory.

"What happened?" I said from beneath my mask. It was fortunate we had found boxes of masks, gloves, and other protective gear in a locked room in the basement.

"April, keep your friend here out of trouble." The white blob I recognized as Drew, placed a gloved hand on Noah's shoulder. Tired green eyes looked at me from above his mask.

"Don't worry, I will," I said moving into Drew's place next to Noah and wrapping my arm around his waist as he draped his over my shoulder.

"Sorry, I'd help you get him to his room, but I've got to get back."

"Thanks, Drew," Noah said with a nod of his head.

"Just do what I said and it should be fine." Drew turned and headed down the stairwell.

I helped Noah through the door into the corridor. "So, what happened?" I said as he hobbled beside me.

"Nothing," he said.

I stopped. "Nothing? Come on, you can barely walk."

"Don't worry, I can walk just fine." Noah lifted his arm from my shoulders, and before I could stop him, he limped away.

"Noah!" I scolded, but he continued walking. His gait transformed from a limp to a normal stroll.

Noah turned, and the corners of his mouth pulled into an impish smile. "Like I said, just fine. Now take me to my room." He held up his arm, and I returned to my place beneath it and wrapped my arm around his waist.

Once back in Noah's room I flopped down on his bed. "Explain," I said, folding my arms.

"Well, I couldn't let you have all the fun."

I cocked my head and raised my eyebrows.

"Look," Noah sat beside me, "you had a plan to find out how many had died and how many are sick. I helped you with the second half." He smiled.

"What did you find out?" My voice rose with anticipation.

"First, you tell me what you discovered."

I pushed myself back further on the bed and leaned against the wall. "Well, first of all, Hester guarded the front door."

"What?"

"Yup. She asked me where I was heading so I told her I needed air. She didn't seem to care that I went out."

"Weird. So, what did you find outside?"

"There are five bodies."

"Five?"

I nodded.

"That's more than what we guessed."

I nodded again.

"Shit!" he said above a whisper.

"How many sick?" The bed jostled, and Noah move in beside me. I leaned my head on his shoulder and closed my eyes.

"Three."

"Three!" I sat forward, and my eyes sprang open like an old doll's.

"All of them are in isolation rooms in the quarantine area. There's only one iso room left."

"Are you sure they were all sick?"

Noah nodded.

"How did you see them?" I didn't think they'd let Noah roam.

"There was some emergency, so I slipped out from behind the curtain area where they'd placed me in the infirmary and did a little investigating. I've never been in there, but it's big with lots of spaces to hide. Anyway, the main door to the quarantine area had a window, so I peeked inside. When I saw no one at the desk, I grabbed a gown and face-shield from the cart outside the door, put them on and went in. I could look into each room, two on one side of the hall and one on the other."

As Noah spoke, I envisioned the rooms. Once through the door marked quarantine, there was a medical station where attending staff monitored patients' vital signs on computer screens and where they kept supplies. From there, a narrow hallway led to the entrance of four isolation chambers con-structed with tempered glass. Rooms one and three were to the left and two and four on the right. "Who was in there?" I said.

Noah shook his head and pulled in his lips. "Esther, from maintenance. Russ from the gardens."

I nodded. I'd expected he had taken ill as I hadn't seen him in the greenhouses in a few days, and it also wasn't a shock Esther had fallen ill. The two of them had grown close.

"And..." Noah paused for a moment, "Archie."

My eyes grew wide. "We need to talk to Marcus."

"Yes, we do," Noah agreed.

Once again, we didn't run into anyone on the way to Marcus' room. Noah raised his hand to knock on the door.

"Wait!" Noah's hand froze in action. "Wouldn't he be in the communications room if Archie. . ." my voice trailed.

Noah shook his head and rapped on the door.

"Who is it?" Marcus called from the other side.

"Noah and April," Noah answered. A few seconds later the door slid open.

Beth emerged from the bathroom. "Oh, hi!" she said.

"Ah, we can come back," Noah said.

Marcus clapped Noah on the back of the shoulder. "No, it's all good." Marcus turned his attention back to Beth and winked.

"Have a seat," Beth said and sat on the bed.

I looked over at the rumpled blankets. "No thanks, the floor's fine."

Beth rolled her eyes as she joined us on the floor in the centre of the small room. "Where's Caleb and Jasmy?" she said to me.

"They're in the kitchen washing dishes."

"So, what brings you two here?" Marcus said.

I looked at Noah. His eyes widened above his mask.

"Shouldn't you be wearing your masks?" I pointed to Beth and Marcus.

"They're too annoying," Beth said.

"Anyway," Noah spoke before I could respond, "we found out some information today."

"Oh! Like what? Hear any more voices in the comms room, April?" Marcus' brown gaze fell on my face. He smiled, but he still hadn't gotten over me accusing his pal, Archie, of being up to something.

"April knows how many have died." Once again Noah interjected before I responded to Marcus.

"How?" Beth said as she leaned forward and stared at me.

"Remember Jasmy said she overheard how they took the dead outside? Well, I found the bodies."

"No one stopped you?" Marcus looked surprised.

I shook my head. "Hester was guarding the door, but she let me go out. Everyone else is either isolating in their rooms or are too busy with extra work."

Beth stretched her too large sweater over her bent knees. "How many then?"

"Five." My voice cracked, and I cleared my throat. The image of plastic-wrapped bodies floated in front of my eyes.

"That's more than..."

"Yes," I interrupted Beth, "more than we thought, more than double what we knew for sure."

Marcus whistled in surprise.

"There's more," Noah spoke. Marcus and Beth turned their attention to Noah. "I got into the infirmary." There was a lengthy pause, and no one broke the silence. After a few moments, Noah continued. "Three more are sick... and Archie is one."

"Are Mom and Dad okay?" Beth looked at me.

"Yes, I saw them both for a bit this morning before I went outside. They're tired, but okay."

"Shit!" Marcus ran a hand through his thick black curls. The muscles in his biceps tensed with the motion.

"When did you see him last?" I asked Marcus.

Marcus shook his head. "I don't know, maybe a few days ago. But he looked fine."

"Did he cough or anything?" Noah said.

"What? I don't remember?"

"Think, Marcus, it's important." I stared at him and waited for him to answer.

Marcus closed his eyes for a moment. "How am I supposed to remember something like that from a few days ago? I guess he might have cleared his throat a few times."

"Are you sure?" Noah said.

"He... no, wait a minute. He coughed. I remember now. He was eating; I thought he'd choked on something. But no, he definitely coughed. It was a real choky cough, you know?"

"Were you wearing a mask?" My heart raced. Obviously, Archie wasn't as he had been eating. And we are to take turns eating so that no two people would have their masks off at the same time.

"Of course," Marcus said, "I..." he stopped.

"What?" Noah said.

Marcus shook his head. "I don't remember." He shrugged. "Anyway, what's the big deal?"

"The big deal is you could have been exposed." I glanced at my mask-less sister; a hand covered her mouth.

"Ya, I'm sure I was, I..." Marcus' dark skin paled.

"Marcus?" Beth's voice filled with an unmistakable worry.

"Wait, I remember," Marcus spoke in a quiet voice. "I was eating too."

Sixteen

History and its Repetition

We hadn't seen our parents in several days apart from the occasional brief meetings in deserted corridors. Their tired eyes said more than the words uttered from behind masks and betrayed the false hope in their voices.

Since learning of Archie's illness, I'd managed two more fact-finding missions outside the compound. On both occasions, I'd discovered another plastic-wrapped body added to the pile. With the death toll mounting and a suspected increase of sick inhabitants, their sudden absence being the only evidence, we had questions. And if the only way to get answers was to ambush our parents, then we would.

Caleb, Beth, and I stood outside our parent's small apartment. Soon the sun would rise and so would they. This was our chance to speak with them before they hurried off to the labs and locked themselves in for the day. Pleasantries could wait, but not our questions.

Caleb reached over my shoulder and knocked.

Dad opened the door. His wrinkled, blue t-shirt hung out over the front of his black sweat-pants, and the sides tucked inside the waistband. Brown disheveled hair stuck out in all directions and he held a face mask over his mouth and nose. Drowsy eyes widened, gazed beyond on us into the corridor, returned to our faces, and crinkled from the smile we could not see under his hand. "What a pleasant surprise. Come in," he said and shut the door as we stepped across the threshold. "Maggie, we have visitors!" Dad called.

Mom emerged from the bedroom that opened into the living/dining area and closed the bedroom door behind her. She adjusted the mask on her face and tied the belt of her green robe tighter around her middle. Her brow knitted together. "Is everything okay?"

"Yes, Mom. We're fine," I said.

Relief crossed her face, and her shoulders relaxed. "Good and I'm glad to see you're all wearing your masks."

"Can we talk with you?" Beth said.

Dad motioned for us to sit on the condo-size, blue couch in the sitting area. "Sure!"

The moment we sat; Caleb asked his rehearsed questions first. "How many are sick? How many dead or dying? How quick is this thing spreading?"

"Well, you don't beat around the bush, do you, son?" Dad carried over a padded dining chair from the round table sitting in front of the window and set in across from us.

Caleb shook his head. "There's no time for that. Not now."

Mom glanced at Dad. "Perhaps now isn't the right time."

I adjusted my mask. "Now is perfect and maybe the only chance we get."

Mom's eyebrows rose. "What do you mean by that?" She sat in an old recliner.

Beth flopped against the backrest of the couch. "Please, Mom, Dad, answer the questions."

They hesitated at first, claiming they didn't want to incite unnecessary panic. I told them it was too late for that. Those of us who didn't know what was going on panicked in our heads, made up scenarios, not knowing what was true and what wasn't. Not understanding had to be worse than knowing. At least if we had an idea, we could do something instead of speculating the worst.

After explaining our feelings and fears, they finally gave us the information we sought. Their words satisfied the need we had to understand and eased our worries.

"So, Archie is alive?" I found it hard to believe, and it confirmed that Esther and Russ had succumbed to the infection.

Mom nodded. "Yes. And he's even improved, but we haven't figured out how yet."

"Marcus will be happy about that," Caleb mumbled.

Beth shot him her icy glare. "Doesn't it show in his blood?" Beth turned her attention back to our parents.

"Unfortunately, he's refusing to cooperate. Says he's tired of being a pin-cushion." Dad stood up from his dining chair and paced the small living area.

"Is this strain more virulent than before?" I thought of Jasper, and how long it took for him to succumb to the illness.

"No, it's about the same. Other than Archie, who is recovering, the longest I've seen was four or five weeks. Some pass much quicker. It all depends on how strong their bodies are to begin with."

"Jasper seemed longer, eight weeks or more. His cough started soon after we arrived at the house which I thought was strange—incubation period and all that." The images of Jasper rolled through my mind like a short film.

"Everyone's different," Dad said as he sat again.

"So, no one young has contracted it, at least not yet?" Caleb asked for the second time. "There are some I haven't seen in a while."

"No, Caleb." Mom reached out and placed her hand on his knee. "So far it has been only the older adults. I think many people are scared and staying in their rooms when they can."

"Which is where you three should be," Dad interrupted.

"Your father is right. Now we have to get back to work." Mom rose to her feet and Dad followed. "And wear your masks at all times, even in your rooms if you visit with someone. There's still a chance of transmission before symptoms."

I looked over at Beth, remembering she and Marcus hadn't been so careful.

"And you'll let us in on any other changes? If anyone else gets sick or dies?" My eyes darted between my parents.

"Yes, Av. We'll do our best to keep you informed as much as we can. We have to have some secrets." Dad winked. His tired eyes smiled for a moment before returning to a look that showed an unsure future.

We stood and allowed our parents to walk us to the door. I still had so many questions, but they would have to wait. For now, I had to wrap my head around the information they had given us. There was hope and that came in the form of a man named Archie; a man I didn't trust.

Two weeks later Archie made a full recovery. After three negative tests for the disease, he returned to work in the comms room. How he'd survived was a mystery as he continued to refuse further blood work. In that same period, though, two more became sick—and both were Butterflies.

The first to fall ill was a girl named Justice, according to Cecil's records. She was one of the unlucky ones. The hypno-drug had wiped her memory, and she remained in a zombie-like trance. Justice had contracted the illness when she wandered away from her room. They found her in the infirmary, in one of the isolation rooms three weeks earlier.

She had not been wearing her mask, and no one saw how she came to be in the infirmary.

The second Butterfly to fall ill was the little redhead boy I so often saw in the cafeteria staring at nothing. His name was Luke and like Justice, he never regained his memories and remained in a trance.

It didn't look good for Justice and Luke or any of us now we knew we were susceptible to the disease.

The fear was palpable. People stayed as far away from each other as possible. While doing chores we kept our distance and conversation to a minimum. Unlike before, we no longer moved freely, and we completed the same tasks with the same residents daily. Inhabitants could only travel between their rooms, place of work, and the cafeteria to pick up food. To keep everyone from gathering at meal time, alphabetical order dictated the schedule. Those who had accommodations in the East corridor had to move to the vacant rooms within the north or south corridors as they came equipped with dumbwaiters and laundry chutes. Lydia and a small kitchen staff moved to the unused suites in the basement, as did Marigold, one other surviving engineer, and two older Butterflies for laundry and maintenance duties. A week later, they locked down the compound. The medical staff and engineers were the only ones with access to the entire facility.

Shut inside my compact room, memories of living in a hypnotic state at C.E.C.I.L., occupied my mind. I anticipated for the door to open to someone dressed in a hazmat suit, pushing a cart into the room. I expected to feel the cold and wet wipe of an alcohol swab on my arm. The thought of needles, filled with trial vaccine or hypno-drug, jabbing my flesh made me cringe. Food arrived via the dumbwaiter as did any communications about our current circumstances or other matters. This time, my existence within the confines of my room did not go unnoticed. I was lucid and aware. This time, I was a part of every passing second while history repeated itself.

Seventeen

Respite

Five weeks, three days, eight hours, and twenty-one minutes—that's how long the imprisonment lasted. It was near the end of March, I'd turned twenty, and we'd survived the crisis.

Five weeks, three days, eight hours, and twenty-one minutes without human contact or conversation. Music playing on an old device was the only time I heard other voices except for mine—and his. Cecil's voice continued to whisper in my ear when I slept. The noise in my head convinced me it was not a dream but a memory. *How many times did I wake up in that locked, upstairs room of the old house to find him loitering about in the dark?*

I'm quiet. My ears prick to the sound of footsteps and a stifled cough. Every muscle in my body twitches, urging me to roll over. I am desperate to know if the late-night visitor is Jasper. But my imagination proves stronger than my desire, and I don't move. It might just as well be Cecil, a little voice inside my head warns. In the same moment, a familiar smell wafts towards me, and I am glad I stayed still. The pointy nail file I'd slid under my mat comes to mind.

I shook the rest of the memory away. On most occasions, he'd left food and other necessities behind, but there was something else. Somehow, he'd planted words in my head. A jumbled mixture of letters and numbers, cryptic messages, and pure drivel, none of which made sense.

Five weeks, three days, eight hours, and twenty-one minutes without Noah—far too long. But he had devised contact between us, so there was that, at least.

The first message had appeared on the tray next to my food, the words *For April*, written on the folded paper. I'd hesitated, worried about its origin and contents. The note caused an occasional glance while I ate. Afterwards, I'd picked up the stationery and turned it around, inspecting it as though the information would pass to me through osmosis. The letter surprised me and reminded me of the one from Jasper that I'd found in the laundry chute so long ago.

A2,

I am sorry I did not answer your question. Your voice caught me off guard. I was not expecting it to return so soon.

It is imperative you never speak while facing the video equipment.

I will see you later. If you must speak keep your back turned to the camera. When I speak to you, I will keep my head lowered and continue with my work. DO NOT react to anything I say.

J.

At the time, I hadn't understood the reason for not looking at the camera. But then I also did not realize that awareness of my surroundings—of me—had just returned.

Whether it was curiosity or courage that persuaded me to read the letter five weeks ago, I can't be sure, but I was glad. Noah's words calmed my busy and agitated mind, and I read the message ten times before I wrote a reply. That was how we communicated. That was what kept me from falling apart.

Five weeks, three days, eight hours, and twenty-one minutes later, I received the last note. That note said I was free.

The door to my room slid open when I approached; the lock now disabled. I stepped out into the corridor and left lunch sitting on the tray—untouched.

My bare feet slapped on the tile as I ran down the hallway towards Noah's room. I pounded on the door and fell into his arms when it opened. He caught me, and we tumbled onto the floor. Our bodies entangled in a heap.

"It's over," he whispered in my ear and planted soft kisses along my neck, prickling my skin.

"For now," I said and covered his lips with mine.

Noah pulled away and sat. "What do you mean 'for now'?"

I sighed and sat beside him. "The only reason it's over is because the virus has run its course. It infected no one else, and those who were sick either died or recovered. Once spring hits and mosquitoes are active again, the virus will come back."

Noah jumped to his feet and pulled me up with him. "Let's go."

My eyes narrowed. "Go where?"

"Find out how many were sick when they locked this place up, how many survived. Or didn't."

People bustled down the corridor in small groups, their chatter bounced off the walls more so than it had in several weeks. While relief showed in the eyes of some, a few looked wary, like they didn't believe the quarantine was over; their masks pulled up over their mouths and noses. Others, like Noah and I, walked in confidence, free from the masks and breathing in unhindered air.

Residents made their way to the basement level and gathered in the cafeteria. I spied my parents across the room as Noah and I took a seat at our usual table, joining Caleb and Jasmy. I hugged my brother and Jasmy, happy to see both of them. People filed into the sizeable room, and I tried to notice who was missing besides the ones I knew about. Before they had confined us to our rooms, seven people had lost their lives. During the lockdown, I had no clue how many more had succumbed, but I was sure we were about to find out.

Marcus and Beth arrived last. An audible breath of relief escaped from my lips the moment I saw them. I released the grip I had on Noah's hand and threw my arms around Beth's neck.

"Oh, thank God!" I whispered. Despite my parents sending the occasional note to let me know my siblings were fine during quarantine, I was relieved to see them.

Beth kissed my cheek. "Happy to see you too."

I hugged Marcus and returned to my place beside Noah.

"Okay, everybody, can we have your attention?" Doctor Reese spoke above both the subdued and exuberant voices of the surviving inhabitants. I wasn't sure if Reese was her first name or her last, but it didn't matter. When she spoke, everyone stopped to listen. The room quieted, and Reese continued. "First, I want to say thank you. Thank you for your patience. I know it has been a difficult five weeks."

Three days, eight hours, and twenty-one minutes, my voice whispered inside my head.

"Your cooperation," Reese went on, "allowed for our team of medical and scientific staff to continue the arduous task of containing the spread of the virus. To treat and help the sick, and to work on a solution."

Dr. Reese waved her hand over the table where my parents sat.

She grew somber. "Good people were lost. And while nine members of this family perished, one survived." Reese held her hand out. Archie rose from the table, nodded his head, and sat again. "Archie's survival gives us hope we can, and will beat this virus. But it will take time. So, I ask all of you that while the disease has been clear of our facility for the last two weeks, that you continue to be cautious. If any of you has even the slightest tickle of a cough, or the hint of a fever, please come to the infirmary immediately. For now, though, we remain cautiously optimistic that the threat of disease is over."

The cafeteria erupted into cheers and whistles. Dr. Reese led everyone in a round of applause as she pointed to the medical team sitting at the table. After a few seconds she held up her hands, and the room quieted.

"In closing, and I don't mean to sound dire, but remember spring is not far away. The virus is still very much alive outside these walls. Unless we can find a new vaccination before the mosquitoes rise from their winter slumber..." She let her voice trail. "Anyway, thank you again. Please enjoy this time to reacquaint yourselves with your friends and family." Dr. Reese sat back down at the table.

People dispersed into smaller groups. Beth, Caleb, and I hugged each other again and then made our way over to the table where our parents stood. They were in deep conversation with a couple of their team members when we approached but stopped the moment they saw us.

"Excuse me," Dad said as he and Mom turned away from their colleagues and faced us. We took turns embracing each other, all of us with watery eyes when we finished.

"Is it really over?" I said.

Dad leaned forward and kissed my forehead. "Yes, for now. No one has been sick in weeks. The disease seems to have run its course."

I nodded. "And except for Archie, everyone who got sick... died. Those aren't good odds. Ninety percent died, my God."

"No, it's not, honey." Dad squeezed my shoulder.

"Mom, you look tired," Caleb said.

Mom looked as though she'd aged ten years as more silver threads weaved through her dark hair. She managed a smile. "Nothing a good sleep won't fix."

"But you're still working on it, right?" Beth said.

"Every day, until we can get this damn thing figured out."

"Why is it taking so long?" My voice sounded more frustrated than I intended.

"This is a complicated virus, honey, and we're limited with what we have here. A lot of the equipment was damaged. We've had to fix, rebuild, and improvise. It has slowed things down."

"But we're making progress." Dad smiled.

"What about Archie?" Caleb said.

Mom and Dad looked at each other. "He finally cooperated about two weeks after he recovered," Dad said.

"And?" My eyebrows rose as I spoke.

"And it was inconclusive." Mom shook her head.

Beth tugged on a piece of her hair. "What do you mean?"

"What your mother means is that we couldn't find any reason his illness wasn't as bad or why he got over it as quickly as he did."

"Marcus and Noah never got sick with the first outbreak, that's how you created a vaccine the first time," Beth said.

Mom rubbed her forehead. "While that's true, neither of them became ill, they had antibodies, which as you know means they had exposure at some point, but never developed illness. This virus has changed again, and we believe they are as susceptible as the rest of us. We tried creating a plasma-derived therapy using Archie's blood, but it didn't work."

I closed my eyes for a moment. "So, you're no closer." When I opened them again, it was to my parents looking at each other.

Mom looked away from Dad and focused her attention on me. "To finding a vaccine—no. A treatment however... well it's too early to tell but we're working on something." Mom smiled.

"Really?" Caleb said.

"Don't tell anyone. That's just between us. Understood?" Dad rubbed his hand through his hair.

I looked at Caleb and Beth, and we all nodded.

Mom yawned. "I hate to break up this family reunion, but I need to take a nap." Her eyes glistened with yawn induced moisture.

Dad mimicked her. "Me too."

We hugged goodbye but promised to meet at dinner. Then the three of us returned to our table and significant others. We sat and talked quietly among ourselves about anything and everything non-virus related.

"What's the matter?" Noah whispered to me after noticing I was no longer a part of the conversation.

I shrugged. "Nothing. Why?"

"You're suddenly very quiet."

I rubbed my hand over the back of my neck; the butterfly tattoo came to mind. "Just listening." I smiled and squeezed his hand. *And thinking,* my internal voice said. My mind replayed Dr. Reese's speech over again, word for word. *Remember, spring is not far away. The virus is very much alive outside these walls.* Her words made my skin prickle. *Will the virus trap us here again? No,* I answered myself. I'd rather die.

Eighteen

Whispered Secrets

"April, are you there?" A distant voice breaks through the haze of sleep. The pungent musk scent of cologne rouses me further.

"Mmm," I groan, then feel my semi-conscious mind drift away again.

"That's a good girl. That hypno-drug is a beautiful thing, never quite leaving the system and making one vulnerable to suggestion. Anyway, it works! Truly it does!" Cecil's whisper turns louder with excitement. "I might even venture to say there exists the possibility of bringing someone back from the brink of death. Of course, I haven't attempted that yet, but soon."

Fingertips brush against my cheek and tuck a piece of hair behind my ear. I try to open my eyelids and tell him to go away, but I am not able. Cecil's voice holds me somewhere between deep sleep and consciousness.

"Let me reveal a little secret, April—our secret." He chuckles. "Only you won't even know. Not yet, anyway." Warm, putrid breath blows over my face, and I can't cover my nose or pull away but have to endure the lingering scent.

"April, secrets are funny things. Sometimes they might be shared among small groups of people, between couples, or

kept solely to one's self. Secrets may hurt or help. Were you aware that your parents have secrets? Does that surprise you?"

"Hmmm." It is the only sound I can make.

"Well, I believe they hid part of the solution somewhere. But what Ian and Maggie don't realize is there's more, another half to the puzzle. That information is something they will need if they ever want to stop the virus once and for all. And that, my dear, is the science I'm prepared to share with you. Too bad good ol' Mom and Dad won't know the wealth of knowledge that will soon be locked deep inside your brain. So, you understand, April, the piece they figured out combined with what I will tell you is the key to solving the mystery of Butterfly Flu. It's all about manipulation, what I do best. Manipulate people, things, minds—viruses. Shall we begin?"

Whispered words echoed in my head. As unconsciousness evaporated and Cecil's whispers faded, my ears tuned in to the tapping on my window.

My eyelids fluttered open. Diffused light spilled into my room, the loud clatter of rain hitting the glass pulled me from bed.

I stared out into the world as sleet pelted against the window. The early morning sun back-lit the grey clouds, and the icy drizzle transformed the glass into a frosted pane.

The pristine white field that stretched across to the forest edge had turned into a patchwork of snow and last year's brown grass. Stiff blades poked through winter's remains. Over the next five to six weeks, the remaining snow and ice would melt away. Trees and flowers would bloom, migrating birds would return, hibernating animals and insects would waken—and the Butterfly Flu would once again become a threat.

Your parents have secrets, Cecil's whispered remarks were clearer than any other he'd spoken.

I disengaged the lock mechanism for the door and hurried up the corridor. My bare feet slapped on the tiles as I ran to my parent's apartment. With each heavy footstep, more of Cecil's words came back.

The hallway outside the apartment was empty and quiet. I knocked on the door, and a few seconds later, it slid open.

"Good morning, April," Mom said from the small couch in the living room. "Why aren't you still asleep? After your birthday celebration last night, we thought for sure you'd sleep until the afternoon. The sun is barely up."

"Because I had a dream," I said and sat in the old, black leather recliner that was too big for the space.

"What a pleasant surprise," Dad said as he entered the living area from the kitchenette with a cup of coffee in each hand. When he reached my mother, he handed one to her. "Can I get you some?" Dad held up his cup.

I shook my head, and he joined my mother. "So, what's this about a dream?" Dad blew over the steaming brew in his cup before taking a sip.

"A dream woke me up this morning." I pulled my legs up and sat cross-legged in the chair. A cold foot tucked under each thigh.

"Honey, you used to have unpleasant dreams when you were little." Mom sipped from her mug adorned with cat pictures, then placed it on the end table. She laced her fingers and rested her clasped hands in her lap.

I shook my head. "No, it's not the same. This is more like a memory."

"Of what?" Dad said.

I sighed. "Ever since we came back here, I've been waking up to the sensation of someone whispering in my ears."

Mom leaned forward. "Who?"

"Cecil."

Dad set his cup on the end table beside him. "Cecil's gone, April. He can't whisper in your ear."

I stopped myself from rolling my eyes. "No, I don't mean now, but when he held us at the house. There were times I'd wake up, and he'd be in the room. Sometimes to bring food and stuff, but I also think it's because he whispered things in my ear while I slept."

Mom's eyes grew large. "What sort of things?"

"That's the problem, I'm not sure exactly. But this morning was the first time I ever remembered his words."

Dad raised his eyebrows. "Oh!"

"Yes, he said you and Mom have secrets."

My parents exchanged glances and then focused their attention on me.

"Well, I imagine there are some. Mind you, I can't remember what that would be right now," Dad said.

Mom nodded. "Most people have some little secrets."

"But he said your secret. . . " I concentrated on the memory, feeling Cecil's hot breath in my ear. "That he believed you figured out part of the solution, and kept it from him, hid it." My eyes flicked back and forth between my parents.

Mom nodded; a look of understanding brightened her eyes. "Well, he knew we could isolate particular proteins to develop an effective vaccine for a little while. And he didn't keep it unknown to us he suspected we were hiding something more, despite our showing him all we had discovered. Everything, that is, but the problem we found with the virus itself. Kind of like finding a switch but not knowing what activates it. And if we figured that out, we felt it would lead to an effective vaccine and treatment. THAT was what we kept from him."

"April," Dad interrupted, "when Cecil told us his scheme, we stored as much as possible on those SD cards. And when we were forced back to the compound, we continued to do so. Whatever we discovered, feasible or not, we recorded that info and then we hid it inside the lockets."

"Cecil couldn't get a hold of those cards. That's why we concealed them and gave them to Jasper to keep." Mom picked up her mug and blew into her coffee.

"Any data we collected in the lab, he locked away. He wouldn't allow us to access it unless it was necessary. Cecil's demands and growing paranoia were troubling," Dad said.

"Whatever we learned about the virus, data that would eventually lead to a successful vaccine and treatment," Mom sipped her coffee, "we copied before Cecil took it from us. But something tipped him off, he just couldn't prove we had anything." Mom looked over at Dad.

Dad placed his hand on her knee. "April, I don't understand how Cecil came to believe we had info he didn't, or that we'd hidden it from him. But he wanted to have complete control of the pathogen and its treatment; it was his baby, his man-made virus gone awry."

Jasper's face flashed in front of me. *It has all gone awry,* he'd said the night he took Beth and I from the compound. "There's more, though." I shook the recollection from my head.

"What do you mean?" Mom said.

"In my dream, or memory, Cecil said there was more to the solution. That you and dad only had half of it."

"And I don't doubt that. It might have to do with the cause of its instability," Dad said to Mom, then turned to me. "In your dream, did Cecil reveal what the rest of the solution was?"

I nodded.

Mom and Dad leaned further forward, and I thought one of them, if not both, would fall off the small couch.

"Where is it?" Mom asked.

I pointed to my head; my parents looked at me with confusion.

"Apparently, it's all in here."

"What?" Dad said.

"It seems Cecil told me all we need to know."

"Oh, my!" Mom covered her mouth with her free hand.

"Well then, perhaps we should get you down to the lab and you can tell us whatever you can. It's fortunate you have such a wonderful memory." Dad smiled.

I half-smiled back. "I may have an excellent memory for everything I experience when I'm awake. Problem is, I have absolutely no idea what he told me. I don't remember any of it."

Mom sat back; her bright eyes dulled for a moment before coming clear again. "You only just remembered this information this morning?"

I nodded.

"But you've sensed it for weeks, and I am sure you'll recall what he told you in a few more." Mom's voice sounded hopeful.

I stared up toward the icy covered glass of their window. A tiny drop of water trickled along the fine cracks in the ice. The sun had emerged and melted away the early morning freezing rain. Spring was approaching. I just hoped whatever secrets Cecil trapped in my head would find a way to escape before it was too late.

Nineteen

Hypnosis

Dad shut the door to an exam room within the infirmary. "Ready?"

"As I'll ever be." Inside, my stomach knotted as I climbed onto the padded examining table. A bright lamp sitting on the desk illuminated the stark room, the overhead lights turned off.

Dad winked as I lay down. A small soft pillow cradled my head. I rested my clasped hands on my belly, took a deep breath, and closed my eyes.

A few days had passed since I'd told my parents about the strange dream. Until we understood what Cecil planted inside my subconscious, there was no point in telling anyone, not even Noah. The thought the answers to the virus might exist within my subconscious was bad enough; I didn't need the added stress of giving the others false hope.

My father had suggested hypnosis and as my mother had minored in psychology, she knew the process. "So, let's see what's inside that beautiful and complex mind of yours," Mom whispered and kissed my forehead. "Take a deep breath, April, and exhale. Focus on my voice, relax, and breathe. Another deep breath and as you exhale, your body grows heavier—your feet... legs... torso... arms...

head... all pressing down into the mattress. Breathe in... and out."

Mom's voice soothed and relaxed me. With every exhale, my body sunk deeper into the padding underneath me. My facial muscles slackened, and the tension in my forehead eased.

"Now, I will count backwards from 10, and I want you to imagine standing at the top of a staircase. With each number, envision yourself stepping down the stairs, each step sending you further into relaxation. At the bottom is a safe place. No one or nothing can hurt you. Imagine a favourite spot, like the beach or anywhere you like to relax. Relax... ten... nine... "

The staircase magically appeared, and I took a step down with each number counted. When I reached the bottom, a beautiful white sand beach stretched for miles in either direction. The sun warmed my arms, but a breeze kept my skin from getting too hot. A white reclining patio chair sat in the sand of the deserted shore, shaded by a matching umbrella.

I settled on the chair and closed my eyes. A warm breeze tickled my skin. The sound of gentle waves and distant seagulls lulled me into deeper relaxation. My mother's voice drifted to my ears, and I wondered if I was under hypnosis. I willed my eyelids to open, but they remained glued shut.

"Remember, April, you are safe, and you will recall everything I ask you and your responses. Are you in a happy place?"

I nodded.

"Good. Okay. Remember you are safe, no one can hurt you. Now, I want you to go back to the house where Cecil imprisoned you, and I want you to imagine the room."

Suddenly, the beach chair in my mind changed into a thin, blue mat. The white sand turned into an old plank floor. Moonlight streaming in through a dirty round window replaced the bright sunshine and clear blue sky. The red umbrella no longer protected me, only a large wooden cabinet stood guard. Inside it hung the clothing of the children used as lab rats to test the efficacy of the many variations of vaccine—the expendable children. My nose wrinkled at the odour of human waste rising from the buckets we used as toilets, the salt air a figment of my imagination. I swallowed the bile that rose in my throat and took in a sharp breath.

"Don't worry, you're safe, April."

My body relaxed, and I felt the hard floor underneath the mat. A dull ache pulsed in my lower back. Behind my closed lids, within the attic room inside my head, I heard his footsteps, and his nonsensical whispers.

"Cecil has just left, what has he said? What did he tell you?" Mom's distant voice caused Cecil to disappear.

Time had no meaning while under hypnosis. It could have been minutes or hours. When I returned to the present, inside the examining room, and to the loving gaze of my parents, I understood what had transpired. My father's weak smile and his gentle touch on my shoulder spoke volumes.

"Did you get it all?" I said to him, hoping something I divulged was conclusive. With no recording device to record the session, he'd scribed what I'd said or at least anything of importance.

Dad closed the notebook. "Yes, Av."

"Maybe we should try again." I swung my legs back onto the bed, now convinced what I'd reported made no sense to anyone.

Mom patted my ankle. "No, honey, that's enough for one day."

"But there's more, I'm sure there is. There has to be." I'd told them what I remembered, what my mind allowed to escape. But from the look on their faces, the information hadn't been what they were hoping for.

"Av, don't worry, this was just the first go, and we can try it again in another couple of days."

"Dad, I can do it again now, really it's okay."

"The truth is," Mom spoke. "I'm tired and hungry. We've already been down here for two hours; people might be looking for any of us."

I sighed. "Fine. Can we try again tomorrow?"

Mom and Dad looked at each other. "Okay, tomorrow," Mom said.

"Good, 'cause I'm sure tomorrow's hypnosis will reveal more. It has to."

"Hypnosis?" Marcus said as he walked into the room.

Mom narrowed her eyes at Marcus. "Weren't you ever taught to knock before entering a room?"

Marcus shrugged. "Sorry, Maggie, didn't think anyone was in here."

Dad smiled. "Do you need something, Marcus?"

Marcus' gaze fell on each of us before he settled back on my father. "Archie needs a bandage. He said he cut his finger, and I've already searched the other rooms."

Mom opened a drawer and pulled out two bandages. "Here you go. And tell Archie to be more careful. There are only so many of these."

Marcus nodded. "See you in the cafeteria?" He said, turning his attention to me.

My eyebrows knitted together. "Cafeteria?" Marcus' question confused me.

"For lunch," he clarified.

"Oh, right... lunch. Yes, be there in a few minutes."

Marcus walked out of the room and closed the door.

I sat on the side of the bed and stared at my dangling feet. Cecil's words faded, but I would never forget them. If only I would have remembered everything at once.

"Why don't you get going before others wonder about your whereabouts." Dad's voice brought me from my thoughts.

I nodded. "So, tomorrow?"

"Sure, Av, we'll try again tomorrow," Dad said.

I jumped down from the bed, hugged my parents, and left the infirmary.

The walk to the cafeteria was brief, and I didn't allow for my preoccupied mind to come up with a reason for my absence should anyone ask.

* * *

"So, you were quiet." Noah wrapped his arms around me and pulled me into a hug.

"When?" I said, my voice muffled by his chest.

"At lunch, you hardly said a word."

"Just thinking about stuff." I envisioned the white sand beach I had earlier as I underwent hypnosis and heard my mother's calming voice. But the soothing atmosphere was fleeting, and it transformed into the dreary attic room. I shuddered.

"Care to share?"

I pulled back and gazed up at him. "Not now, okay, but later."

Noah leaned forward and kissed me. The action caused my legs to wobble; he knew how to make them feel like jelly. "Okay," he said. "But if you take too long, I might have to use torture to get it out of you."

A half-smile tugged at one corner of my lips. "What kind of torture?"

"The kind you can't resist." He pulled me back into his embrace.

I closed my eyes and concentrated on Noah's trail of kisses along my neck. When he reached my ear, my body tensed as his warm breath tickled. And for a moment, I thought Cecil whispered, but it passed, and I relaxed again.

* * *

I did not sleep. What the hypnosis might uncover kept me awake most of the night. But I also worried I would be of no more help than the day before.

My parents were ready for me when I arrived at the altered examination room. Candles burned on a cart set beside the examining table. Instead of the bright desk lamp, two small lamps bathed the room in a dim yellow glow. I squeezed my eyes shut. The yellow light transported me back in time.

The room looks unfamiliar in the yellow glow of the old lamp. In one day, it has changed. It is no longer a place where hope still lives with the sun shining through the window. Instead, it has become a room with dark corners where anything or anyone can hide. I shake at the thought as I glance around the nearly empty room. The only place my eyes don't search is the locked door behind me; it only reminds me of how trapped we are.

"Are you ready, honey?"

I opened my eyes to the concern on my father's face as he waited for my answer. "Yes, I'm fine. Where d'you get those?" I pointed to the lamps.

"From our apartment, see?" Mom lifted a towel she'd placed over the shade, and I recognized the lamp at once.

"Why the towels?" I said.

125

"Oh, it makes the light less harsh, don't you think?"

If only it didn't remind me of the tattered and dented lamp from the attic room. "And the music?" I said as my ears picked up the faint melody playing in the background. I glanced around the room, but I could not find the source.

"We'd found an old CD player back in Kearney and some yoga CDs. I knew it might come in handy. We should get started." Mom patted the examination table.

I kicked off my shoes and climbed on top. My body sunk into the padding; soft coverings caressed my skin.

"We used all the blankets we had to make it softer and added a layer of memory foam from a cot in an unoccupied suite." Mom said as I nestled into comfort.

"It's nice," I said and closed my eyes. "Scented candles?" A faint and pleasant smell floated in the air.

"Yes, lavender and vanilla. Do you like?" Mom's voice soothed.

"Mmm." My body sunk deeper into the blankets.

"Are you ready?"

"Mmm," I repeated.

"Let's begin."

The voice drifting to my ears was mine, but not the words. Even my laugh had changed. It was almost maniacal, like Cecil possessed me, like he knew they would try to unlock the secrets stored somewhere in my brain. The words taunted and teased but revealed little. And after some time, my mother eased me back from hypnosis.

"I'm sorry." I swung my feet over the edge of the bed and looked at my hands as I woke from the trance.

"Sweetheart, don't worry about it. You may not have spilled all the secrets, but we got something and that is a start." Dad held up the notebook he'd been writing in while I was under hypnosis.

"Your father's right." Mom blew out the candles. "Every bit of information is an enormous help."

"Still..." I let my voice trail.

"Still—nothing. We'll give it a few more days, and we'll try again." Dad touched my shoulder. The room grew much brighter as Mom removed the towels covering the lamps.

"But do we have time?" The warmer weather was coming fast.

"We have all the time in the world." Dad flashed a smile.

I cocked my head and folded my arms. "Really?"

"No," he said in a more serious manner, "but we'll make do with whatever we have. We can't rush this no matter how urgent." Dad placed his hand on my back, and the three of us left the room.

My parents whispered as we walked up the stairs, but I paid no attention to their voices. I only heard Cecil's laugh in my ears. Hypnosis didn't seem to work, and if I didn't remember soon, whatever time we had left would be short.

Twenty

Disappearing Act

Bright sunshine highlighted the green trees, and the grass seemed to grow before me as the blades soaked in the light and warmth. The black glass of the solar panels gleamed under the sun's brilliance.

A fly landed on the window. Tiny legs washed over bulging compound eyes. Translucent wings fluttered, and the insect flew away.

Cecil's dead clouded grey eyes flashed in front of me. Flies walked over his face and nestled in his hair. The echoed buzzing of more flies trapped in a bucket of waste played inside my head. I shut my eyes and covered my ears until the memory faded.

My hand flattened against the window. I wanted out.

* * *

"Have you noticed," Caleb said as he moved a can of corn to grab a tin of peas instead, "there seems to be fewer cans of food in here."

"Well, the stock is bound to diminish. No one has gone out on a supply run for months. A good thing the greenhouses have had a great yield." I went back to packing a box with the cans Caleb handed to me.

"Exactly. Such a good yield we've hardly had to use canned goods all winter."

I concentrated my thoughts on the shelves and sorted through memories of stocking them last fall. "You're right," I said as I compared the visions with what was in front of me.

"So, who do you suppose has been in here?" Caleb looked around the room.

I shook my head. "Maybe we should check the freezers too."

The store room containing the freezers was next to dry storage. I waited in the hall with the box of cans in my hands as Caleb unlocked the door.

Six large freezers lined the walls. Three chest freezers stored meat and three uprights kept few vegetables and loaves of homemade bread as we ate most upon harvest and consumed baked goods daily.

Caleb opened the lid to one of the meat freezers. "Let's see."

The freezer was about three quarters full of frozen meat packed into heavy plastic bags and other packaging. Apart from what we'd removed over the weeks, there wasn't anything else missing. I shrugged. "That looks fine." Caleb shut the lid and moved on to the next, and it was the same as the other.

Caleb closed the door on the last upright freezer. "Well, that's the last."

"The freezers all seem fine."

Caleb nodded. "Still, we should track things better."

I cocked my head. "Really? You don't trust my memory?" I gave a half-smile.

"Yes, but recording what we take out and having kitchen staff sign it will make tracking the food easier."

"You're right. And since it's your idea, you can create the list. Now we need to get these to the kitchen before Lydia starts looking for them."

Caleb locked the door to the freezer room and stuffed the key into his pocket. "We should mention this to someone," Caleb whispered as we walked into the kitchen.

"No, not yet anyway. We need more evidence than thinking a few cans of food are missing. No point in upsetting anyone."

A not so cheerful voice yelled as we stepped through the door. "Well, it's about time."

"Sorry, Lydia." I held out the box, and she took it from my hands and placed it on the stainless-steel prep table.

Lydia raised her brown eyebrows and waited for an explanation. She folded her arms. The dragon tattooed on her right arm glared at me with beady little eyes, and its nose moved as the muscles beneath contracted.

"Sorry, my fault," Caleb interjected. "I wanted to show April something before coming here."

"Hmph! It's always your fault." Lydia sniffed and furrowed her brow.

Caleb shrugged. "What can I say, one-track mind."

"Whatever." Lydia dismissed us with a flick of her hand, fingernails chewed down as far as possible, disfigured each of her fingertips. She turned back to the box of cans and ignored us.

"Caleb, you've got to stop doing that," I whispered as I pushed open the door.

Caleb batted his blue eyes. "Doing what?"

I rolled mine. "Always telling Lydia it's your fault and pissing her off. She will complain and next thing I'll be doing this job with someone else."

"Ah, don't worry, Lydia's no threat."

"Ever notice the size of her arms? She could lift you up with one hand and hold you above her head if she wanted."

"Nah, she likes me." Caleb winked as we stepped into the cafeteria.

Caleb and I sat at our usual table and waited for the others. "So, think it happened during the quarantine?"

I stopped inspecting my fingernails and looked at my brother. "What? When the food disappeared?"

"Yes. Never mind, I'll ask Lydia."

"And just what are you going to ask? Didn't we agree not to mention it yet?"

"How often, during isolation, someone went into the storage room, that's all." Caleb stood from the table.

"What? Now?"

"Yup! Anyway, I might not get another chance." He walked away before I could say anything else.

Caleb had yet to return by the time the rest of the group gathered at the table. Even Marcus arrived before my brother. I fielded their questions as to his whereabouts with shrugs and shakes of my head, avoiding further interrogation as we lined up for lunch. Caleb returned moments after we all sat back down and started eating.

"Aren't you getting any food?" I said, noting Caleb did not have a tray.

"Already ate," he said.

"How d'you manage that?" Noah wiped his mouth with his hand.

"Lydia fed me in the kitchen."

I glared at my brother.

"Told you not to worry about it." Caleb winked at me.

"So, I heard something kinda interesting." Marcus drank from a large cup of water.

"Hang on, Marcus. Why were you in the kitchen?" Beth questioned. She sat on Caleb's right side and turned her body to face him.

Our table grew silent. Marcus moved closer to Beth and looked around her at Caleb. Jasmy, seated on my brother's other side, put her sandwich down and focused her attention. Noah pushed his tray over to his right and folded his hands on the table in front of him and leaned forward. "Yes, tell us," he said.

I glared at my brother across from me and gently kicked him under the table as a warning.

"April and I noticed some food missing from storage so I asked Lydia how much she'd taken out during quarantine."

I slumped back in my chair and deflated. I should have kicked him harder.

"Don't worry, April, I didn't tell her we were missing any. I told her I needed the info for our inventory control. She said she'd figured on that and kept a list." Caleb pulled out a folded piece of paper from his pocket and set it on the table in front of him.

"Were you going to tell us?" Beth said.

My eyes fixed on the folded paper Caleb had pushed in front of me. I didn't have to look up at my sister to see her glare. I felt it burning a hole in the top of my head.

"Relax, we just noticed it today," Caleb answered Beth.

"Just today? We've been out of quarantine for two weeks now."

I picked up the paper and unfolded it. "She barely took anything," I said as I read Lydia's neat handwriting and tossed the list back on the table.

"She said she didn't have to. The yield from the greenhouses was enough, and she had plenty of supplies in the pantry, refrigerator, and walk-in freezer. They didn't need much from the extra storage area." Caleb retrieved the paper and stuffed it into his pocket. "Just like now. Today was the first time we had to go into the dry storage since quarantine."

"What does that mean?" Jasmy's soft voice broke the temporary silence that had fallen on the table.

"Well, it means," I sighed, "that someone may have stolen the food."

"But you can't be sure of that," Noah spoke.

"Between Lydia's list and what I remember was in there before, I'm sure."

"This might not be related, but I heard something else might be missing." Marcus said.

"Really! What?" For a moment, I focused my attention on Marcus.

"A wheelchair. Overheard Drew mention something about not being able to find the one with the squeaky wheel kept in the infirmary."

"Well I doubt it's related, someone probably put it somewhere else. The food though, we should tell someone, Mom and Dad." Beth stabbed three peas with her fork and scrunched her face before putting them in her mouth and swallowing them whole.

"No!" All eyes glued to my face. I lowered my voice. "We need physical proof. Caleb and I will monitor the room. Once we've gathered enough evidence, then we'll say something. Until then, no one says a word." My heart fluttered.

Beth saluted. "Yes, ma'am."

I cocked my head. "Beth."

She held up her hands. "Don't worry. I won't say a friggin' word. Again. Come on Marcus." Beth grabbed her tray and stood up with Marcus trailing behind her.

"Looks like we have another secret to hold on to." Noah sat back in his chair and stretched his arms over his head.

"Not for long, just until we're certain." I pushed my tray away with my half-eaten lunch.

"Wait, I thought you were sure," Noah said. His voice tainted with a hint of disapproval.

"Yes, I am, but my memory won't be proof enough for everyone. So, we need solid evidence." I rubbed my forehead.

"April, if Caleb hadn't mentioned it, would you have told me at least?"

Caleb's chair squeaked across the floor as he pushed away from the table. "Time for us to go. Not getting involved in your squabble. Come on Jasmy." Caleb held out his hand to Jasmy. They were both out of sight before I could even register what was happening.

"Well?" Noah sounded impatient.

I shook my head. "Not right away. I've learned since telling everyone about what I'm sure I overheard with Archie, that unless there's absolute proof, no one will believe. Marcus taught me that."

Noah nodded. "Sure, I get that, but there's something else you aren't telling me. What about the hypnosis?"

"What?" My heart thudded.

"Marcus told me he walked in on you and your parents the other day. Said you mentioned tomorrow's hypnosis, and that you looked secretive. What's going on with you?"

"Good, 'cause I'm sure tomorrow's hypnosis will reveal more. It has to." My voice replayed inside my head, and my cheeks flushed. "Nothing's going on." I dropped my gaze to my clasped hands.

"Really? And here I thought you wouldn't hide anything from me. Got to get to the greenhouse. Aya's starting today." Noah reached for his tray.

The mention of Aya conjured her dark flawless skin, stunning green eyes that pulled you in to her gaze, and her not-quite-bald, perfectly shaped head. The young woman was striking with personality and confidence to match. Even her full name, Ayanna, was beautiful. She was Cecil's perfect specimen. I shook my head and fixed my attention back on Noah. "Wait! Can't we discuss this?" I rested my hand on his arm.

"What's there to discuss? I asked you what's going on and you said nothing, and I know that's not true. So, clearly, you don't trust me."

"Of course, I trust you."

"Well, you have a funny way of showing it. I've got to go."

"Noah, I'm sorry, I..."

Noah turned back. "No, April, I'm sorry for believing you wouldn't keep secrets from me." Noah didn't wait for any response, and he walked away.

Everyone has secrets. Cecil's voice whispered inside my head.

"Oh, shut up!" Heads turned and looked at me.

I stared at my hands for a moment. Noah was right. I had secrets—too many to tell, too many to keep, and too many to have to remember.

Twenty-One

Clarity

The silver-toned box sat on the bookshelf between two enormous scientific volumes I remembered from home. They were a few of the possessions my parents brought to the Contagion Eradication Centre for Intelligent Life when they'd first agreed to work with Cecil at the compound. But they didn't realize at the time they would become imprisoned there.

The box, like my head, also held secrets. On top of it was my grandfather's pearl-handled pocketknife. The same one Caleb used to carve his alphanumeric message inside the wardrobe at the old house. At the time, he was just coming out from under the influence of the hypno-drug.

"Go before too late," I whispered as I picked up the knife and envisioned the carving of the characters G-O-B-4-2-L-8. Beth and I had found the knife inside a shoebox within the cabinet and used it to escape from the same old house weeks later. Caleb still didn't remember carving the cryptic warning or placing the pocketknife inside the carton hidden in the wardrobe.

The pearl covering on the handle was off centre, held in place by a small, rusty screw at one end. I pushed the piece over a bit to show the recessed area underneath. The space was empty, the key once hidden inside, now placed elsewhere. It was not a regular key, but one my father fashioned with what looked like an infinite symbol welded perpendicular to a short stem. The knife was another instrument used for hiding surprises.

I put the pocketknife back on the shelf and picked up the silver box. My fingers traced over the butterfly engraving; leftover soot smeared across my fingertip. The black smudge reminded me of the fires set at C.E.C.I.L. First, by Jasper to let everyone free and destroy what Cecil built. Then later, smaller ones we presumed set by Cecil on one of his many returns to the compound as he searched for the secrets he was sure my parents hid. My parents had concealed the metal container inside the framework of a couch he set on fire along with other items in the small apartment.

The unlocked box opened with ease. Inside, my and Beth's gold, heart-shaped lockets nestled in the indentations created for them in a metal tray. The tray was the only way to open the refashioned lockets with the help of the infinite key which lay loose between them. I picked up the key and pressed the end into its matching infinite-shaped slot. This actioned tiny, flattened steel pins to spring from the sides of the indentations in the tray. The pins entered a narrow slit along the edge of each locket and the hearts popped open.

"Sorry, I took so long. I couldn't find the tea you like." Mom stepped out of her bedroom and into the compact living room. "But then I remembered I stored it on the shelf in my closet." She grinned and held up the box of lemon herbal tea.

"Aren't you worried someone might find this?" I shut the golden hearts and closed the lid on the silver box.

Mom walked over to the kitchenette. "No. Besides no one is looking for it and no one would think anything hiding such important information would be out in the open."

"Hidden in plain sight," I commented and replaced the box on the shelf.

"Exactly!"

"Mom."

"Yes, honey?"

"I never told her; you know."

"Told who, what?" She called out over the sound of the running tap as she filled an old kettle.

"Beth, about her locket. Not until much later."

Mom turned. "That's why we told you all those years ago. We knew you could keep a secret." She smiled.

"Even when Beth discovered mine around my neck back at that old house, I didn't tell her she had one exactly the same. Not until we found the silver box; I had to tell her then."

A snippet of our conversation popped into my head.

"This heart was a gift from them for my thirteenth birthday."

"And mine?" Beth rubbed her bare neck.

"There was one for you, but it was a secret, until you turned thirteen."

"So, why didn't you tell her when you first remembered there was a locket for her too? You could have told her then." Mom grabbed two cups from a cupboard.

"Because she didn't remember the necklace from before, and I didn't want to upset her. It was bad enough that I suddenly had something to remind me of you and Dad and she still had nothing, not even memories. Even my old pyjamas from home had hung inside the old wardrobe." *THOSE PY-JAMAS ARE YOURS!* Beth yelled the day we'd discovered them. "There was nothing of hers in that cabinet," I continued. "And in the shoebox, besides the pocketknife—Caleb's

138

old teddy. Though when we first found it, neither of us remembered the stuffed toy."

"How about some of those cookies that Lydia makes?" She changed the subject, and I nodded.

"Why is that, Mom?"

"What, honey?"

"Why wasn't there anything of Beth's? Parts of that night are still a blur."

The kettle whistled. Mom placed tea bags in each mug and poured in the boiling water. "Here." She handed me a cup and sat beside me. She placed a plate of cookies on the table.

"Haven't we discussed the night of our abduction?"

"Yes, but not in significant detail, and I feel like something is missing from that night. What has come back to me, is I remember visiting the compound before we ended up staying permanently and against our will. I guess it was early days, and sometimes, the three of us spent the night or weekend. I remember being mad you wouldn't let me stay at home by myself. Most of the time, though, we stayed at Gran's." I thought of my grandmother, while we didn't speak of it, we all knew she'd suffered the same fate as everyone else.

"Well, in the beginning you were only fourteen and your father and I had to be away for days sometimes weeks at a time. There was no way we would have left you by yourself. When you turned sixteen, we were on the verge of a pandemic not caused by the virus we'd set out to work on but an entirely different one. One that appeared, it seemed, without warning, a new pathogen. The best thing was for you to stay with us, or your grandmother's in the country. At least there, you were only an hour drive away from the compound. Are you sure you want to rehash this?"

I nodded.

Mom sighed, then blew on her tea before taking a small sip. "Ooh! Much too hot!" She set the cup on the table.

I laced my fingers and squeezed the heels of my hands together, wanting my mother to get to that night, but I waited patiently. *Patience is a virtue;* my father's words whispered in my head. I couldn't help but roll my eyes.

"Okay, where do I start?" My mother said. "Your father and I returned to the compound for another stint. When we learned it would be at least a month, the longest rotation yet, your father left to get the three of you from your grandmother's. We couldn't leave you that long," she began. Her words prompted me to pay close attention. "A few days after he returned, Cecil told us only those he deemed worthy would stay at the compound. A global pandemic was imminent, and this unknown virus spread faster than anything we'd seen. How could it not? Mosquitoes infected people who passed it on to others. Anyway, Cecil's reasoning was unacceptable to us, and we refused to play a part in his insanity, so we resigned. He tried to convince us to stay. Before leaving, we saved the information we'd learned without his knowledge and wanted to share the discoveries with the National Microbiology Laboratory in Winnipeg. We had options." Mom took a sip of tea. "It didn't take us long to grab our suitcases and get out of there and drive home."

"And Gran? Why didn't we get her?"

Mom's eyes misted. "The intention was once we had everything in place, we would pick her up the next morning and take her with us."

"But you never got the chance."

Mom shook her head.

"Then what?" I said.

"Well, I remember it was close to dinner by the time we arrived home. Takeout restaurants, grocery and pharmaceutical stores were the only things open, and they had reduced hours. People locked themselves in their homes; others had moved further away, hoping to escape the disease by going to the country. The virus scared everyone. Anyhow, your father called his contacts and made plans while I scraped up something to eat. After supper, you asked me for a needle and thread."

"Because I wanted to sew on a button to replace the eye on Caleb's bear." The memory now clearer than ever.

"Yes, it upset him losing the teddy's eye, and you wanted to fix it. He was only eight."

"Grandpa gave him that bear."

"That's why he was so attached."

I nodded. Our maternal grandparents had been a huge part of our lives. When Grandpa died, it was a tough time for Beth, Caleb, and me, being the first family death, we'd experienced.

"Anyway, you planned on fixing it after your bath."

"Then I put on my orange pyjamas, placed the button in the little pocket and went to my room with the bear and sewing kit." The fine tendrils of memory grew.

Mom brushed away cookie crumbs from her lap. "Your intention was to fix the bear before Caleb fell asleep."

I reached up toward my empty neck. "I always wore the necklace, even to bed."

"Every day since your birthday."

"And Beth? Where was she?"

"Beth was in a foul mood."

I chuckled. "Doesn't surprise me."

"I can't quite remember why, but when she saw you in your pyjamas, it seemed to push her over the edge and she stormed off to her room."

"'Cause I wore them more to aggravate her than because I liked them." I tapped my fingertips against my forehead.

"Well," Mom waved her hand in the air, "I retrieved the bear from you and told you to fix the eye in the morning. We said goodnight, and I left. Then I checked in on Beth who was asleep, checked on Caleb and tucked the bear under his arm, and then your father and I turned in."

"Maybe two hours after we fell asleep, we woke up to Cecil and his thugs standing in our bedroom. Archie was with Cecil that night."

My eyes widened in disbelief. "What? He helped abduct us?"

Mom pressed her lips together and narrowed her eyes. She spoke with a tight voice. "Like so many, he was following orders, thinking it was for the best. Cecil said he wasn't taking no for an answer, and we were helping him and moving into the compound, permanently. He promised us no harm would come to any of you if we did as told. We had no choice, and his thugs led us to a waiting car in the middle of the night with only the clothes on our backs. Ian and I pleaded to have all of you ride with us, but Cecil refused, promising you'd be right behind in the van. Back then, we knew nothing of the hypno-drug he'd created to keep you and the other children under his control. And he used it on you that night and every night after." Mom wiped at her eyes. "The only reason you and Caleb had items from the house was because you had them with you in bed. Beth, I recall, did not sleep with any stuffed toys, and I think she had fallen asleep in her clothes. I imagine once we reached the compound, they destroyed the clothing. As for your pyjamas, who knows why they kept them."

I sat in silence, my memories from that night as clear as if it had happened only yesterday. My body remembered too. The pressure on my arms and legs as they held me, the tape over my lips, the sharp poke in my arm, the paralysis of limbs, and of mind. Cecil's *move them out* cry resounded in my head.

Twenty-Two

Night Whispers

There was scant conversation amongst our group as we sat at our usual table in the cafeteria. Forks scraped over plates, and we shoveled food into our mouths.

"So," Caleb said after he swallowed his last mouthful. "There's no more canned peas in the stockroom."

Beth wrinkled her nose. "Hmph, isn't that a shame." Peas were her least favourite.

"And almost out of canned beans too," Caleb continued.

"Plenty of fresh vegetables in the greenhouses," Noah added, speaking for the first time since we'd started eating.

"And there's a supply run coming up soon, so I'm sure we'll find more food." I looked at Noah when I spoke, but he kept his focus on his plate.

"Are you going?" Marcus said to me.

"Well... I don't know if I'll be going yet, but... " I didn't want to go, though it was my turn. It wasn't only because the vaccine no longer protected against the mutated version of the Butterfly Flu, but I hoped to have another hypnosis session. Two weeks passed since the last one, and we were no closer to uncovering the mysteries buried inside my brain. I couldn't help but think the next time would be different.

"If you go, you'll have to wear one of those hazmat suits," Beth said.

"That will be okay, right?" Jasmy joined the conversation.

I shrugged. "Guess so."

"Don't worry, it'll be fine." Noah pushed his plate aside.

The silence returned to the table and one by one the others dispersed until only Beth and I remained in our chairs.

"Sooo, I've noticed things between you and Noah seem a little... off. What happened between the two of you?"

"The quick version, I kept something from him, personal stuff, and he's not happy about it." I hadn't told Beth about my hypnosis sessions either, though I'm sure Marcus told her what he'd overheard since he'd told Noah.

"Only because he cares about you, and he's worried. All of us are." Concern registered on Beth's face.

"Beth, I'm fine, really. There's just some stuff I have to work through on my own."

"Hey, I get it. And things between you and Noah will get better." My sister offered words of encouragement.

"Really? 'Cause he's hardly spoken to me the last three days. 'Don't worry, it'll be fine' are the most words he's strung together and directed at me." I pushed around what I left of my lunch with my fork.

Beth nodded. "But it's something. And if you think about it, even if it didn't exactly sound like it, he was reassuring you. Noah will come around." Beth patted my hand and rose from the table.

I pushed my tray away and stared at the mural on the wall in front of me. Captivated by the painting, I wished I could step inside and escape to a free and safe world. Beth's "see you later" drifted to my ears. I raised the fingers of my left hand in a week wave of goodbye and drifted back to my daydream.

* * *

My eyelids fluttered open. The full moon outside bathed my room in a soft glow. Several days had passed since the last time I woke in the early morning hours as I learned to live with Cecil's mysterious whispers. Though in two more days I hoped we'd learn the meaning in its entirety.

Fragments of nonsensical dreams faded as I sat up, wide awake. There was no point in trying to sleep. A pre-dawn stroll, something I hadn't done in a while, would be the quickest way to settle my brain enough to fall asleep. I shed my pyjamas, and pulled on yesterday's clothing, then stepped out into the corridor.

As I approached Noah's room, I slowed and trailed my fingertips across the door. Part of me hoped he hadn't locked it and it would glide open with my touch, but it remained sealed.

I glanced at the closed door of my parent's apartment as I padded through the exit connecting the north and east halls and continued my stroll along the eastern corridor. At the far end I made a right turn and walked through the entrance to the southern hallway. There was an eerie peacefulness in the compound in the middle of the night. When I reached the end, I turned right again into the western hallway and headed down the stairs. I hesitated a second at the entry to the main level as I considered walking by my old room for a moment. Just as quickly I changed my mind and continued down the stairwell on my way to the cafeteria.

The mumbled words floating through the air were difficult to understand. I tiptoed from the cafeteria to find the source, recalling the memory of overhearing Archie and a mysterious voice. If it was Archie again, somehow, I'd finally get the proof he communicated with someone outside the compound.

A quiet chuckle echoed. The yellow light in the communications room glowed out into the dark hallway. I stood outside the open door with my back against the wall and listened to the hushed discussion. My heart thumped.

Archie's voice came from the room. Another, more muffled tone responded. I held my breath and focused my attention on the conversation.

"What's that? Please repeat. Over" Archie said in a louder voice.

Static emanated from the room, followed by a strange voice. "How much longer?"

"The radio!" I whispered in a voice barely audible to my ears and inched closer to the open door. I knew I could peek around the frame and investigate the room without being caught. Archie sat at the desk with his back to the entrance. But I closed my eyes and listened instead; the risk of him catching me was too great.

"Not much longer. Over," Archie said.

"Didn't you say that last week, and the week before that? I'm gettin' tired of waitin'," the radio voice responded followed by a loud crackle.

"Look, it's not as simple as you think. There's got to be a foolproof plan, and I almost have one worked out. Over."

The radio crackled again. "What's there to plan? Just–" More static interrupted the radio voice. "... girl and..."

"Hang on, you're breaking up again. Over. Stupid radio," Archie grumbled. A bang made me jump. "Come on!"

I peeked into the room. As assumed, Archie sat at the desk with his back to the door. He slapped the side of the radio. His back straightened for a moment, then he returned to hitting the radio and adjusting the knob.

My heart beat in my ears as I pressed myself against the wall. I closed my eyes and exhaled a slow breath.

The radio popped, and the voice came back. "Well, you better come up with the rest of your plan and soon. I killed four mosquitos today."

"What are you worried about? You're protected. Over."

"Ha! So, you keep sayin'. And if it don't last, then what? You didn't even get any."

Archie sighed. "Nope, but I'm living proof the other stuff worked, and once you survive, you're immune. What more proof do you need? Over."

The radio cut out again. "... need is... girl... so we can..." More snaps and pops interrupted his words.

"Damn radio!" Archie said and by the sound that followed I knew he'd hit the side of the equipment again, though much harder.

"When?" The voice came back loud and clear.

I jumped and gasped. My hand flew to my mouth, and I readied myself to run. My heart raced as I waited for a response of any kind from Archie.

There was a long pause before Archie spoke. "Maybe sooner than you think."

I slinked away from the communications room and into the shadows as I hurried back to my room. I'd heard enough. While I wasn't sure what Archie and the voice spoke about, the fact he hid communicating with someone outside the compound was proof not to trust him. He had concealed making contact, and that information should not be unknown.

I climbed into bed still dressed and closed my eyes. While I couldn't wait to tell what I'd learned, I wouldn't be hasty. I needed to think about what to say. It would still be my word against his. Conversations rolled around in my head and no sleep position was comfortable. Ruminating thwarted every attempt to rest. But eventually, exhaustion prevailed, and I drifted off into a dreamless and whisper free sleep.

Twenty-Three

Traitor

There wasn't enough time for terror or panic to set in as the shadowy figure that stood over my bed disturbed my sleep. Before my brain registered the presence was real, a sharp poke in my arm delivered me into a strange state of unconsciousness. And it felt like I swam inside a kaleidoscope.

A haze clouded my thoughts and stunted my emotions. Much like a fevered sleep, I drifted in and out of consciousness. Each time I floated toward awareness, I forced myself to concentrate on what I heard and sensed. Voices echoed in my skull and whispered in my ears, but neither were comprehensible. In a seated position, my head hung forward, lolling from side to side, and my body jostled. I perceived forward movement as stale air flowed through my nostrils with every shallow inhale. An annoying squeak and a strange crunching sound rose from beneath me, reminding me of rubber tires on a bumpy gravel road. I gave up on the fight to stay semi-alert and yielded to darkness.

Mere hours or days could have passed before my eyelids fluttered open again. I blinked several times and squeezed them shut. I rubbed at my closed lids and tried to bring my silent brain back to life. When I opened them again, the first thing that came into focus was a rough wood floor with marks in groups of five scratched into the board. My finger-tips brushed over the notches, and my brow furrowed as I worked to clear the fuzziness in my brain and understand why the marks looked familiar. A second later, I recalled scratching them with an old nail file to count the days of my and Beth's captivity.

The sudden realization caused my stomach to churn. I sat up, flung back the heavy grey blanket covering me, and scooted backward into the corner of the room and leaned against the wall. I drew my knees to my chest and buried my head under my folded arms. "This is just an awful dream," I whispered and rocked; my back hit the wall with each backward motion.

After several moments, I raised my head; my eyes darted around the room. This was not an unpleasant dream, but a nightmare. The horrible reality of the room stretched out in front of me, highlighted by the light shining in through a round window. I trembled, both from cold and fear. A numbness crawled up from my feet and settled in my head. Coloured spots filled my eyes and disappeared behind a white film as my lids closed. Quickened breaths matched the rhythm of a racing heart. "No!" I cried and crumpled onto my side, allowing darkness to carry me away.

A sweet hickory scent filled my nose, and I pushed myself into a seated position. I rested my head against the rough wall behind me. I didn't need to open my eyes to see I existed within a nightmare. The odour permeated the air, and my stomach turned; I opened my eyes.

A white bowl sat in the middle of the room; a wisp of steam curled and rose from the contents. The crumpled grey blanket laid beside it.

"Pfft," I uttered in indignation, refusing the offering someone had left. Instead, I concentrated on my surroundings.

The attic room was the same, but different. Other than a space heater with its electric cord threaded through a hole in the wall and a blue flashlight sitting beside it, the room was empty. Someone removed the enormous wardrobe that had stood sentry under the window. From my vantage point, it seemed someone also patched over the hole in the floor through which Beth and I had escaped not quite a year earlier. Boards no longer covered the window.

Another difference, and one that caused me to rise to my feet and investigate, was the knob that stuck out from the centre of the wall on my left.

The doorknob beckoned me, and I placed my hand on the piece of metal and turned, but it did not budge.

The faint scent wafting from the bowl on the floor caught my attention again, and I went to inspect its contents. Beans floated in a brown sauce, an unwelcome sight that stirred up an unpleasant memory. The thought of eating turned my stomach. While I wouldn't starve myself, I didn't trust that the food was simply nourishment. I would wait until I met my captor, for now the questions I had were more important than sustenance.

While waiting, I inspected the room. The old window was much cleaner than when Beth and I inhabited the place, and new caulking replaced what I'd pulled out in our attempt to escape through the window.

My eyes travelled to the floor. New boards replaced the ones we'd removed. With no tools at my disposal, I would not be leaving through a hole in the floor again. It seemed the only means of escaping was through the door.

The doorknob captured my attention again. Before, when Cecil trapped Beth and I in this room, no doorknob existed. At least now, the exit was less inconspicuous.

Clutching the metal knob, I jiggled it gently at first, but then with more force.

My hands curled into fists, and I gritted my teeth as anger succeeded the fear I initially felt. If I allowed for it to resurface it would surely take over, and I would stay imprisoned.

Blood pooled into my cheeks and earlobes, warming my skin as rage replaced anger when no one came to my calls. I stomped toward the bowl, picked it up and launched it at the door. The white bowl disintegrated, and its contents splattered. Beans and sauce oozed down the door, and fragments of stoneware littered the floor.

I stood with folded arms and glared at the exit. Whoever had trapped me would have to respond to me now. The sun beam shining through the window behind me warmed the top of my head and radiated through the rest of my body. Each beat of my heart thumped in my ears as I stared at the doorknob and waited.

The click of a key in a lock quickened my pulse. I inhaled a deep breath and held it as the knob turned. The door squeaked at the hinges. The sound surprised me as it had never made such a noise. No one could sneak in or out of that room now. Whoever stood on the other side continued to push open the door in deliberate and agonizing slow motion. My knuckles whitened as fists clenched tighter and fingernails dug into my palms.

There was no pre-conceived notion, no inkling, no telltale signs, no extrasensory perception, no reason to think I would know my captor. And yet when the door finally stood open, my eyes met with traitorous ones. The half-smile said more than any words uttered from between those lips.

We stared in silence for what seemed like several minutes, though in reality only seconds passed.

"Hello, April."

He deserved no salutation of any kind, and so I opted for just the name, and even that caused bile to rise in my throat.

"Archie."

Twenty-Four

Reincarnate

The distrust and distaste I had for the man now made sense. There was something about him I hadn't liked from the first time we'd met. The way his tiny pinched nose sat in the middle of his round face annoyed me. Everything screamed not to trust him, his mannerisms, his voice, his past as Cecil's thug. And yet people did.

Archie looked at the old plank floor. "Looks like you weren't hungry." He flicked at a bean stuck on the edge of the door, and it landed in front of him. "No worries, but you'll have to clean up the mess. Lots of supplies out in the hallway for that."

"Why am I here and how the hell did you get into my bedroom? The mechanism was locked."

Archie pointed to shards of glass scattered near the exit, ignoring me. "Don't walk too close to the door, wouldn't want you to cut your feet."

I kept my focus on his face as my bare toes wiggled a little. "Are you going to answer my questions?" My pulse quickened.

"Better take care of that first, that sauce will be harder to clean off when it dries." Archie stepped out into the hallway.

Run, my brain shouted, but before my feet received the message, he was back in sight with a broom, dustpan, and a handful of rags.

"Let's make a deal, I'll sweep up the glass since you don't have shoes but the beans, that's your mess." He tossed the rags onto the floor.

Dust rose like smoke as he swept up the pieces of the broken bowl. "There, that's better." Archie leaned the broom and dustpan against the wall. "Now, get to your cleaning."

"Not until you answer my questions." I pressed my lips together and scowled.

"One question, and yes, your door was locked." He reached into his shirt pocket and produced an ID card, "But this is a master key, and it gets me into any room I want." He winked, and it sickened me.

"How do you have that? Where did it come from?" While it didn't seem unreasonable a master key existed, I'd never heard of anyone having one. Though Cecil must have.

"Tsk, tsk, one question. Now clean." Archie pointed to the mess.

For a moment, my gaze fell on the broom next to the door, then I looked away, not wanting to draw attention to the cleaning tool I hoped to turn into a weapon. I moved toward the rags scattered on the floor and bent to take one.

Archie stepped further into the room. "Sorry about the beans, there were so many in dry storage."

I visualized the storeroom and recalled the conversation between Caleb and I about the missing stock. "So, you took the food?"

Archie shrugged. "Thought no one would notice. Guess I was wrong. Then again, you really have quite a memory." He folded his arms and rested them on his protruding gut. A smug smile pulled at one side of his thin-lipped mouth.

I shuffled closer to the door and wiped the sauce and beans onto the floor, flinging some of them closer toward the broom. Archie's body remained relaxed as he stood in the centre of the room. My proximity to the open door didn't seem to bother him.

When I finished wiping down the door, I threw the dirty cloth onto the floor and grabbed a cleaner one. I moved closer to the broom and crouched, wiping up the mess with the towel. "Looks like you missed a piece of glass." I pointed toward the corner of the room. When Archie looked in the direction, I seized the broom behind me and jabbed the end of the wood handle into his soft gut. Archie bent over and gasped.

This time was no hesitation, and I ran from the room. My heart raced as my feet hastened me down the stairs.

It would have been a quicker exit to turn left and run out the front door. But I turned to the right instead, toward the compact kitchen at the back of the house.

The image of Jasper's lifeless body flashed in my head as I hurried along the narrow hall and past the small bedroom where he'd died. All the while, my ears waited for the sound of Archie's footsteps behind me.

I stepped over the threshold of the kitchen, and my body came to an abrupt halt. In front of me was a ghost from my past, and he stared at me from his seat at the kitchen table, his wicked grin greeting me. He folded his arms and leaned back in the wood chair. The front legs hovered over the worn, black and white checkered tile as he balanced on the back legs.

"So, I don't know if you've been formally introduced." The sound of Archie's voice in my ear startled me, and I jumped. I stepped further into the kitchen and leaned against the counter. The drawer to my left was open slightly, and I glimpsed the blade of a knife.

The chair clunked on the floor as the ghost rose and towered in front of me. He kept his arms folded and tucked his hands into the armpits of his stained blue shirt. "No, not formally," he said, and his wicked grin broadened into a sinister toothy smile that did not touch his dull grey eyes. A piece of one front tooth was missing, causing the remaining part to resemble a fang. He held out his hand, chewed fingernails rimmed with dirt, as though to shake mine. Then he laughed and combed his fingers through his slicked, shoulder-length brown hair streaked with white. A pungent odour wafted from his armpit with his movement.

"But you're dead," I said, finally finding my voice.

The ghost reached into his breast pocket and fidgeted with something behind the blue material. "Hmph. Well, I was pretty banged up, but dead—no. Not like your friend, brains leaking out his ears." He wrinkled his face in disgust, but once again the emotion didn't display in his eyes.

The ghost's words transported me to the past, and for a split second the events of that day unfolded and I relived every moment.

My heart pounds in my chest as I carefully reach for my pack and the one thing I hope to trade for my brother's life. My eyes fix on Caleb wrapped in his captor's grasp. In my periphery, a flash of movement draws my attention and all I can do is watch. Everything slows and I'm paralyzed. I can't move. I can't scream. Shaun is running straight for Caleb and his captor. A loud boom interrupts the deafening quiet. The captor shoves Caleb backward as Shaun collides with him and the two of them fall over the cliff ledge. Beth screams and the passing of time returns to normal. My feet spring me forward as I spy Caleb's hands clinging to the rocky ledge, his knuckles whitening. It is only then that I notice Marcus kneeling on the ground, his hands covering

Caia's chest, blood gushing between his fingers and a puddle flowing out beneath her. There is nothing I can do. Beth cries out Shaun's name, but no reply comes from below. Caleb's fingers claw at the ground, and I am there to help. He's the only one I can save.

"Enough with the pleasant chit-chat." Archie said, pulling me out from my memories. "Banks, why don't you show our guest what we've done with the place, then get her ready, but hurry. I've got to get back."

My eyes darted from Archie to the man he'd called Banks, and I scrutinized his face. *Is it just a coincidence he shares the same last name as Cecil—this man I once called The Collector?*

Twenty-Five

Gus

The small and only two-piece bathroom in the house was cleaner than when I'd last seen it, though not by much. However, a working toilet and the fact that they allowed me to use it was far better than what Cecil permitted. Memories of having to use a bucket played in my head as I devised several plans of escape while washing my hands in the water that dribbled from the faucet.

"Hurry up!"

The pounding on the door stopped the ideas forming in my head and brought me back to reality. I stared at myself in the hazy mirror. "No matter what, we're getting out of here or die trying," I whispered to my reflection.

"Come on!" The door moved under his pounding fists.

I opened the door and stepped out into the narrow, paneled hall. Banks filled the hallway, blocking my view of the living room and front entrance. If I wanted to run, it would have to be out through the back door in the kitchen a few steps behind me.

"When I told ya you had two minutes, I meant it. Next time, I will remove the door." He flicked at the top hinge with his finger. "Put this on." Banks handed me a white safety suit like the one he was wearing.

Suddenly, I remembered the conversation I'd overheard between Archie and another over the radio, and I realized it had been Banks on the other end. "Where are we going?" I said as I pulled on the large boots attached to the pant legs. The words spoken between Banks and Archie continued to play in my mind, and it puzzled me. *Why is he wearing a safety suit?*

"Out."

I pulled the rest of the garb on, jamming my hands into the gloves fixed at the end of the sleeves. Then I pulled the hood up over my head and tucked my hair inside, zipping the suit up to my chin. "What about my face?"

Banks handed me a mask which covered my entire head and attached to the suit with some sticky material, sealing it entirely. The plastic window in front of my eyes fogged a little as I breathed.

Banks pulled on his mask and made a motion for me to lead the way toward the kitchen and the back door. The door was no longer a direct exit. Instead, a small vestibule with two more doors extended from the original exit at the back of the house. The area was like a containment room and we had to close one door before opening the next. Bottles of bug killing spray filled the small entrance.

"Well, it's about time," Archie said from the fenced-in yard as we stepped outdoors. "What do you think?" he said as he waved a hand around at the fence, and he too was wearing a suit.

Are they wearing them for protection or is it for show? Once again, the conversation I'd overheard replayed in my head.

"What are you worried about? You're protected." Archie had said into the radio's mic.

"Ha! So, you keep sayin'. And if it don't last, then what? You didn't even get any."

I focused on the sound of the voice playing in my head and confirmed it was Banks.

Archie sighed. "Nope, but I'm living proof the other stuff worked, and once you survive, you're immune. What more proof do you need?" According to Archie, it seemed there was no reason for them to fear the virus.

The conversation in my head faded as I focused on the high fence topped with barbed wire surrounding the yard. Dew on the grass glinted in the late morning sun. "Why are you showing me this?"

"In case you get any ideas," Archie said.

"There's always the front door."

Banks chuckled. "Nailed it shut."

"Take her inside." Archie turned and walked to the end of the yard to the shed and stepped inside.

"Have you unsealed it? The tunnel to the compound?" I said.

"And no one will ever find out." Banks grabbed my arm and tugged me ahead of him, then he gave me a push forward.

Once we entered the vestibule, Banks sealed the outside door and sprayed with insecticide. After several seconds, he opened the second door. The tight space was barely large enough for two people. Then he opened the door to the kitchen. He grabbed a bottle of insecticide from the counter and sprayed within the compact space and sealed the kitchen door. While my captor inspected the seal, my eyes caught sight of an open drawer to my right.

The knife blade gleamed from inside the drawer. I kept my eyes on Banks as my gloved hand inched toward the shining object.

"That should do it, just in case." Banks spoke, and I withdrew my hand before he turned.

He unfastened his mask and removed his protective gear. "Take yours off."

My heart thumped as I pealed out from the suit.

" 'Squitoes aren't too plentiful just yet, but they're comin'. Weather's gettin' warmer every day. So, my suggestion is not to venture out in the early morning or dusk. Understand?"

My brow furrowed. *Does he expect me to come and go as I please?* The confusion must have shown on my face because he answered my wondering thoughts.

"Nah, you're trapped here, but not like before. See, you can leave your room to go out in the yard or use the bathroom. Heck, you can even make your own meals. But you won't be escaping from here until we have what we want."

"And what's that?" I said as I stepped out of the boots and completely freed myself from the suit.

"The information you got trapped in your head."

I narrowed my gaze.

"Yes, I know all about it." The corner of his lip pulled into a lopsided grin, exposing his fang-like broken tooth.

"What do you want with it?"

"Well, let's just say insurance."

"Well, good luck with trying to get it out of my head. Whatever is in there refuses to come out."

"Oh, it'll come out all right. All it takes is the right combination, the key."

"And you have said key?" I was skeptical but asked anyway.

Banks smiled. "We all got secrets, April, and that one's mine."

"What's your first name?" I folded my arms and leaned against the kitchen counter. My suspicion about his identity was not only because of his surname, but there was also a resemblance I could not deny. My throat tightened, and I swallowed hard.

Banks pulled off his suit and laid it on the table. The boots rested on the floor underneath; the sleeves stretched out in front, with the gloves resting one atop the other. In that position, the suit reminded me of a much more macabre scene. Cecil's dead body sat in the kitchen chair and slumped over the table in the same way. I blinked away the image and looked back at Banks, waiting for his answer.

"Gus," he said, stretching out the s and hissing like a snake.

"Gus," I repeated, "and that stands for. . . " I knew what it was but wanted him to say it and confirm what my memory told me.

"Gossamer."

"Gossamer Banks," I whispered, and Banks smiled. I closed my eyes and envisioned the manifesto. Beth had found the book. Believing it was something else, she'd buried it inside her backpack and forgot about it until we reunited with our parents. Cecil's words spread out over the pages, his tactics, his aides, the names of the residents. My father had read parts of it to us, shown us other pages and those imprinted in my brain. "You're his brother. Cecil's brother." I heard my father's voice as he'd read the entry about Cecil's brother, Gossamer, who lived at the compound but confined to his room. *He was a dangerous man,* Dad said, *a psychopath.*

Banks chuckled. "The one and only. Now why don't you make us somethin' to eat." He brushed his hair away from his eyes.

I turned away from him and stared down at the counter. My eyes once again fell on the open drawer.

"And stop contemplating about that knife. It'll only do you more harm than good."

I envisioned an excerpt from Cecil's manifesto.

So many extraordinary people out there. People who will make this world much better with their intelligence and their talents. Talents the skeptics don't believe exist. Talents like Gus's. Gus, who knows what people are thinking before they do.

"I know your secret," I said.

"Do you? Enlighten me." He sounded more like Cecil now.

"Telepathy." My voice was not as strong as I hoped it would be.

Gus clapped his hands. "Bravo! We'd make an impressive team with your incredible memory, and my ability to read thoughts, pull hidden memories from one's subconscious."

I shook my head.

"In time, April, in time. Now how about makin' that dinner? I'm starving."

I turned around again and closed my eyes. The knife in the drawer came to mind, and so too did more of Cecil's writings about his brother.

"Again, with the knife." Gus chuckled behind me.

Somehow, I would have to make my mind blank, as blank as it was back at the compound when I'd only existed. Gus couldn't get inside my head. If my family could not reach the information locked inside my brain, neither could he.

"Oh, but I can, April, and I will."

I looked up at the open cabinet above me and stared at a can of beans.

"That's fine." Gus said, and I reached for the can.

I clenched my fist. It was bad enough that I had so many memories to contend with. Cecil's whispers in my ear, trapped information. And now Gus was in there too, rifling around in anything and everything that wasn't his business. My head was too full, and it was about to explode.

I pulled open the drawer further and grabbed the can opener lying beside the knife. Gus chuckled behind me.

Twenty-Six

At His Mercy

Sleep would not come. There was too much to consider, too much to plan. Gus had locked the door to the attic room, so while roaming around the house was permissible during the day, night was entirely different.

Moonlight fell across my lap as I sat on the floor in the middle of the room and stared up at the window. Twenty-four hours since my abduction, everyone had to know I was missing. *Or do they think I ran away? Are my parents searching for me? Is Noah? Would they bother to come to the old house?*

Archie had returned to the compound hours earlier, and I wondered if he helped in the effort to find me. If he was, he'd lead searchers in opposite directions, tell crazy lies. Maybe they weren't even looking. Maybe Archie had told them I'd confided in him and said I wanted to go. *Did he tell them he'd tried to convince me to stay, but I was adamant?* A lie like that, was close to the truth. When we first moved back to the compound, I had wanted to leave. If you stayed close enough to the truth, lies were believable.

I slammed my palm against the floor. "Bastard!" The expletive spilled out between gritted teeth. My thoughts turned to Gus. *Can he 'hear' my mind while I am upstairs, or do we have to be in the same room? Can he read them when I sleep?*

I took a chance and devised ways of escaping, but every idea seemed futile. Other thoughts tried to interrupt, but I pushed them away in case Gus was 'listening'.

Noah's face drifted in front of my eyes, and I squeezed them shut. I would not think of him or anyone. I needed to be strong, and that meant nourishment and rest and no emotional responses. With that in mind, I lay on the floor and pulled a covering up to my chin. The soft, grey blanket warmed my cool skin. My focus rested on the round window and the untouchable moon which from my position on the hard floor was now visible. As my thoughts settled, I resolved to strengthen my mind and body and look for means to escape. "And demand a mattress," I whispered and closed my eyes.

* * *

At the first thread of daylight, I began the process I hoped would lead to freedom.

Exercise reminded me of the daily and monotonous circuit training I performed in the forest simulation room while under the influence of the hypno-drug and during my awakening. For months after, I avoided any form of physical activity except for walking. But, when winter came, I developed a new routine, one that I managed, and I intended to continue while in captivity. Over the last four months, the regime had proved beneficial as my physical strength developed.

Perspiration dripped from my temples with the last set of push-ups. The lock clicked, and the door swung open on its squeaky hinges. I swept my dampened hair off the back of my neck with one hand, wiped the sweat off my face and cleared my mind before Gus walked into the room. His hair pulled back into a tangled, short ponytail.

"Just to let you know, I won't be makin' breakfast so you can fix your own. Told Archie this wasn't no damn hotel. What's the matter with you?" He scrutinized my face.

I deliberated on the colour white, conjuring a foggy image. "Nothing. Why?"

"'Cause your face is all red."

White, white, white. "I was hurrying." *White, white.* I dropped my hair.

He folded his arms. "What for?"

"Because my shirt got twisted, and I took it off during the night. I was struggling to put it back on as you were coming in." I imagined the lie in my head and tugged at the hem of the t-shirt.

Half of Gus's mouth pulled into a smile. He must have 'seen' my imaginings. "Next time, I'll knock."

White, white, I concentrated on a blank screen and Gus's smile vanished as the false images I projected faded.

I folded my arms. "Now, I want a mattress."

"Do you?"

White, white. "Yes."

"Guess I can do that. Breakfast first though, I'm hungry." He turned, and I followed Gus out the door.

Like hell I'm making yours, I glared at the back of his head forcing my intention into his brain as we walked down the stairs.

"If you want that mattress, you will."

There was no need to see his face to know he smirked with satisfaction.

I washed the last breakfast dish while Gus sat at the table. Apparently, not only was I held hostage for the buried knowledge inside my head, but I was also the domestic help. "Is that how you did it then?"

"Did what?"

I turned and leaned against the counter. "Found us in the forest because you followed our thoughts?"

Gus reached into his breast pocket and pulled out a small gold chain and wove it between his fingers. "Hmph! If only it were that easy. No, my dear brother used some of that drug he'd concocted on me. Guess it was easier to keep me locked up in my room at the compound with that crap in my system. Stuff made me unable to get into people's heads. After some time though... " he tapped his forehead, "things started working better by the time I caught up to your bunch. Course, I didn't have full use of my telepathy then. That didn't come back until later."

Again, my father's reading of Cecil's manifesto came to mind. *White, white,* I refocused and cleared the thought away, not allowing anything to come forth.

Gus's eyes narrowed at that same moment, like he'd seen what I recalled and wondered what it meant before it disappeared.

"So, it really was the food that lured the others to where you could find them."

Gus nodded.

"And how did you find us then, if you couldn't use telepathy?"

He shrugged and held the chain in front of his eyes. A golden heart charm dangled from the chain and swayed back and forth. "Well, I wouldn't say that entirely. There was a hint of telepathy, and your bunch was not as blank as the others. Anyway, once I got close enough, I sensed your thoughts, but did not understand them. Recognize this?" Gus looked away from the object in his hand and stared at me.

I recognized it. Beth and I had found the piece of golden jewelry inside one of the decorated shoeboxes hidden in the wardrobe during our captivity. I nodded. The gesture more of an impulse reaction than a confirmation as the smirk on his face told me he'd read my thoughts. I resumed my interrogation. "Did you know Shaun would charge at you that day?" The image of Shaun throwing himself at Gus popped into my head. The gunshot resounded like it just happened, and I jumped.

"That boy was blank. When he reacted, he just did. There was no time for his brain to register. Course, he caught me off guard. Not too many people have done that. Better go wash up now." The sudden change of subject ended my questioning.

Gus stayed at the kitchen table as I walked down the hall. Once inside the washroom, I replayed breakfast in my mind, sure he'd be 'listening'. Meaningless things and silly memories rolled through my thoughts while I searched the compact room.

A banana bread recipe popped into my head as I tugged on the window sash, and when it didn't open, I remembered my eighth birthday party.

Lyrics from an old nursery rhyme sang in elementary school was the memory of choice when I opened the medicine cabinet. I envisioned painting the murals at the compound, reliving each colour choice and brush stroke as I rifled through the contents. When my favourite movie replayed inside my head, I found a drug I didn't expect, though hoped to find. My eyes fell on the sharp instrument needed for its delivery, still encased in sterile wrapping. Then I recalled my tenth-grade report card, and I remembered every grade and remark as I tucked the drug and needle into the hidden pocket inside my sweats. I took inventory of the alcohol-swabs, bandages, and other first-aid supplies before closing the cabinet door.

I used the facilities, washed my hands, and splashed water on my face while concentrating on the unimportant. The rust stains around the drain, the chipped paint on the wall, all the bathroom's details occupied my brain.

"It's hot in that bathroom," I said to Gus as he rose from the kitchen table. "And I tried to open the window but..." I kept my thoughts on the action.

"Well, thanks to you, I've got Twinkle Little Star as an earworm. Anyway, you might as well go upstairs, it's started to rain. Grab a book or two from the living room." Gus indicated for me to walk ahead of him. He went into the bathroom as I continued down the hall toward the living room. But instead of going into the room, I walked to the front door, grabbed the doorknob, and pulled.

The door didn't budge.

"Told ya, we nailed it shut." Gus yelled from the bathroom.

My focus trained on the ceiling. Sheets of plywood replaced the tiles Beth and I damaged when we escaped from the attic room through a stovepipe hole we found in the floor under the wardrobe.

"That's solid too!" Gus yelled again.

My eyes wandered from the ceiling to the cobwebs in the far corner of the wood paneled room. The space looked more like a catchall area rather than a place to sit. I followed the cobweb down the wall to some old camping gear piled in the corner.

Disheartened, I stared out the front window. The rain outside pelted the ground. While the porch roof protected the window, the occasional gust of wind blew the rain sideways, and it sprayed against the glass. I placed my fingertip on the cold, hard shield and traced a raindrop as it trickled along the windowpane.

I grabbed a book with a tattered cover from a pile on an end table beside a brown couch. At the other end, sat a wheelchair, the acronym C.E.C.I.L. printed on the backrest.

"I'm going upstairs." I called to the closed bathroom door as I stood in the hallway.

The door swung open, and I jumped back.

"Good for you."

"What about the mattress? I can't sleep on that floor again."

"Pfft! Take the couch cushions. I don't sit in there."

"Hey, what happened to them, the others wandering in the woods?" A question I'd thought to ask earlier popped back into my head.

"The ones I gathered?" He folded his arms and leaned up against the bathroom doorjamb.

I nodded.

"Well, you don't really want to know," he said. He was right, I didn't. "But you're curious anyway, and afraid of the truth at the same time."

I stared at him, not knowing how to respond.

"Their minds were too far gone. There was nothing anyone could do. Call it being merciful."

Twenty-Seven

Risky Business

I lay on my makeshift bed and sank into its comfort. A fresh-smelling, spare blanket wrapped around the couch cushions took care of the scratchy, brown material and masked the dusty smell of the old fabric. The book I chose from the end table downstairs rested on the floor beside me. The wind rattled the roof and whipped the rain at the unprotected window as the day's events played in my thoughts. The compact heater vibrated, and while it didn't heat the room it was enough to take the dampness out of the air.

Gus read my thoughts while behind the closed door of the bathroom, not too far away from where he sat in the kitchen. But I needed to test how much further his tele-pathic skill reached. *Call it being merciful*, played through my mind as I ruminated on our earlier conversation. Gus had smiled as though he'd enjoyed whatever mercy he'd enacted, but as always, his eyes remained unaffected.

The rain drummed on the metal roof. I rolled onto my stomach, not wanting to stare up at the rafters any longer. The objects I'd taken earlier and hid in the inside pocket of my sweatpants drove into my pelvic bone and made me wince. Digging into the pocket, I pulled out the glass vial and syringe.

The small bottle was familiar, and I remembered the effect of the liquid it contained. My fingers curled around the glass vial and held it against my palm. There was no forgetting the drug received at C.E.C.I.L. Even in a diluted state it was effective. I'd realized that when it took weeks for the effects of my last dose to disappear. The risk was considerable, but one I was glad to take. I shook the bottle. Tiny bubbles floated up to the surface and popped.

Gus should have been up the stairs and barging into the room, ripping the bottle from my hand and scooping the packaged syringe up off the floor. He should have been confining me and locking the door both day and night. He should have known what I thought and planned. But instead of heavy steps on the stairs, there was only violent rain on the roof. Instead of Gus throwing the door open, there was only gusting wind that rattled the window. Instead of his fingers clawing and prying the bottle from my grasp, mine gently set the vial on the floor beside its plastic wrapped companion. The risk had been grand, but the result outweighed it. Up in the attic room with Gus in the kitchen, my thoughts were mine.

My fingers searched for the zipper along the edge of the cushion. When I found it, I unzipped the cover and tucked the bottle and syringe against the foam insert. A mark on the floor peeked out from underneath the cushion and distracted me. I rubbed my finger over the rough gouge. The scratch had been the last I'd dug into the floorboard, and I remembered its creation as much as the first.

"Reminiscing?"

Startled by the intrusion, I rolled over and faced the door with my hand against my chest. *How long has he been watching me?* The usual squeaky hinges had not given me any advanced warning of his entry. "Crap, you scared me." My voice cracked.

"Cause you were deep in thought, almost like in a trance."

My heart skipped at his words. "Well, I was–"

"Remembering when you were here the last time. Okay, I get it."

I pushed myself up into a seated position. "What do you want?" My ears tuned into the sound of the rain and the wind knocking at the window behind me.

"Don't you know?"

My focus remained on the storm as I shook my head.

"Lunch."

"Not hungry." I stretched out onto my back.

"That's fine, but I'm not asking if you are."

"Pfft! You're a big boy, and I'm sure you can handle it." My pulse raced with my impertinence, and I counted the rafters to calm myself. There were six of them, the same six there'd always been. One, two, three...

"Stop counting!"

Twinkle, twinkle, my insolence continued inside my head. I knew I shouldn't push him, having seen what he could do.

Gus placed his hands over his ears as though I'd sang the words out loud. "STOP!"

"Why don't you just do your thing, get the information buried in my head and let me go."

Gus shrugged. "Gotta wait till Archie comes back."

"So, call him on your radio and get him over here." My voice was flat and unemotional.

"That's not how it works. Archie calls me. For now, anyway."

"So, what? It could be days before he shows up again?"

"Or weeks."

I turned my head to look at him for a second, then resumed gazing up at the rafters. Another gust of wind rattled the window. *Oh, how the north wind doth blow*, I recited inside my head.

175

"What is that?"

"A nursery rhyme."

"Humph. So, you're not hungry?"

"No." In my periphery, he turned toward the door and stepped out into the hall. I turned my head in time to see him reach back and pull the door shut.

My thoughts concentrated on another poem regarding wind. After several minutes, I rose to my feet and walked to the door. It squeaked open to an empty hallway. I closed it and returned to the cushions; the hard lump pushed into my butt cheek, and I shifted.

The risk was considerable, as my plan developed in my head, but a blank mind would be the only way to keep him out.

Twenty-Eight

The Best Laid Plans

My racing heart woke me. "Stop!" I whispered and laced my fingers behind the back of my head, pressing my forearms against my ears. The thumping grew louder with each troubling thought as I rocked back and forth in the dark. *It's okay, sh, Mom and Dad will find me.* A long deep inhale filled my lungs then slowly escaped from my pursed lips. The pounding intensified.

I will get out of here. I chanted inside my head as I paced the room. Tingles travelled over my body; adrenaline coursed through my veins. A scream rose to my lips, but I did not let any sound escape.

The pacing helped my agitated body but did nothing to quiet my heart. Plunking down on the cushions, I closed my eyes. *Slow down,* I begged my heart, fearing it would explode at any second. *Sh! Sh!* I wrapped my arms around myself and imagined Noah. *Sh!* I rocked. Deep inhales and controlled exhales diminished the pounding in my ears. But my imagination wandered away from Noah and turned to worrying thoughts, and my heart responded with another flutter and a burst of speed. *Please, stop!* I rocked and forced Noah back to the front of my mind. This time I would not let go. *Sh! That's it.* I continued the soothing motion. I exhaled, my heart slowed, and I concentrated on Noah.

Curled up in a tight ball, a tingle crept from my feet to my head. The sound of my heartbeat reverberated off the cushion. *Sh!* My body eased another notch, and the thumping quieted. An uncontrollable shiver took over as the agitation subsided, and my hands searched for the blanket. Noah's face sharpened behind my eyelids, and I imagined his arms around me as my hand stroked my shoulder. A final violent tremble convulsed my entire body as I exhaled the last of the nervous energy. Noah's image faded as exhaustion took over. Under the blanket my muscles relaxed, and my heart resumed regular and unnoticeable beats.

I woke to daylight streaming in through the window and the faint sound of birdsongs. Last night's panic attack left me frazzled; thoughts of freedom still on my mind. I rose and stood beneath the round glass, stretched out my fingers, and touched the window ledge. "I am getting out of here."

* * *

"What's the matter with you?" Gus's voice startled me.

"Nothing." I turned away from the kitchen counter, a cup of tea in each hand, and set one on the table.

Gus sat across from me. The image of Cecil's dead face superimposed over his for a moment. I blinked the vision away and took a sip of tea.

"Well, you didn't sleep well. That I can see."

Last night's panic attack ensured I hadn't. "No, I didn't." An unexpected yawn caused my eyes to water, though it had no effect on Gus. Unlike most people, he seemed immune to the contagious nature of yawning. The entry in Cecil's manifesto devoted to his brother and detailing his psychopathy came to mind.

"No matter, you'll sleep sound tonight. Arch is bringin' in a mattress."

We hadn't seen or heard from Archie in three weeks. But yesterday, he'd finally communicated again with Gus on the radio. Archie had been busy. Dressed in protective clothing, select members with Archie as their leader, had been out searching for me every day. My parents took turns leading another group, which included Noah. When one went out, the other stayed behind to continue their work. Archie led no one toward the house. And when anyone suggested exploring the property, he told them he'd searched already and there was no sign I'd been there. He said the search would only go on for one more week. They would no longer waste resources looking for someone who didn't want finding. Someone who'd left on her own volition; a story he'd concocted and assured was true. I did not believe him. My family wouldn't give up that easily, even if they believed I didn't want anyone to find me.

Archie arrived by noon. As promised, he carried in a mattress through the wide-open doors of the vestibule and kitchen. Much to Gus's annoyance. From across the room, I recognized the mattress as belonging to a cot Cecil had brought for Beth and me a year earlier.

"Here. Wouldn't want our *guest* to be uncomfortable." Archie's voice snapped me out of my memories. "And you could have got this, it was in the shed, under your chainsaw." He glared at Gus.

"Oh, yeah! That reminds me of a pile o' wood I cut out by your place. Amazing I even got that old thing running with the gas I had. Didn't last long though, only got a bit sawed up before it died." Gus smirked as he looked at me. "Used a piece of orange cloth to mark where I left it too."

I envisioned the small stack of wood hidden under brush next to the wall surrounding the compound. My eyes widened. "By the –"

"Here, take it up to your room. Gus and I need to have a talk." Archie interrupted and shoved the small and dirty mattress toward me. Bits of grass and mud covered the edge, and a streak of grease stained the top.

Gus nodded.

Tired from lack of sleep, I struggled with the mattress as I pulled it up the stairs, almost losing my balance in the process. Once inside the room, I dropped it into place and set the cushions I'd been sleeping on, on top of it. There was no way I would sleep on that filthy thing.

I took a moment and inspected my new bed. A lump caught my attention, and it was a welcome sight. I reached over and lay my hand on the bottle hidden inside the couch cushion. My well-developed plan was about to begin, and it had to work. But before it could, I had to get downstairs and find out what my captors discussed. With a quiet mind, I tiptoed down the stairs and stood in the hallway leading to the kitchen. The conversation drifted to my ears.

"How?" Gus said.

"We all had on protective gear, but one could have come inside unnoticed."

"So, they've cancelled further searches?"

"They have, for now, though her friends and family aren't in agreement. Her mother is beside herself with worry."

"And you said some are sick?"

I held my breath at Gus's words.

"Yup, two right now."

"Lydia and... who's the other?" Gus said.

My eyes closed, and I focused on nothing, ears trained on their quiet voices.

There was a lengthy pause before Archie spoke. And while it was difficult to hear, I was certain he'd said Aya.

The veil shielding my thoughts fell with the name, but I quickly cleared my mind. While Aya wasn't part of my close group, she had become a friend as we worked alongside each other in the greenhouses. The disease may have spared my loved ones, but who knew how long their fortune would last.

"Look, we gotta get whatever's locked up in her head. Without it..." Gus didn't finish his sentence.

"Okay, we'll start as soon as I finish this glass of water," Archie said. I took a step back, forcing my mind to stay thoughtless.

Each careful placement of my foot ensured a silent ascent. I'd learned days ago where the wrong step elicited a squeak, though I thought the sound of my racing heart might give me away. Safely back in my room, I allowed my thoughts to flow as I paced. Soon, Gus and Archie would try to extract the information buried deep in my subconscious with whatever method they had devised. At the sound of a loud creaky step, I flopped down on my makeshift bed and picked up a book. I had just flipped open to a page when they entered the room. I pretended the words enthralled me and did not look in their direction. The vial inside the cushion pressed into my thigh. My heart fluttered and stomach tensed. Scrambled thoughts rolled through my head despite my attempts to stop them. I would not get the chance to make my mind permanently blank before my kidnapers invaded it.

"Interesting book?" Archie said.

Before I answered, Gus did for me. "Doesn't seem to be. She can't get past the paragraph she's trying to read. Too much going on in her head. Isn't that right?"

I stared at Gus. He folded his arms over his chest and sneered, exposing his fang.

"Oh? What's going on in there?" Archie said.

Gus locked his eyes on mine. "Hard to sort out, too many conversations, too many images." The men stepped further into the room and stood in front of me.

I slammed the book closed. "What do you want?"

"Well, I think you already know that." Archie spoke first.

"April, it's time." Gus produced a syringe and a small bottle from his pocket.

I dropped the book and sat up on the bed. "What's that?" My pulse raced.

"Just something to make you relax," Archie answered my question.

My eyes darted between them as Gus prepared the injection. "Don't worry," Gus said, "you'll remember everything when we're done. Even the things buried inside your brain. Isn't that what you want?"

I jumped to my feet; my gaze locked on the psychopath. "Don't you mean the information you want? I thought you were the key."

"Oh, I am. This is just to help. Another concoction made up by my dear late brother. I'll be able to monitor your thoughts and memories. And then there are the passwords."

My brow furrowed; hands curled into fists at my side. "Passwords? What do you mean?"

"Well, your mind is like a complex computer with intricate programs. Cecil *implanted* passwords and those will let us in," Archie said.

"Okay, let's go." Gus reached over and caught my right arm while Archie seized my left. I tore away from their grasps and bolted for the door. Just as my hand grabbed the doorknob, Archie's snake tattooed arm wrapped around my waist and pulled me away. I writhed in his clutches, and we fell backward. Instead of my head hitting the wood floor, Archie's face cushioned the blow, and he groaned underneath me. He wrapped one arm around my midriff and the other across my chest as I lay flat on my back on top of him.

"Let me go!" I screamed, trying to free myself from his grasp. While he was on the chubby side, he was strong and my thrashing proved futile.

"Maybe. You. Could. Help?" Archie panted underneath my struggles.

"Nah, you've got this. Besides, this is most entertaining." Gus snickered.

Archie's grip tightened across my chest, and I bent my head forward, sinking my teeth into the snake tattoo.

"Fuck!" Archie yelled and flung me over onto my back. This time my skull connected with the plank floor. He straddled my waist and pinned my right arm under his knee. He grabbed my left wrist and stretched my arm above my head. "Hurry!" Blood dripped from his nose.

The point of a needle entered the vein on the inside of my elbow, and Gus pushed down on the plunger.

The room undulated, canned voices whispered in my ears and inside my head. They lowered my body onto the cushions, and my legs straightened. A strange floating sensation flowed and ebbed from the top of my head down to my feet and then back up again like ocean tides. The lump in the cushion pressed into my leg, and I closed my eyes.

Twenty-Nine

Accessed Information

Tap, tap, tap.

I stretch my arms above my head; snaps and pops ripple up my spine. A quiet snort from somewhere in the room makes me smile, and I roll onto my side. A solid lump shoves into my hip, and my eyelids spring open.

Rain drums on the steel roof overhead. The sound reverberates in the dark. I rub the sleep from my eyes and sit. Where am I?

My first musing is of my bedroom back home, but that quickly changes into memories of a white chamber. I scan the darkness, but no tiny red camera light pierces the black. The thought shifts again, and I understand where I am, the room at the top of the stairs in the old house.

Moonlight filters in through the rain splashed window, casting strange shadows on the walls. The hammering overhead fades into a patter and then ends with a final tap.

A tall cabinet stands sentry below the window; moonbeams dust across its top. The presence of the sizeable piece of furniture causes my eyes to narrow. I rise and tiptoe toward it; the ghostly object appears solid. I stretch out my hand, expecting to feel the smooth wood beneath my fingertips, but the apparition of the cabinet wavers and dissolves into the moonlight.

Beth's voice echoes from behind me, and I turn to see a black form lying on the floor by the makeshift bed. I approach and just like the cabinet, Beth vanishes.

I exhale a loud breath, frustrated by the visions and sounds. "What next?"

"Next? Next you divulge what you observe."

Almost a year has passed since hearing his actual voice and not the ghostly whispers. But I recognize it the second the sound enters my ears. Cecil stands in the doorway; strange light glows behind him. He waves his hand toward the corner of the room. "Why don't we have a seat?" A table and chair materialize from out of the shadows, and he walks towards it and sits.

The bed appears more real. "No, I'll sit here," I say and sit on the cushions, pulling a blanket over my lap.

"Suit yourself." Cecil stretches his arms back and rests his silver dusted head in his clasped hands. The chair's front legs lift off the floor.

"What is this place?" I say.

Cecil leans forward. The chair's feet clunk on the floorboards, and he places his elbows on the table with his hands folded in front of him. "What do you want it to be?"

I shake my head, refusing to answer, I will not fall for any silly games.

"This is your room, of course. Well, not really. Things have changed a little. This place is so much emptier now."

"This is not my room," I say.

"Isn't it?"

I shake my head again.

"How do you know?"

"Because you're here, even though you're dead." My blunt statement catches him off guard as he takes a moment to respond.

"Am I?" The moonlight highlights the rising of his eyebrows, and he stretches. Cecil's gigantic shadow stirs a second later. My eyelids close like a nod in confirmation. "That may be physically true. But inside your mind," he taps his index finger to his temple, "I am very much alive."

"How do I get you out?"

Cecil leans forward and snickers. "Well, you don't. That's the wonderful thing about hyperthymesia; nothing ever leaves. That is why I chose you to tell secrets to."

"When you visited Beth and I while we slept, when you left food, or took away things." I thought back to our captivity and the morning I'd awoken to find the table gone and a huge cardboard box in its place. Staring at the newest piece of furniture in our room, I'd called to Beth to wake. At that moment, I realized that my night hadn't been as sleepless as I'd first believed. Somehow, Cecil replaced the table and chairs with two small stools and the cardboard box.

"Yes. . . " he hesitates, "but before that too."

"At C.E.C.I.L.?" The idea pops into my head. But before he can confirm, the hint of a hazy memory of him visiting my room at the compound resurfaces.

"See, you already know the answer to that question." He reads my mind.

"Is that all?"

"What do you think?"

I close my eyes. In the dark behind my lids, I sift through memories, pushing them around until I find something. "You've been in my head for a long time, before any of this started."

"Brilliant ideas require years of planning and preparation. And you, my dear, were, still are, a big component to the plan. I had to share important things with someone who would never forget. Could never forget. I had to tell someone my intentions."

"But why? You don't forget either." My parents had told me months ago that Cecil also had an amazing memory, something few people knew.

"For situations such as this, that were out of my control."

My eyes narrow as they lock onto Cecil's. "Your death?"

"Precisely."

"So, over all these years, what did you implant in my head?"

"Well, I shared with you what I'd written in my manifesto. How the global pandemic of 2020, Covid-19, provided the ideal cover and opportunity. While everyone else worked on finding treatments and vaccines, I began designing a unique pestilence. There was already fear of swine and avian flu developing into another pandemic. Preoccupied people and global stupidity gave me the idea to rid the world of humans exhibiting such behaviour. Then I told you how I developed this most perfect bunyavirus, complete with formulas and diagrams."

There is a brief flash of an image, things I don't recognize. My brow furrows.

"April, you need not understand all the science to record everything. It will be just like tracing a picture or copying text. But since you're a smart young lady, I'll give you some background that might help."

"I created a new RNA virus belonging to the Bunyaviridae family. This genetically modified virus would change the world, but I needed the perfect vector for transmission, and so I infected a mosquito. When the insect feeds, it infects its prey. But I desired for more than a mosquito to pass along this pathogen. I also wanted human-to-human transmission, and that was not an easy manipulation. Insect born viruses infect the blood, but I needed a contagious respiratory infection, so I investigated hantavirus. Do you know what that is?"

"Yes. My mother told me rodents can carry it."

"Precisely. Anyway, this pathogen can cause hantavirus pulmonary syndrome. Now the North American strain is not infectious, however, person-to-person transmission existed in a South American variation. Long story short, I created a virus transmitted by mosquitoes, causing respiratory distress and contagious between humans. Thus, was born my unknown novel virus. But there was no way I could enact my plan all by myself. So, I enlisted some like-minded people, and they helped me to find brilliant children and young adults with promising futures. And once I rid the world of ignorance, only the best would reproduce. Oh, there were flaws, and maybe my dream of a perfect and intelligent society was far-fetched, but I had to try. And admit it, this virus of mine did the job."

"You're a monster."

Cecil smiled. "Thank you. Now, where was I before your virology lesson? Right. Your brain holds everything there is to understand about the bunyavirus I developed. And while your parents may have figured out bits and pieces, and could temporarily come up with a vaccine, it was I who solved the actual problem. While I had intimate knowledge of this pathogen, there was an issue with the viral mutation rate. The replication was much faster than expected and made this thing continue to mutate almost constantly, making all vaccines eventually inactive. That's what happens when you manipulate nature. Sometimes it fights back. Most viruses don't mutate into increasingly stronger variations, usually they stay the same or sometimes weaken. Viruses want to survive as much as we do, if they kill all their hosts... Let's just say that wouldn't be good for the virus. The Butterfly

Flu went rogue, and even I couldn't resolve the problem. But one day, after the fire, while I was searching the compound, it suddenly occurred to me what I needed to do. I started using the equipment left behind at C.E.C.I.L. and, after some trial and error, finally developed not only a reliable vaccine but also a viable treatment."

"But if you had all this knowledge, why were you still seeking information from us? Why did you think we had secrets?"

Cecil shifts in his chair and combs his fingers through his white hair. "Because, I suspected your parents understood what the problem was with the virus and would come up with what I eventually did. About that, I had no doubt. And that would have ruined everything. I wanted all the information they learned so I could destroy it. The pathogen was mine to control."

"So, you implanted all your recent work in my head too?"

"Every bit."

"And you developed a new vaccine and a treatment? Created it with the equipment in the lab?"

"Yes, that's the thing about RNA vaccines, they are quick to produce and laboratory based. Mind you, I only made a small sample. Enough to vaccinate Gus and myself, and I gave him the vial with the one dose of treatment I had produced and told him to keep it safe. Then I destroyed the remaining equipment at C.E.C.I.L. So, you see, April, without that information locked in your head..."

He doesn't finish, but he doesn't have to. The virus had mutated again. And unless my parents soon figure out the answer buried in my brain; we have no chance.

I stare down at my hands and wiggle my fingers. Something presses into the back of my thigh. 'What's she saying', whispers in my ears but I ignore the indistinct voice. "So, this is some weird space inside my head." I look up at Cecil *as I realize what I am experiencing is not reality, not a dream, but a significant memory.*

"This can be wherever or whatever you want it to be."
He leans back in the chair; once again the front feet rise off the floor.

"And you, you're just a mixture of the memories of you which you planted in my head, and my memories of you and everything that happened after. You're neither real nor a dream—a nightmare." I correct.

He smirks.

"And the whispers I hear now, the voices that are wondering what I'm talking about, it's them, Archie and Gus outside my head." I close my eyes and Gus and Archie's faces come into focus.

"Well, I think I'll be going. Looks like you have this under control. Besides, you have lots of work to do." Cecil rises from the chair and walks back toward the open door. A strange glow pulses from the entrance as he approaches. The table and chair melt into the shadows. My eyes dart around the room. Handwriting covers the walls, formulas, and instructions. Everything Cecil had planted in my brain is clear and in front of me.

"Don't come back," I call to the shadow in the doorway.

"Tsk, tsk," he clicks his tongue. "Now you know that's not possible. For as long as you live, I will stay in your head." Cecil laughs and closes the door.

I rise to my feet and turn a slow circle. The moonlight highlights every bit of data, the missing pieces of the puzzle scribbled on the walls of the room. I study the words, numbers, and diagrams, storing the science in easy to reach places within my mind. When I finish, I lay on the imagined cushions and drift into consciousness.

Two faces hovered over me. Their expressions of anticipation easily identified even in my post-sleep, post-dream, post-whatever-it-was state. A hard lump forced into the back of my thigh, and I almost withdrew it before remembering what it was.

"Get away," I mumbled to the disembodied heads floating in my field of vision.

The heads pulled away as I sat up, covering the vial hidden inside the cushion with my right hand. With my left I rubbed my forehead, erasing the remaining fog.

Archie glared. "For your sake, I hope you remembered something." Dried blood streaked across his cheek.

I glared back. "What do you mean?"

"Well, he means–" Gus began.

"What I mean," Archie interrupted and threw a notebook down beside me, "is you didn't tell us anything. Mumbled a few times, but that was all."

The walls of words and formulas flashed in front of me. "Look, I told you everything I saw."

"Nope! Everything is still in there." He pointed to my head.

"Couldn't you read my thoughts and write them down yourself?"

Anger flickered in his eyes. "That was the plan, but there was nothin'. That drug I gave you to relax must mask thoughts. Even now, your thoughts are too hazy to focus on anything."

I envisioned the now accessible information knowing Gus, for the moment, couldn't 'see' what was in my mind. When I cleared my head, I glanced at the blank notebook.

"You write everything down, everything you remember and leave nothing out." Archie pointed at the notebook as he walked toward the door, Gus ahead of him. He stopped and turned back. "The lives of everyone you love are at stake, and you will never step outside of this room again if you don't." The door squeaked closed, and the audible click of the lock on the other side let me know he meant what he said.

Thirty

Double Cross

I stared at the blank pages of the notebook until the thin blue lines merged with the white background. At first, I considered writing everything in the same jumbled manner Cecil's secrets formed in my brain, spewing the words out in random fashion. Instead, I organized the information and, with great attention to detail, began the arduous task of transferring the knowledge to paper.

When my neck ached from my hunched position, I lay prone on my bed, the notebook in front of me on the floor at the end of the cushions. Both my arms hung over the edge while I scribbled words and numbers onto the paper. When I filled both sides of fifteen pages, I stopped. With notebook in hand, I stood at the locked door.

"Are you done?" Archie said as he opened the door after several minutes of my incessant knocking.

I flexed and curled the fingers of my writing hand and rubbed my wrist. "No, I'm thirsty."

Archie yelled to Gus and moments later he appeared with a cup of water.

"Don't knock again until you're finished." Archie closed the door. The click of the lock caused goosebumps to erupt on my arms.

Time passed, and with the lack of sunshine on this stormy day, it was difficult to estimate how many hours ticked by since I'd written the first of Cecil's words. Eventually, the rain ceased, but wind continued to rattle the window. I doodled in absent-mindedness, filling the margins of the pages I'd already filled with my documentation. The pause in my writing started further procrastination as another plan formed in my head and distracted me. I could not let Archie and Gus have what they wanted. My pulse raced, and sweat dampened the hair at the back of my neck as I contemplated what I needed to do. I picked up the notebook and read over my last notes before reaching for the pen.

When I finished, when all the formulas and instructions covered several pages, I tore the papers from the notebook. I ripped off the corner of the last page, jotted a brief instruction, and tucked the scrap of paper into the inside pocket of my pants. I folded the sheets of paper in half and placed them inside the cushion. Then I began re-writing the formulas and instructions, minus the doodles. Cecil had divulged the science in significant detail, even including the hazards of inaccuracy that would render the treatment or vaccine ineffective. I considered adding the misinformation but decided it would be of no use. Archie had no intention of giving the information to anyone, not without payment of some kind. Gus had said it was for insurance. So, giving them something useless served no purpose. There had to be one viable document out there for someone to use. As far as what was in my head, it would stay there. I did not see an escape in my future, nor were they going to release me. I knew too much. The only chance was to hide the other copy and keep the instructions to its whereabouts in my pocket. If someone found me later, they would find that document.

My stomach rumbled, and I stretched the kinks from my back and rubbed my aching neck. The second rendition had taken less than half the time, but I didn't alert Archie or Gus. I wanted to enjoy whatever daylight, though overcast, that I could.

A confident smirk played on my lips as I considered my ploy for a moment. Then I veiled my thoughts with the wonderful memories of my life. For the first time, it made me happy to remember every detail of those moments. I laughed out loud, not caring if Archie heard me or Gus 'saw' what I thought.

Every so often a not-so-pleasant memory came to mind, and while I initially blocked it, I soon realized that those ruminations also shaped me.

For as long as you live, April, I will always be with you, Cecil's voice whispered inside my head. A smug smile crossed my face. "Not for long," I whispered back.

The door squeaked open behind me, but I continued to stare up toward the window and glimpsed the swirling clouds.

"Are you finished?"

I detected a hint of impatience in Archie's voice and nodded, keeping my gaze on the stormy sky outside. "Yes," I said and reached inside the pocket of my sweats, grasping the glass vial of the hypno-drug.

"So, that's everything then?" He picked up the notebook. "Looks like some pages are missing."

I pointed to the wads of paper on the floor. "Rough draft," I said, "but it's all in there." Noah came to mind. Then another memory replaced him, and I let it play in my head. When it faded, I spoke again. "Gus, he gave you the treatment to hold on to, and that's how you survived the virus."

A smile crept across Archie's face. "If it weren't for Gus, I wouldn't be here today. Now, I've got to get back for my shift in the comms room. But I'll check this, and If something seems funny or incomplete, I'll be back and Gus can do more digging. If not, I'll radio Gus and tell him to let you go."

I turned and faced Archie. Light from the hallway spilled into the room through the open door. "Will he?" There was no way they were just going to let me go, not now.

Archie smiled and shrugged. "Sure, though he won't allow you to go back to the compound, you know too much. And anyway, I think he misses 'collecting'. Either way, Gus will search your mind or search for you out there." Archie pointed toward the window with his chin. "And I'm sure he'll enjoy the pursuit." He held up the notebook and walked out of the room, leaving the door open.

There was no way Gus would get back into my head or hunt for me. What I held in my hand would prevent either from happening.

* * *

I leaned against the kitchen counter. "When is he supposed to contact you again?"

Gus stared up at me from his usual spot at the table. "What exactly do you mean?" He narrowed his eyes.

Details of the compact kitchen filled my mind as I suspected Gus would try to read my thoughts. Every once in a while, I threw in the image of Cecil's dead grey eyes and the flies that crawled over his face. "Exactly what I said. Archie told me he'd contact you to let me go." I folded my arms and leaned against the counter.

"In a hurry to leave? And here I thought you enjoyed my company."

"Hardly." I channeled my sister's boldness.

"Feelin's mutual. Anyway, it'll be more fun when you leave. Thrill of the hunt and all that."

I swallowed back a moment of fear.

Gus smiled. "Don't worry, I'm just as anxious."

A crackle of static interrupted our conversation. "Right on time." Gus rose from the table and walked past me and out into the hall.

I followed behind him and stopped as he opened the bedroom door. I hadn't seen that room since Jasper had died inside it, and I didn't care to see it now.

"Where are you goin'?" Gus called. "Don't you want to hear the news yourself?"

"Upstairs," I called back, "I'm sure you'll tell me."

Gus's laughter followed behind me as I made my way back to the room.

What little daylight streamed through the window faded fast. The black clouds blocked any light from the rising moon and first evening stars and plunged the room into darkness.

The flashlight beam had a way of making a dismal room appear more eerie. I imagined creatures lurking in the shadows, ready and waiting to show themselves to the unsuspecting. The only comforting part was the dazzling display of dust particles undulating in the glow. I kept my focus on the dust from my spot on the cushions.

"Well, it looks like you're a free girl." Gus's voice startled me. Light streamed in through the open door where his ominous silhouette stood. Though shrouded in darkness, I sensed his grin. "Aren't you gonna say somethin'?"

My eyes and mind focused on the dust once again, and I pretended they were tiny fairies. "What's there to say?" I swirled the particles with my finger and watched as they undulated fervently in the temporary movement of air currents.

"Thought you'd be happy with your newfound freedom." He didn't hide his sarcasm.

"Hmph, freedom." I imagined myself skipping and laughing down the trail back to the compound, though I suspected that's not what he had in mind.

"Suppose you're right. It won't be like that. But you'll be free for a little while. I'll give you a head start. And if I don't get you, Butterfly Flu will."

"Aren't you afraid?" I looked away from the tiny specks, each one a small world with inhabitants of their own. I wondered if the dust mites got dizzy.

"Of what?"

"The mosquitoes." I had nothing to lose.

"No. I've taken the last vaccine Cecil concocted."

"What if it doesn't work?"

"Well, it does."

"Sure, the treatment helped Archie. But you don't know how efficient the vaccine is. Maybe the virus will change again. The vaccine we had is failing now. It could be yours will too. Anyway, you didn't look so sure a few weeks ago when we were both wearing protective gear the last time we were outside."

"That was all pretend, didn't want you to think we had nothing to worry about. And I'm confident in the vaccine because my brother created it, because he was the only one who really knew how. You leave tomorrow morning at dawn. Better get some sleep." Gus closed the door and locked it.

Thirty-One

The Abyss

The glass vial glinted in the beam from the flashlight. Clear liquid sloshed inside the bottle as I gave it a shake. The anguish building inside me would soon be over, and I took comfort in that thought. Physically, my body would be the same. But the amount of hypno-drug I was about to inject would likely take away my memories for a long while, perhaps forever. Forgetting my family or Noah or any of the happier times in my life was not something I desired. But I wanted to forget Cecil's voice, and I didn't want to relive terrible moments as though they were just happening. But mostly, if I forgot, maybe Gus would leave me alone. I wouldn't be much fun to hunt if he found me unconscious in the morning. And while I knew too much, soon I wouldn't remember.

I planned on a dose as substantial as the one given to me the night of my kidnapping and imprisonment at C.E.C.I.L. According to the manifesto, the hypno-drug designed by Cecil combined a drug called Midazolam, a hypnotic-sedative with a psychotropic he concocted. Cecil's designer drug boosted the amnesic effects of the Midazolam and allowed for mind control. It would take about fifteen minutes for the sedation to kick in after administration. Once conscious again, the resulting trance-like-state would fade with time, and I would be myself except with no recollections. At least that's what I hoped. If the first dose wasn't enough, and I found myself aware with memories intact, there was ample supply to fill the syringe two more times.

Beneath the protective cap, the point of the needle waited to meet my tender flesh. There was no doubt I could administer the initial dose. But a second, should the first shot not accomplish my desired outcome, of that I was unsure. The timing was crucial as it took from one to six hours for the effect of unconsciousness to wear off after the injection. This depended not only on the measured quantity, but on the person receiving the drug. Everyone was different regarding the pharmacodynamics, according to Cecil's information. Either I would wake a mute, susceptible to hypnotic suggestion with no memories or find myself groggy but lucid.

My heart tried to talk me out of my decision. But Cecil's whispers inside my head strengthened my resolve and convinced my heart. There was no other choice. I lay on my bed and closed my eyes, needing a moment of rest to calm my racing thoughts.

After what seemed about an hour, I sat up. "Forgive me," I whispered. The plea was both to myself for my inability to lie still any longer and to my family and Noah for lacking strength.

It seemed a strange and surreal dream as I drew the plunger and watched the liquid fill the plastic tube. The blue-white light from the flashlight beam gave the act an even more dreamlike quality.

I tapped the syringe, releasing tiny air bubbles, placed the cap back on the needle and set it on the cushion beside me. My shaking fingers tucked the vial inside the hidden pocket of my sweatpants along with the note I'd scribbled earlier. I pulled out one of two alcohol swabs I'd taken from the medicine cabinet the night before.

The injection would be in my outer right thigh on the same side as the pocket. I practiced pulling down the waistband with my left hand far enough to expose the area below my hip. Then I pretended to clean the site with the swab and tucked the imaginary wipe and its packaging into the hand holding the waistband. I rehearsed uncapping the needle and delivering the injection. While I had time to tuck the evidence back inside my pocket, I wanted to make sure everything went smoothly. I'd never given myself a needle of any kind before, and the act itself was as disquieting as the outcome.

April, there is so much I will share with you, Cecil's whisper interrupted my rehearsal. I squeezed my eyelids shut to squelch the flow of memories, but it did not work. Instead, his whispers came louder and faster. Words and sentences blended with each other, echoed, then faded, as though someone played with a volume control inside my head. *Bunyaviridae is a massive family... human-to-human transmission... global pandemic... ha, ha, ha... tsk, tsk, tsk, April... everyone has secrets... You're staying here until you rot!*

"STOP!" I spoke through clenched teeth. Cecil's laughter filled my head, then faded into silence. I exhaled, more convinced I held the answer to quieting his voice in my hand.

There was a sudden flutter in my chest when I finished the third and final run-through. Sweat dampened the hair at my temples, and I inhaled as much oxygen as my lungs could hold and held my breath before allowing it to escape. A star outside the window caught my attention. Within hours, the sun would rise and wake the sleeping world, but would I?

The dress rehearsal over, I hooked my thumb of my left hand under the waistband and exposed my leg. Tiny bumps rose on my skin as I blotted a small area with the swab. The smell of alcohol pricked my nose. I tucked the packaging and used swab into my palm, then placed the cap of the syringe between my knuckles and pulled the needle free.

My right hand shook a little as I held it over the bared area. "Relax," I whispered. Then, before I could think, sunk the point into my flesh. I blinked at the quick sting, and my thumb pushed down on the plunger, slow and even as though I'd made a habit of giving injections. The thought of Beth, and how she'd love to be doing this, popped into my head.

I exhaled the breath I held and pulled the syringe free. My hand shook as my other brought the cap closer to the needle's point. With the cap in place, I tucked the syringe, the swab, and its wrapping into my pocket. I rested on the cushions and stared up at the rafters overhead, counting the beams as I had so many times before. Memories of my life swirled in my head as tears leaked from my eyes. It was too late to regret my action. A dizzying fog replaced my memories. Heavy eyelids closed and though I tried to lift them, I could not. Voices echoed in my skull in a mounting din, then became silent. Muscles relaxed, and my body fell into a deep abyss.

Thirty-Two

Gone

Unrecognizable faces hovered overhead. Rich brown, vibrant green, icy-blue, and other various shades of eyes stared. Eyelids blinked, pupils darted, and turned towards one another before returning their gaze on the object of their attention. The eyes spoke silent words. Each pair displayed sympathy, refracted light, and held something familiar. Lips in hues from pink to plum squeezed together, holding back words and emotion.

A hand floated upward, my hand, and blocked out the intrusive and monitoring glares. I tested the fingers, spread them wide, curled them into a fist, and splayed them open again before dropping my hand from sight. The action caused strange, delicate whispers of unrecognizable words to spill from the lips of the faces still hovering. But the fog returned and darkness fell.

* * *

"What's goin' on?" A strange and scratchy voice interrupted the hum of overhead lights. My hand moved to my throat, realizing the voice was mine.

A figure standing at the end of the bed spun around, and a lock of dark, wavy hair caught in her open mouth. She brushed the piece away as she moved over beside me and sat in a chair.

I blinked.

"April?" The girl questioned in a somewhat shrill voice as though unsure she had the correct name.

My hands shot up and protected my sensitive ears. "Quiet, please," I whispered.

"Sorry," she said. "Are you okay?"

I narrowed my gaze and studied her face. Piercing blue orbs stared back. "Beth?"

Beth leaned forward and kissed my cheek. "Thank God!" She smiled. "Everyone will be so happy you're aware and you recognize me."

"Who's everyone?" I sat up and leaned against the wall at the head of the bed.

Beth reached for my hand and gave it a light squeeze. "What do you remember?" The question was like turning a key in a locked door. One tug was all it took to free whatever was on the other side.

I shrugged, wanting to keep the door locked for a moment longer, unsure of what was on the other side and whether I wanted to set it free.

Beth squeezed my hand again. "Don't worry," she said. "Tell me whatever you can."

That was the tug. The door creaked open and memories spilled forth. Most were clear, though some I couldn't quite grasp or define, and I suspected those were the most recent. Images, sounds, tastes, smells—almost everything I had experienced came rushing out at once. I squeezed my eyes shut and mentally closed the door.

"Well, a lot, actually," I said, rubbing my forehead.

"But?" Beth prompted.

"Some things aren't so clear. How long have I been here?"

Beth dropped my hand and sat back in the chair. Her gaze darkened, and she glanced at the window. Her eyes welled, and she closed them, but a drop leaked out from between long lashes. "April, so much has happened."

My heart skipped. "What, Beth?"

"Sorry I'm late... April?" The sound of a surprised voice shifted my focus from my sister's emotional face to the visitor who'd just entered my room. "Beth, you're supposed to alert us." The expression on Caleb's face changed into several emotions, then finally rested on irritated as he sat beside me and leaned in for a hug. I didn't know how long it had been, but he appeared taller than what I'd remembered.

Beth folded her arms. "How can you tell April isn't just like before?"

Caleb shook his head, pulled away, and straightened. "Clearly not. Before, April looked like a zombie. Awake, but not there. Now, you can see awareness in her eyes." Caleb smiled.

"What do you mean, before? How long have I been here?" I said.

Caleb's eyes narrowed. "What have you said?" he asked Beth.

Beth shook her head. "Calm down. April just woke up a few minutes ago, and I haven't had a freakin' chance to say anything."

Caleb folded his arms. "Why didn't you alert us?"

My eyes darted between the two as I took in their exchange.

Beth glared at Caleb. "Did you not listen? She. Just. Woke. Up!"

"Still, the second you realized her awareness, you–"

"Um, hello!" I said louder than intended. Beth and Caleb looked at me. "Hi! Remember me?" I smiled and waved. "First, quit talking like I'm not in the room."

Caleb rested his hand on my knee. "Sorry."

"Me too." Beth leaned back in the chair.

"Now, who wants to tell me something—anything? Or answer my first question. How long have I been here?"

Beth and Caleb exchanged looks. "Almost six weeks," Beth said.

I gasped. "Six weeks? Where's Mom and Dad?"

"Hang on." Caleb jumped from the bed and picked up the bag he'd left at the door.

I strained my ears as he muttered a few words seemingly to himself, then dropped the bag. He returned to the bed with a satisfied grin on his face.

"What was that about?" I said and tapped my fingers on my leg.

Caleb stared at me. "How are you feeling?"

I sighed in exasperation and ignored my brother's question. "What's going on?" I pointed to Caleb's bag by the door.

"Walkie," he said.

My focus switched from the bag to the doorway as my mother, Marcus, Jasmy, and trailing a few feet behind, Noah, stepped into the room.

"April! Oh, thank God!" Mom replaced Caleb on the bed. I leaned forward, and she hugged me and kissed my cheek. She pulled away after several seconds and held me at arms-length. Mom brushed the hair from my eyes and held my face in her hands. "Are you okay?" Her eyebrows drew together.

I nodded. It was all I could do, for the second I opened my mouth, I wouldn't be able to contain my emotions.

Marcus and Jasmy took turns greeting me and offering well wishes. Noah smiled, and my abdominal muscles quivered in response. He took me in his arms, and my heart skipped. I closed my eyes, inhaled a deep breath, and held it. When he pulled away, I exhaled.

"Where's Dad?" I said to Mom, seated at the end of the bed.

Her eyes darkened and filled with something I'd seen before but didn't quite understand. She averted her gaze as an uncomfortable silence filled the room. After a moment, she smiled, though it did not reach her eyes. "Right now, you are my priority."

"Dad's okay, right?" I searched my mother's face for an answer before she spoke.

Mom's forced smile faded, and a shadow crossed her eyes again.

"Dad's fine." Beth spoke, and I turned toward my sister. "He's fine," she said again. Her gaze left mine for a moment and found our mother's before returning to me.

My muscles relaxed, and I stared at my hands. "So, I'll see Dad later," I said more to myself than to anyone else in the room. But my words sounded more like a wish than a confident statement. The return of uncomfortable silence forced my attention back to the others. "Since everyone else is here. . . " I looked around at the eyes staring at me. Goosebumps travelled up my arms as the memory of the watchful camera came to mind. I blinked away the thought. "Would someone please tell me what has happened?"

Caleb spoke. "What's the last thing you remember?" He stood beside the bed, holding Jasmy's hand. Beth still sat in the chair at the head of the bed with Marcus standing behind her, his hands resting on her shoulders. It seemed their relationship had changed. Behind them stood Noah, and our eyes locked on each other's for a moment.

A loud sigh escaped my lips. It was clear I would not be getting any information from this group until I answered their questions. Several memories of different clarity fought for attention. I focused on the clearest and pulled it out from the cluster of others. "Archie is dangerous and not to be trusted."

Marcus nodded. "Yup, we figured that out. Sorry for doubting you, April."

"Marcus turned him in." Beth reached up and placed a hand on top of Marcus' still resting on her shoulder.

"What happened?" I wanted to tell them about Gus too, but needed to know if we were safe from Archie first.

Marcus shrugged. "Headed to the telecoms room one night 'cause I couldn't sleep. There were voices coming from inside, and I thought someone else was there with Archie. When I walked in, he was alone. He switched off that radio quick, and I pretended like nothing happened. I think he was suspicious at first, but after a bit he seemed to relax. That night I told Caleb and Beth, and they weren't too happy about me waking them, but I had to tell someone."

"Then they showed up at my room and told me everything," Mom said. "So, I kept as close of an eye on Archie as possible without making him suspicious. Two days later, Caleb was in the right place."

"What do you mean?" I said and looked to my brother for further explanation.

Caleb rubbed his chin. "I was in the food supply rooms, checking on the stores. The list, by the way, worked, and nothing else disappeared. Anyway, I heard a noise out in the hall that wasn't the usual kind. The supply room door was closed, so I opened it a crack and peeked out."

I sat straighter. "And?"

"Archie. Only he wasn't coming down the hall from the cafeteria but was at the other end by the sealed door.

His back was to me, and he was easing the not-so-sealed-anymore door closed."

"And Archie didn't see you?"

Caleb shook his head. "No, I quietly shut the supply door. Arch wasn't aware I was inside the room."

"Where is he now?" The room fell silent. All eyes took turns staring at one another as though each pair urged someone else to speak first.

Noah sighed. "Archie's gone," he said.

"What do you mean, gone? Like in left?" My stomach rolled at the thought. The air in the room grew heavy. Jasmy's wide eyes stared up at Caleb; she clenched his arm and her knuckles turned white.

"No, he didn't leave." Mom's soft voice floated through the tension.

"Someone tell me what happened?" I said after several more seconds of silence followed my mother's statement. Now, no one wanted to look anywhere except at the floor.

"Archie's dead." Beth was blunt.

"How?" The revelation both shocked and relieved me.

Beth sighed. Marcus' hands gripped her shoulders. "Dad... " she stared at her clasped hands in her lap.

I threw back the blankets and kicked my legs over the side of the bed. "Move, I'm going to see Dad. Where is he?" I glared at Beth as she was the only one willing to offer information.

"No, you can't." Caleb's voice cracked. Jasmy wrapped her arms around his waist and leaned into him.

"Yes, I'm going." I stood up and closed my eyes; the room spun from the sudden movement, and my knees buckled. I sat back on the bed.

Mom stood by me and faced the others. "Could you give us a moment?"

Beth leaned around our mother and kissed my forehead before rising from the chair. Two by two, the couples filed out of the room with Noah trailing behind.

"Stay, Noah," Mom said.

Noah's back stiffened as he faced the open door. He stepped backward, and the door closed as he joined my mother at my bedside. Mom sat on the edge of the bed while Noah sat where Beth had.

"So, Marcus and Beth..." I said to Noah, wanting to prolong whatever it was my mother was going to tell me.

Noah Shrugged. "Just," he said.

"Are you okay with that?" I turned my attention to my mother.

Mom nodded. "I have to be," she said in a quiet voice and reached forward to take my hand. Her eyes welled, and she cleared her throat. "April, your father," she began and her gaze drifted to our joined hands for a moment. She forced a half-smile. "Your father..." A strength returned to her voice, though it seemed fragile. She tightened her grip.

My eyes burned, and my throat ached. While I did not understand what my mother was trying to say, my body prepared for the worst. "Did Dad... did he really kill Archie?" My father hardly raised his voice, and it seemed impossible he could kill someone.

Mom shook her head. "April, we don't know what happened." She closed her eyes for a moment and took a deep breath.

I rubbed my forehead with my fingertips; my body tensed. "Mom, I'm confused."

Mom took another deep breath. "After Caleb told me what he saw, I confronted Archie."

"So, you and Dad?"

Mom shook her head. "Just me, but I told your dad everything. Anyway, Archie denied it at first. Then he confessed, said he was trying to clear the tunnel in case we needed another exit. He'd said the tunnel wasn't close to being finished, and he didn't tell anyone what he was doing."

"Did you ask about the radio?"

Mom nodded. "Archie swore he'd contacted no one and said that you and Marcus only overheard him talking to himself. He showed me the radio, and he flipped through all the channels. Anyway, by the end of the conversation, Archie said he would stop working on the tunnel, that he'd re-seal it. Three weeks later, Noah caught him coming out of the tunnel again."

I turned to look at Noah. He'd been so quiet if it hadn't been for seeing him in my peripheral vision, I would have forgotten he was in the room.

Noah cleared his throat. "I was helping Caleb at the supply room and we heard the door opening to the tunnel. We ducked back inside the room and closed the door a bit. Archie was too busy flipping through a notebook in his hands to notice the door was open as he walked by. Then he went into the comms room. He was in there it must have been an hour, but we waited. Anyway, we heard him then on the radio. He wasn't speaking too loudly but we knew he spoke to someone. When he stepped out, he had the notebook in his hands. Caleb and I blocked his way and asked him what he was doing. Told him we saw him coming out of the tunnel earlier and heard him on the radio. He said he was sealing the tunnel up for good on the other side of the door. Caleb snatched the notebook from his hand, but Archie didn't even try to take it back. Instead, he rushed past us. We didn't go after him until Caleb noticed your handwriting inside. We didn't know which way he went and figured he headed back to his room."

"But he didn't though, did he?" I took a deep breath, held it, and exhaled a steady stream of air. My heart rate slowed.

Noah shook his head. "After searching for about ten minutes on his floor, Jasmy came to us and said she'd heard yelling coming from the infirmary. Caleb and I got your mom from her room and we went to the infirmary together."

"Where was Dad? Was he in a lab?" My pulse raced.

"There were patients in the infirmary," Mom said. "Only I could enter so I pulled on my suit and–"

"Yes, I remember. There were two patients with the virus." Noah and mom stared at me. "I overheard Archie and Gus talking one day, and Archie said two were sick." I closed my eyes as the conversation replayed in my head. "Lydia and... Archie whispered Aya, I'm sure of it. How did they get sick?"

Noah's forehead wrinkled. "Lydia was bitten by a mosquito. There was a tear in her suit." Noah dropped his gaze to the floor for a moment. "Who's Gus?"

"Later. Sorry, Mom, please finish."

Mom's eyes glistened. She blinked several times and cleared her throat. "When I entered the room, Archie was on the floor—dead or dying, his throat cut, a scalpel beside him. There wasn't anything I could do. We don't know where the scalpel came from. There are theories but... "

"This happened inside the lab? Where was Dad? Didn't he explain what happened?"

Mom reached over and grabbed my other hand. "Honey, it wasn't in the lab."

My brow furrowed. "What do you mean?"

Mom looked toward Noah, then back to me. "The room was a quarantine room in the infirmary."

"Dad was in with Lydia and Aya? Didn't they see what happened?"

Mom closed her eyes and took a deep breath. "Archie was wrong, or lied. Aya wasn't a patient; it was your father."

When she opened her eyes again a tear rolled down her cheek.

My stomach knotted and chin quivered. "But he's okay now. Dad's better, right?" My mom turned into a blurry form, and I rubbed my eyes. A warm hand, Noah's, touched my back.

Mom's head rotated in slow motion, first to the right, then left, and back to centre. Her eyelids closed then opened, in time with a breath in and a breath out. Her lips moved and formed around soundless words, and I leaned forward, trying to see, trying to hear.

"What?" My voice pierced through the heavy veil of sorrow that had fallen over the room.

Mom's blinks returned to normal; her warm hands squeezed mine; her lips formed around words; the words reached my ears. "No, honey, he's not. Dad's gone."

Thirty-Three

Missing Memories

At the back of the courtyard, through the gate in the concrete block wall, lay the small cemetery. The wall acted as a
backdrop to thirteen wood crosses, seven on one side of the
gate and six on the other. Grass and wildflowers grew over
the top of the mounds in front of the markers, the vegetation
thicker on some than others. The smell of wet earth from the
early morning rain permeated the air. Though a cloudburst
had started the day, the sun now shone, promising a bright
and humid day. A brown rabbit hopped out from the field
and stood on top of the furthest grave and nibbled on a
patch of clover, oblivious to my presence.

His grave marker looked no different from any other, and
it was no more special. But it should have been. He was
my dad.

The name Ian R. Linden carved into the wooden cross
made my throat ache. Etched below the moniker was his
birth and death date. Suddenly, everything was real. I pulled
my gaze away and observed the other crosses. While their
appearance was similar, there was one noticeable difference.
The others were desolate, with few to stand over them and
mourn for the body below. Perhaps the odd co-worker or

friend stopped by, but Dad's cross served as a reminder to his entire family.

A week had passed since learning of his death, and this was my first visit to his grave, despite my attempt on the day Mom and Noah had given me the new. But I hadn't believed them, didn't want to, though my heart knew it was true. Every day seemed an eternity until I could finally say goodbye.

A mosquito crawled along the cross. My thumb crushed its bloated body; the popping sensation underneath was satisfying. I drew my thumb along the horizontal section of the cross, smearing blood into the wood. A red welt rose on my bare arm, and a half-smile tugged at the corner of my lip. The bug had dined for the last time.

There was no concern for the growing itchy spot on my arm. I'd received the newest vaccine prepared using the data hidden inside the cushion and found by my rescuers after they discovered the note in my pocket. Though Caleb snatched the identical information from Archie, it proved useless as it seemed a page was missing. Unfortunately, it had been too late for my father. My mother hoped he'd survive long enough to receive the treatment, but the virus took him a few days before the serum was ready. I curled my fingers into a fist. Had we been able to access the information I had buried in my subconscious sooner, he would still be alive.

A cough pulled my attention away from the grave, and my eyes met with Lydia's as she stood at another marker. One of the other kitchen staff stood by her side, supporting her. Though still weakened from the virus, she'd regained strength over the last several days.

Lydia gave a weak smile before dropping her regard back to the marker. I tried to smile back, and while in my mind I did, the physical show of happiness for her recovery never appeared on my face. Instead, I stared at Lydia for a second longer and then returned my attention to my father's grave.

A gentle June breeze fluttered my hair. My eyes closed, and I tipped my head back, allowing the sun to warm me. Birds sang, insects buzzed, and the breeze hushed. Pictures and images rolled behind my closed eyelids. Memories from the past, both distant and recent, flipped along like the pages of a book as I recalled voices, words, and emotions. I dug, searched, and replayed every moment from the second I'd found myself held captive to the present. And then I flipped through my memories again.

Remembering Cecil's whispered words was not only beneficial for humanity by revealing what was necessary to complete the vaccine and treatment, but also for me. I no longer heard his voice in my ears unless I wanted to—and I did not.

Caleb said I was lucky. The dose of the hypno-drug had kept me in a trancelike state for almost six weeks, yet did not erase my earlier memories. But there was no recollection of anything that happened over that time. Everything I knew from that missing period was only what my family and friends recounted. The memories were not mine but a compilation of everyone else's. No, I didn't think I was lucky.

The slow-motion recollection of smearing blood over the cross and Lydia's pitying gaze and fragile smile signaled the end of the most recent memories. The movie inside my head had played three times and not one repeat provided any additional information. And so, I began again, only this time I focused on the time lost and everyone else's words and recollections. I hoped something would spark even the faintest of memories.

Beth told me I'd seen our father, spent time with him during that first week after my rescue. Mom had dressed me in a protective suit and guided me to a chair by his bed, and there I sat for one, sometimes two hours a day. Mom said he'd smile from behind his oxygen mask and reach for my glove-covered hand. I didn't remember any of it, and it killed me.

The day he left us; we were all there. Mom said I stood by Dad's head on one side of the bed and she on the other, Beth beside me and Caleb beside her. They'd taken turns saying goodbye. He'd slipped into unconsciousness the day before, and so they could only hope he heard our words of love.

Mute from the moment they saved me, I spoke that day. Despite the deep sorrow in the room, my voice had been a light in the dark, a sign of hope my awareness had returned and my memory was intact. *What did I say,* I asked mom as she recalled the occasion. Mom had shaken her head and exhaled a shaky breath. After a minute, she cleared her throat. *You told him not to go, that you loved him.*

I reached out and placed my hand on top of the cross, willing myself to remember. But someone else's images and words were all that came to mind. And they weren't good enough.

"Did you talk to me, Dad?" I whispered to the mound of dirt. "There was more than just a smile behind that oxygen mask. I may not have spoken, but you must have." I closed my eyes again and summoned the picture Mom had placed in my head.

My heart skipped, and I spun around as a hand rested on my shoulder. I stared into Noah's eyes. The image in my head faded along with what I thought might be my memory, but it was nothing more than an inkling. "Sorry. I didn't mean to scare you," Noah said.

My voice cracked. "It's okay."

"Here." He set his pack down and pulled out a cloth from an outside pocket. My brow furrowed at the offered swatch. "Don't worry, it's clean, just wrinkled."

"But I don't..."

Noah wiped under his eye. I mirrored his action and studied my wet fingertips. Unnoticed tears streamed down my cheeks.

I dried my face with the cloth and handed it back. Not wanting him to look at me, I stared down at the ground. "Are you going again?" A hard lump of dirt lay among the green blades of grass. The piece came from the mound of dirt that covered my father's grave.

"Yes."

"He's dangerous."

"Please look at me." Noah lifted my chin until our eyes met. "April, we know, and that's why we have to find him."

"But it's been six weeks, Noah. He's long gone."

Noah shook his head. "No, he's not that far away. The man's a psychopath, and he's out there." Noah looked toward the forest across the field.

Goosebumps covered the back of my neck. I'd known of the danger he posed, but Cecil's manifesto revealed Gus was much more. Incarcerated in a mental health hospital for the criminally insane, Cecil somehow got his brother released. Gus's talent for mind-reading made him a candidate for Cecil's new civilization. A world filled with the exceptionally gifted, intelligent, and those possessing unexplainable abilities, even if they were demented.

I folded my arms. "How can you be so sure?"

"Jasmy. She senses he's near—waiting."

"Pfft!"

"What? Are you questioning her skill, Miss Remember-absolutely-everything-in-her-life?"

My cheeks burned at Noah's words despite his charming smile. "If her skills are so great, why didn't you find me sooner?"

Noah took my hands. "April, you know Jasmy just recently became stronger. If she could have sensed you sooner,

218

she would have. She has been building on her ability for months, and you were her first success."

I lowered my gaze. "Sorry."

"Don't be." Noah tucked a piece of hair behind my ear. "Now, I've got to go." He leaned forward and brushed his lips against mine.

"Be careful."

Noah smiled and picked his bag up off the ground. As he walked away, his words replayed in my head. *Miss Remember-absolutely-everything-in-her-life.*

I turned and looked at my father's grave. "Everything except for my last moments with you," I whispered.

Thirty-Four

Plan

I was the last member of the group to arrive at the cafeteria. Whispered words added to the eerie vibe already in the room. A battery-operated lantern sat in the middle of the table. The glow cast large, inky shadows, and they stretched up the mural painted walls and covered the ceiling. It was the middle of the night and no one would bother us during our meeting.

As I approached the table, my eyes narrowed. Seven bodies huddled over the lantern.

Noah looked up from the others; the light brightened his face. "Hey, I thought you would sleep through this." He smiled at me and pulled out a chair beside him. I sat, and my attention focused on the two new members.

I nodded at Aya and Khelden. Aya raised her hand from the tabletop in acknowledgement. Sitting beside Khelden, the top of her nearly bald head just reached his shoulder. Khelden gave a slight nod, animating his cowlick, and it addressed me with more exuberance.

Like us, apart from Marcus and Noah, they were Butterflies, rescued from the forest. What their particular talents were, I did not know. It wasn't something any of us spoke about—ever. It was like everyone wanted to forget about whatever made them desirable in Cecil's eyes. Whatever talent had made him destroy or try to destroy humanity as it had existed, though, I couldn't forget mine if I tried. Even now, we still did not have a sense as to the impact Butterfly Flu had had on the rest of the world. For all we knew, life continued as normal beyond the stretch of terrain we'd covered and searched. But that did not explain why we had contacted no one with the radio, or why no one had found us.

A pencil rolled back and forth between Beth's hands, resting flat on the table. First toward one hand and then to the other. The soft sound was almost imperceptible in the quiet room.

"So, I thought you'd given that up?" I said to Beth, quite surprised she showed her talent without reservation.

Beth shrugged, and the pencil stopped. "This is who I am, I might as well embrace it, use it for the greater good."

Her words made me think of our father. I nodded. "Maybe."

"Anyway," Beth said, "we need to find Gus and using our gifts might be the only way."

Jasmy's soft voice interrupted the stillness that had fallen on the room. "Gus is still out there." Everyone's eyes rested on her face.

"Let's all take turns and tell everyone about our particular gifts," Noah said. "April, you first."

I looked at Noah and rolled my eyes. "Okay, well, I remember things." My voice came out empty as my focus drifted between the newcomers.

"What kinda things?" Khelden spoke.

"Everything."

"So, everything, everything..." Aya added.

I nodded. *Except for six weeks of my life*, my annoyed-self whispered in my head.

"That'd be cool, wish I could do that." Khelden said; his cowlick bobbed.

I shook my head. "No, you don't."

Aya rubbed her hand across the short, dark bristles on the top of her perfectly shaped head. "Yes, I agree."

"With who?" Khelden and I said at the same time.

Aya looked at me, then nodded in Khelden's direction. "With him. You'd never lose anything, perfect grades in school, important dates, punchlines to jokes." She listed her points on her fingers.

I gave a half-smile, not bothering to match her list with the not-so-great things. "Okay, your turn," I said to Jasmy.

"Well, I have clairsentience, a kind of heightened empathy."

"What do you mean, heightened?" I said.

"So, I can sense different vibrations, changes in energy."

"Okay, I don't get it." Khelden laced his fingers and stretched his arms out in front of him.

"Everything has a distinct vibration. I can pick up on that and understand an emotion, or where something is."

"Or someone?" I said.

Jasmy nodded. "Yes, sometimes, but it depends on how close. Apparently, my ability is unique."

"In what way?" Noah said.

Jasmy shrugged. "In that I have a stronger intuition than most."

"Doesn't it overwhelm you?" I said.

"That's why I meditate—a lot." Jasmy's mouth drew up in a shy smile.

My eyes widened with interest. "Does it work?"

"If it didn't, I could not handle this place." Jasmy smiled again.

I took her words and tucked them away. Not that I needed to. Meditation was something I might want to try.

Caleb spoke next and explained his uncanny sense of direction. After Caleb, it was Aya's turn.

"Medium," she said as she rubbed the back of her neck. Aya held up her hands. "Now, before anyone tells me they don't believe, that it's all a scam..."

"Seriously?" Beth interrupted, "you just saw a pencil roll around between my hands, I would be the last to accuse you of a scam."

"Hey, I'm cool with it," Marcus said. "We gotta talk later."

Aya looked past Marcus to the darkness behind his shoulder, smiled and nodded her head. "Yes, I think we do."

Khelden shrugged. "Math whiz."

My eyebrows rose. He didn't look like a math whiz, not that I had an idea what one looked like.

"Yes, I know, unbelievable," Khelden focused his gaze on my face. "One day I was an ordinary kid playing hockey. Then boom, wake up after a blow to the head and suddenly, I'm a math genius."

Beth flicked the stilled pencil with her finger, and it rolled toward Khelden. "So, a savant."

"Guess so. Not so smart with anything else, but math..." Khelden nodded.

"Well, you've seen what I can do." The pencil rolled back toward Beth on its own and spun in circles.

"That is so wild." Khelden folded his arms on the table and leaned forward for a closer look.

"But I prefer biology and science. This is just some trick, a nuisance, but it might come in handy."

We stared at the pencil for a few seconds longer, it's spinning almost hypnotizing.

"What about you?" Khelden pointed his chin in Marcus' direction.

"Me, I'm just ordinary. No butterfly tattoo here," Marcus brushed a hand over the back of his neck. "Turns out I was immune to the major outbreak that took everyone I knew and more. I came across the compound after I'd left home. My blood was the first try at a vaccine. It was a success at first until–"

"Why'd he bother?" Aya interrupted.

"What?" Marcus said.

"Well, he gave you the formula, or whatever, to treat this virus," Aya stared at me, "so why use Marcus' blood if Cecil figured it wouldn't work. If he had the..." She waved her hand through the air as if to catch the word that had escaped her. "Cure." She rolled her eyes as she spoke.

"'Cause, he didn't know." I shrugged. "Not then. He created the virus, but it got out of hand. Our father..." I swallowed the lump that formed the moment I spoke of him. My eyes glued to Aya's face. I couldn't look at my siblings. "They found notes and Cecil was concerned he wouldn't be able to fight the virus he'd created. So, while our parents did their research, Cecil quietly did his own too. He'd continued after everyone escaped from the compound, and it was from that research that he regained control. Who better to understand the design but the creator himself?"

Aya nodded. "So, Cecil was coming closer to resolving this... DNA virus and let everyone else think they were making progress, when they weren't."

"Bunyavirus with single-stranded RNA," Beth spoke. All eyes focused on her. She shrugged. "It was unstable, that's why it mutated so often. Told you, I am more into biology and stuff."

Marcus continued. "Anyway, it mutated. So then..."

"Then it was my turn," Noah said. "Yup, I'm like Marcus, and they used my blood too."

The eight of us sat in the lantern-lit cafeteria, forming a plan to catch Gus. What we'd do with him afterward, we had no clue, but we concluded we had to stop him before he hurt anyone else. So, while everyone contributed ideas to that issue, I reflected on events from the last several weeks.

With a new and effective vaccine and an antiviral that worked, more people left the compound to enjoy the weather. Teams went out in the solar-powered cars on more recon and recovery missions to towns and villages they had not yet searched. Some of these outings lasted more than a day as they explored further away from the compound. Each time a mission returned; it was always the same—no survivors.

Our food storage shelves benefited from the trips as we filled them again with non-perishables. The missions also recovered plenty of other useful items, such as medical supplies and weapons. The latter stored in a locked room and overseen by Noah and Hester.

Hester had at least ten years on Noah. Though quiet and laid back, she did not allow anyone to bully her. I learned Cecil had brought her to the compound as part of his security team. While her training had not been in security, she had expert knowledge in self-defence tactics. And when I learned this, I asked Hester to show me a few things. After what happened with Archie and Gus, I never wanted to feel helpless again. But it was all in secret. It was during one of my instructions I learned she had accompanied my mother with Cecil when they returned to our old house the day after our abduction.

"There's only one way to catch him." Marcus spoke to Noah as though they were the only two in the room. Their conversation ended my ruminating.

Noah nodded. "We have to draw him to us."

"How?" Aya said. She laced her fingers and forced the backs of her hands toward each other. Her knuckles cracked in succession.

"Bait." Khelden spoke. His attention focused on a spot on the table in front of him.

Marcus and Noah nodded in unison. I narrowed my eyes. It seemed the two of them had already discussed the plan at length.

"And who's the bait?" Caleb said.

My eyes caught Beth's. I couldn't tell if she too was in on the idea or if she was as uninformed as Caleb and I.

A sure and quiet voice interrupted the heavy silence that had followed Caleb's question.

"Me," Jasmy said.

"What!" Caleb stared at Jasmy in disbelief.

Jasmy sighed. "It has to be me. I'm the only one who can sense when he's near."

"Don't worry, she won't be alone. So, everyone agrees?" Noah said. His voice pulled me away from my thoughts, and I looked around the table. Everyone but Caleb, Beth, and I nodded in slow, unenthusiastic agreement. Caleb stared at his hands clasped in front of him. Beth opened her mouth as if to speak, but then closed it again and pressed her lips together. As much as we wanted the task at hand to be over, no one looked forward to the potential danger of collecting The Collector.

Thirty-Five

The Collector Strikes

"Wake up, April. We have to go."

Noah's desperate pleas roused me from my sleep. "What time is it? What's happened?" I sat on the edge of my bed and rubbed the sleep from my eyes. A yawn muffled Noah's explanation as he tried to wedge shoes onto my feet. "What did you say?" I said when I'd finished yawning.

"There's been an attack."

"What?" I pushed his hand away and finished putting on my shoes.

Noah held out a blue sweater. "Here."

"Can't I get dressed first?" I started pulling my bare foot out of a shoe, wanting to put on at least a pair of sweats over my thin PJ bottoms.

Noah shook the sweater at me. "There's no time."

I snatched it from his hands. Before I pulled it on, he grabbed my hand and tugged me toward the door. As I stumbled, my foot came out of my shoe. "Hold on," I scolded and wiggled my foot back inside and straightened my sweater.

While the corridor was empty, voices and footsteps echoed from the stairwell at the far end, and we made our way toward the sound.

A cacophony of excited conversations drifted through the air as residents filed into the cafeteria. The room filled with speculation as we waited for someone to tell us what had happened. My mother, Reese, Lydia, a lab tech named Max, and Hester stood at the back against the wall. They waited patiently as the rest of the stragglers entered the cafeteria and the whispers subsided.

"I'm sorry," my mother began, "for disrupting your sleep," her eyes met mine for a moment, "or interrupting your work. However, there has been a serious incident and rather than allowing rumours to grow, I would much rather you all know the truth now."

The gathered crowed erupted into another round of anxiety-filled dialogue, interrupting my mother. Once again, she waited before continuing.

"With our newfound freedom comes danger as we venture outside this building and beyond the walls." She took a deep breath. "This morning, one of our Butterflies, wandered away from the courtyard."

My breath hitched. Butterflies, those who'd never regained awareness, needed supervision, especially while outside. They had a powerful desire to return to the woods and wander the trails.

"Lydia?" Mom spoke and placed a hand on Lydia's back, encouraging her. Lydia nodded with glistening eyes.

"This was my fault," she began. "I brought Ingrid outside to the courtyard to enjoy the sunshine. The gate at the end was closed. I..." She paused and looked at my mother, who nodded.

"I became distracted by the small herb garden I'd planted. When I looked up again, Ingrid was nowhere in sight and the gate was open." Lydia stared at her feet.

Max continued the story. "Hester and I were inside the doors talking when we heard a commotion." He paused and rubbed his stubbled cheek. "We immediately went outside to see what was going on. Lydia explained the situation, and along with a few others we headed out in search of Ingrid, while Lydia returned to the compound for more help." Max looked at Hester and she took up the briefing.

"As we neared the forest edge, I caught sight of Ingrid. She was easy to spot in her bright pink shirt." Hester cast her gaze to the floor for a moment before returning her focus to the crowd in front of her. "She had just entered the forest, so I called to the others, and we hurried forward before she walked deeper into the bush." She cleared her throat and shook her head. "Before we could. . . " Hester hesitated and looked at Max. "Before we reached her, someone grabbed Ingrid. He put her over his shoulder and looked back at me. He wore a dirty blue shirt and had brown hair pulled into a scraggly ponytail. That's the only description I have. With all the underbrush, it was difficult to gain any ground. I kept focus on Ingrid's pink t-shirt, but after a few minutes they disappeared, and we lost sight of them."

"That's got to be Gus," I whispered.

"Why aren't you out there still looking for her?" A voice from the crowd cried out. I looked in the voice's direction and back to my mother and the others.

"Recon Group Two had just returned from their assignment when Lydia found me, and they are out there now," Reese spoke.

Murmurs exploded once again.

"If anyone," this time my mother called out, not waiting for the crowd to settle, "would like to join the search, they could use more help."

The room quieted for a second, long enough for the sound of the cafeteria door banging closed behind us to make us turn toward the noise.

Three people stood at the back, having just entered the room. Black uniforms gave them away as Recon Group Two. The team lead stood ahead of the others and shook his head. A small, purple teddy bear dangled by its foot from his hand. Dirt dusted the fur of the stuffed toy. A silver medallion hanging from a light purple ribbon tied around the bear's neck glinted under the cafeteria light. My breath caught at the memory of the bear I'd left behind in Kearney. The teddy belonged to the previous inhabitant of the bedroom I had occupied for a short time after our parents and Noah rescued us from the forest. The last time I'd seen it was when I placed the stuffed toy back on its perch on the white dresser in the bedroom.

Mom's gaze fell on my face, and I read the sadness in her piercing blue eyes. For a moment, her eyelids fell shut and then opened again to a sober and crestfallen room. "We must remain vigilant at all times. No one is to leave the grounds alone. No one is to leave without the knowledge of others. No one—until we have dealt with this threat." Mom focused on Noah standing beside me, and he nodded.

"These are troublesome times," my mother continued with a solemn tone. "Danger is everywhere. Until we contact others, we cannot understand how much the world has changed and how much we've lost."

I dropped my gaze as my eyes welled. The crack in my mother's voice intended not just for Ingrid but also for her personal loss. Noah squeezed my hand as it had not gone unnoticed by others in the room.

"The missions in the last few weeks have revealed no more survivors. With each venture further away comes the potential for more danger, but it also brings hope. The surrounding towns and villages have revealed only a small picture of what we suspect elsewhere." Mom made eye contact with many in the room, and then she focused on the recon group at the cafeteria's entrance, directing her last words at them. "Gather supplies, rest, regroup, and recruit—in three days, you will head to Huntsville."

Thirty-Six

Change of Plans

They'd locked the front entrance of the compound, and apart from the recon teams, no one could go out the front door. And as for the exit in the courtyard, chains and locks kept anyone from opening the gate.

Recon Group Two grew by six new members, four fully recovered Butterflies in their early twenties and two in their late teens. They assembled their supplies and prepared to set out for Huntsville. The large town was located a little over an hour south of the compound and was the biggest settled area the recon group would search. While Recon Two's leaving occupied everyone else, our small gang assembled one last time before setting out on our own undertaking. Most of the recon teams' new members had volunteered, which left our bunch intact as there was no doubt, they would have recruited a few of us. We now focused our attention on a dangerous problem—Gus.

"Look, you don't have to do this." I overheard Caleb say as I joined him and Jasmy at our usual meeting place. Unlike last time, I was not the last to arrive. "April, you're early," Caleb said, sounding as though I'd interrupted an important conversation. Jasmy smiled at me from across the table.

"Not as early as you," I said.

Caleb made an annoyed sound, barely audible but loud enough to show his exasperation.

Before I could ask about what I walked in on, though I had a good idea, the rest of the group filed into the cafeteria.

"These middle-of-the-night meetings are killing me," Khelden complained as he pulled out a chair beside Caleb and stretched out his long legs.

"Aww, what's the matter Khel? Not getting your beauty sleep?" Beth said from her place at my left.

"Pfft, you should worry." Khelden said with a half-smile and tossed his head back, making his cow lick bounce.

"Go to hell." Beth flipped her dark waves with her hand and winked. A smirk played on her lips.

"This shouldn't take too long and then you can both get your beauty sleep. We have to change plans." Noah spoke from my right. His hand rubbed my back.

"What do you mean?" Caleb said.

Marcus cleared his throat. "Seems, April, has another theory."

I tapped my fingers on my forehead. "Yes, I do. Gus isn't hanging out in the woods. That teddy bear found by Recon Two was a message, and it came from the house we stayed at in Kearney. More specifically, the room I slept in."

There was a moment of surprised gasps and unbelievable whispers.

Beth spoke when everyone quieted. "Shit! Are you sure?"

I nodded. "Yes. I asked to take a closer look. There was a letter J in the middle of the medallion, just like on the stuffed bear in Kearney." The moment I first saw the engraving replayed in my head.

Khelden folded his arms. "But how can you be sure it's exactly the same?" Aya, seated on the other side of Khelden, punched him in the shoulder. "Ow!" He unfurled his arms and rubbed the injured area. "What was that for?"

Aya rolled her eyes. "Seriously, you think she wouldn't be sure? A person who remembers everything?"

Khelden's cheeks pinkened, and he swept his cowlick from his eyes. "Uh, I guess she would."

"Why do you think it was a message? Did he spy on us when we lived there? And how the hell would he know it was your room?" Questions spilled out of Beth's mouth.

"No, Beth, he didn't spy on us. But I do think he got it out of my head, read my thoughts when he abducted me. And why would he leave that bear behind if it wasn't a message? Gus knew I'd recognize it. He wants us to find him. And he's waiting in Kearney."

"Did Mom recognize the teddy bear?" Caleb said.

I shrugged. "Not that I'm aware of."

"So, what now? Same plan, but we go to Kearney?" Marcus scratched his chin.

Noah stretched his arms behind his head and tilted his chair on the back legs. "Same plan, different location."

"And they will let us take vehicles?" Jasmy's question quieted the room.

The front legs of Noah's chair clunked back on the floor. "Guess we'll have to walk there. There's no way we can take a car. Anyway, it's not that far away, a half-day's walk. Definitely doable."

"We can't just walk out the front door, it's locked," Beth said.

"No, we can't, and we don't have to." Caleb stood up and dug into his pants pocket and pulled out a key. "This unlocks the padlock on the door leading to the tunnel."

I reached over and took it from his hand. "How did you get this?"

"I've had it since we caught Archie using that door. No one ever asked me for it, so I've kept it. Just in case." He smiled.

After an hour of discussion, we agreed on the change of plan, though Caleb had several reservations about Jasmy's role as bait. But after much argument and deliberation, he had no choice than to go along with the plan. Jasmy had no doubts and no intention of allowing him to talk her out of it. Jasmy's determination and argument for being the only one able to keep her mind clear for more than a few minutes at a time won out. Gus's ability to get inside someone's head and read their thoughts made him a hard person to catch.

Dawn arrived three hours after our middle-of-the-night meeting. A few remaining stars twinkled in the dark sky as the sun broke the horizon. I stood on my bed, closed my eyes, and rested my forehead against the cool glass of my window. The second my skin touched the hard surface, it transported me back to the room in the house. The memory played, sinking me deeper into my rumination.

Stop! I told myself and opened my eyes, forcing my attention on my senses. The smooth and cold glass beneath my forehead; the faint scent of roses as a piece of my hair hung across my face; a residual minty taste in my mouth from brushing my teeth the night before; crickets chirping outside the window; and the dark forest in the distance. All to keep me in the present.

As the sky lightened, I pulled on my clothes and left my room. Jasmy, Caleb, and I planned to meet at the storeroom to gather supplies before breakfast.

"So, I tried it this morning," I said to Jasmy as we filled our packs with foodstuffs while Caleb stood guard outside.

Jasmy stopped mid-packing of a can of peaches. The label barely clung to the can, and she pulled it off. "Meditation?"

I shook my head. "No, the other thing, switching my focus."

"And, did it work?" Jasmy crumpled the label, then placed the can inside the pack.

"Wait, we won't know what that is!" I said, pointing to the bag.

Jasmy shrugged. "A surprise. So, back to my question, did it work?"

"Yes, it was easy."

"But..." Jasmy rummaged through the shelves, grabbing two bags of rice. Recent successful recon missions had filled the supply room, giving her plenty of choice.

Now it was my turn to stop mid-pack, and I inspected a box of bandages in my hand by giving it a shake. "Just... it was easy this morning, but I worry about the next time and the time after that."

Jasmy placed her hand on my arm. "Once my brother told me the only moment to focus on is right now. We cannot change the past. The future is unknown. Unless you are like a... is anyone here, you know, can see into the future?"

I considered what the members of our group could do, and while we had special talents, no one had that ability. "Not among us, anyway. Some other Butterflies, maybe. But the rest seem gifted more in things like music and art or have high IQs. At least on observation."

"Like you are gifted in art," Jasmy said.

"Thank you!" I smiled. "And you are wise for your age. What is that anyway?"

Jasmy smiled. "Fourteen. Fifteen in about two months."

"Oh, so my brother likes older women." I teased.

Jasmy giggled. "He has an old soul, like me, or so they tell me. Back to your murals, the enormous butterfly is amazing."

"Oh, you've seen that?" My eyes widened as I didn't believe anyone ever ventured down the short central corridor. There was no need.

"Yes, many people have, once word got out." Jasmy went back to packing. "Everyone is impressed. Really, it truly is amazing." She stopped for a moment and smiled at me.

We finished filling all six packs in silence, and I kept my focus on the present. But the memories of Beth and I loading our packs to escape the old house tried to sabotage my thoughts once or twice.

"Done!" I said and closed the last backpack. Each one held anywhere from eight to a dozen cans. Along with the food, we packed a can opener, a small pot, first aid supplies, matches, flashlight batteries, and an extra t-shirt for each of us. We'd fill our individual water canteens before leaving. "Okay, Caleb!" I called my brother back into the room. The three of us picked up a backpack in each hand and carried them to the door leading to the tunnel. Archie never sealed it off, and neither had anyone else.

Caleb produced the key from his pocket and unlocked the padlock on the door.

"So, you haven't told us how you actually got that key," I whispered.

Caleb placed his finger to his lips. "Sh! It's a secret."

I rolled my eyes.

The door opened with a groan, and we placed the bags inside the dark tunnel. We would retrieve them before sunrise the following morning on our way out of the compound.

Caleb re-locked the padlock. The resulting click evoked the image of the lock on the cabinet doors in the old house and the day Beth and I first unlocked it. And once again I slid back into the past. But the image melted inside my head as I strengthened and shifted my focus.

"Meet you back here in about four hours." Caleb took Jasmy's hand. "April, you got that?" he said and pointed to the supply room.

I nodded. "No worries, I'll lock up."

Caleb dipped his chin, and the two of them walked away, leaving me to wonder when my little brother had grown up.

After a quick inspection of the supply room, I locked the door and returned upstairs. There was more to do before we left, but something else suddenly needed my attention.

* * *

The door closed behind me with a soft click. For a moment I allowed the darkness to engulf me, and when I could take no more, I flicked on the flashlight.

My footsteps echoed as I walked down the corridor. The fingertips of my left hand trailed along the wall, bumping over grooves and small imperfections. I kept the flashlight trained on the wall to my right.

When the beam caught the image, I stopped. Leaning against the wall behind me, I shined the light on the mural of the large and colourful butterfly. The painting was one I hadn't seen since the night I finished it. The memory of every brush stroke played like a video recording. I traced the light over the butterfly in the same way as the paintbrush. This was more than the image of an ordinary butterfly, but a tribute. Instead of colourful spots on the wings, I'd painted tiny portraits of the children and young adults Cecil had gathered. While I painted some by memory, most of the likenesses came from photographs found in the manifesto.

My hand stopped at the first miniature on the butterfly's left wing. Shaun's amber eyes seemed to refract the light from my flashlight. I moved the beam over to the next image. Caia's spikey short hair was the first thing I saw. I wanted to reach out and smooth down the unruly pieces. As my light fell on each portrait, I gave it an equal amount of time.

I'd captured every single Butterfly Cecil had trapped within the compound's walls—his cocoon. It was as though drawing them on the wings gave them the freedom they'd deserved.

The light trailed down to the final two pictures at the bottom of the right wing. The image of myself never looked right in my eyes, though I'd heard read before that seeing your own form never looked right.

I took a deep breath and held it before allowing it to escape. The angle of my wrist tilted lower, and the light illuminated the last representation, though he was not a Butterfly. Deep brown eyes peered out from beneath his black side-swept fringe. I had taken such care in making sure every bit of this portrait was perfect.

I squeezed away the burning at the back of my eyes. "Oh, Jasper," I whispered.

Thirty-Seven

Before We Go

There was an ominous atmosphere surrounding the closed door to Cecil's residence at the compound. I raised my fist and tapped a light rhythm, knowing that no one would answer. Not because the sound was barely audible, but because the apartment was vacant. I thought of Cecil's dead body slumped over the kitchen table. Ignoring the disturbing vision, I laid my hand flat against the door. *When one door closes...,* Dad's voice whispered inside my head. But deeper in my mind there was another indistinct whisper, what I considered a residual echo of Cecil. I shifted my thoughts.

Doors, I hated them, and I hated feeling trapped behind them even more. The airy whoosh of those that slid caused goosebumps to rise, and wooden doors that creaked made me jittery. Worse still were doors that opened without a sound—quiet and unsuspecting. And I despised doors that locked away secrets and ones that opened to nothing but death and grief.

More intruding memories swirled inside my head and fought for attention. But I focused on breathing and tamped them down. One by one, the images disintegrated until my mind was a blank canvas. I walked away from the door to

Cecil's apartment. There was one more door I had to visit in this corridor, but that one would open to my knocking.

"April! What a pleasant surprise, I'm so happy you popped by." Mom kissed my cheek as I stepped over the threshold.

"Hi, Mom, do you have a minute?"

"Of course, honey. Is something wrong?" Mom stepped back, allowing me further into the small apartment.

Signs of my father were everywhere. Slippers peeked out from under the couch; his journal sat on the coffee table. A pencil stuck out from between the pages. I swallowed the tightness in my throat as I passed my hand over Dad's navy-blue sweater hanging over the back of a chair.

Mom's voice startled me. "Seems I still can't put any of your dad's things away."

"Don't worry, Mom. There are no set rules. When the time is right, you'll know."

Mom hugged me. "When did you become so wise?" She broke away and rested her hands on my shoulders. "Well, you are your father's daughter." A wistful smile crossed her face. "So, what's going on?" Mom tilted her head.

"Can we sit?" I stepped toward the couch and sat before she answered.

Mom joined me. "This sounds serious."

Yes, it was serious, but I wasn't there to tell her anything about us leaving. She could not know what we planned. And by the time she or anyone else found out, we'd be well on our way. "No, not really, I just wanted to tell you I'm learning to keep my memories in check. Jasmy helped me and it's working. And even though I still need more practice, things are getting better."

Mom's eyes brightened. "That's excellent news," she said. "How?"

"Meditation, focus, stuff like that." I lowered my eyes. "What you and Dad said I should try but didn't. I should have listened sooner."

"Oh, April, you're doing it now, that's the main thing."

"I guess. Anyway, I'm okay."

"Yes, you are." She smiled again. "Tea?" Mom said and patted my knee as she rose.

While there was plenty to do before we left the next morning, I wanted to spend as much time as possible with my mother, and I accepted her offer.

A knock caused Mom to switch directions from the kitchenette and answer the door. "Two more of my favourites," Mom said as Beth and Caleb stepped inside the apartment. "I was just putting on some tea, would you like some?" She said.

They nodded and joined me on the couch as Mom headed into the kitchenette.

Beth's eyebrows rose in a silent question, and I shook my head in response. I'd said nothing. Caleb didn't see the exchange and whispered too loudly. "Did you tell Mom anything?"

"Tell me what?" Mom stood in front of us with her arms crossed. "This is a little unusual that the three of you are here for no particular reason."

"Coincidence, Mom." Caleb smiled and cocked his head.

Mom's eyebrows rose. "Mm-hmm, that boyish charm might work on Jasmy but–"

"We're going out," Beth interrupted.

I looked at Beth, my mouth half open. The idea not to tell was no longer a part of the plan.

"Out?" Mom said and sat in the chair.

"Yes, out."

"And how do you propose to do that, we locked the exits?" Her piercing eyes narrowed.

Beth sat straighter and pushed her shoulders back. "Through the tunnel." She glanced at Caleb and me, "We, and a few others, are going to the old house."

"The tunnel? So, you're here to ask me for the key to the door?" Mom looked at me.

"Ah, Mom, you don't have the key, I do," Caleb confessed.

Mom's face contorted into a confused look. "What? How? Did you take it without asking?"

"No, you never had it. See, when I found the key on Archie's desk in the comms room, I mixed it up with a spare I had for the storage room by accident. That's the one I gave you. I didn't know until a while later, but then I thought it was better. With the food going missing from the storeroom, I thought the spare key was safer locked up in your room, and I kept the one for the tunnel."

Mom turned her questioning back to Beth. "Why on Earth do you want to go out?"

"Because we need to get out of here for a few days."

"A few days? With Gus out there, lurking about." Mom shook her head. "No, I don't think so."

"Don't worry, we'll be fine. And like Dad always said, there is strength in numbers." A reassuring smile crossed Beth's face.

"Sorry, but no. What the others do, well I can't stop them. But I can stop you. I've already lost your father, I'm not willing to risk losing the three of you either."

"Mom, you can't stop me, I'm an adult." This was not the conversation I planned on having.

"That might be true, April, but I never imagined you'd want to go back there again."

"No, but I need to. I have to face my fears."

"And what if he's there? What if Gus has a gun? Did you forget he killed two of your friends, and your brother almost

243

fell to his death?" Regret flashed in my mother's eyes the second she'd asked if I forgot.

The movie in my head played, but I stopped it. "He won't be there."

"How can you be so sure? He grabbed poor Ingrid less than two kilometres from here."

"Mom, I promise we'll be careful. But I need this. We need this." I looked at Beth and Caleb.

Mom sighed. "The three of you have been through so much, and I just want to protect you."

"We understand, but we'll be fine," Caleb said.

"Hang on, I didn't say you could go, Caleb. You're only thirteen."

"Fourteen in a few months and wise beyond my years." Caleb smiled.

"We'll watch him. And besides, he can take care of himself. Remember, he was the first one to escape Cecil last year. He wandered the woods alone for weeks before we found him." Beth reminded our mother of Caleb's resilience and survival skills.

Mom sighed. "I admire the strength and bravery you all have. No mother could be prouder." She paused and pressed her fingertips against her forehead. "I can't change your mind or stop you, short of locking you in your rooms. Can I?"

We shook our heads.

"And your responsibilities?"

"Taken care of," Beth said.

Mom closed her eyes. She took a deep breath and exhaled. "Things are so different now," she said more to herself. Her eyelids fluttered open, and she looked at Beth again. Her gaze calmer than a few seconds ago. "Take a walkie."

"But I thought the recon team took all of them," I said.

"Not all." Mom went into her bedroom and returned moments later with two radios. "Leave this on channel three and call if you need help." She handed me the walkie.

After that, Mom didn't press anymore. Instead, we talked of better times. Happy memories filled my head. We laughed at remembered antics and Dad's penchant use of idioms and expressions. We spoke of him and shared our fondest recollections. And while everyone else had a special memory of their last time with him, I still had nothing.

"When are you leaving?" Mom said after we'd composed ourselves from a bout of laughter that left us wiping our eyes.

I cleared my throat. "Early tomorrow morning."

"A few days at the most?" Mom's question sounded more like she feared it would be longer.

"Yes," Caleb said with conviction.

Mom nodded. "Well, I still don't like the idea, but promise you'll be careful, stick together, don't go off on your own. Now," she stood up, "get going, I'm sure there's a lot to do before you head out, and I might change my mind about allowing it."

We embraced Mom at the door; the hugs lasted longer than usual. "I have a feeling," she said as she hugged Caleb, "that I won't be seeing any of you in the morning. Be safe, and I love you."

I couldn't help but sense she understood there was more to our half-truth. And I couldn't help but sense our leaving would change us somehow.

Thirty-Eight

The Hunt

No one said anything as Marcus unlocked the padlock and opened the door to the tunnel. An earthy scent hung in the stale air as we stepped into the dark. I stared ahead. The light shining in from the corridor behind me reflected off the damp reinforced rock and dirt walls of the shaft at the entrance. But it did not stretch down the passageway, and the details faded into the black.

The door closed and for a split-second darkness engulfed us. The click of three flashlights echoed inside the chamber.

We plodded through the tunnel. Light beams bounced off the walls and floor, leading the way. The rock walls amplified every sound we made.

"Anyone think he could be hiding in this tunnel right now?" Aya whispered behind me as I walked beside Noah. The passage was wide enough to walk through in pairs.

"Doubt it," someone, I think Marcus, answered from further behind.

"Gus is not here," Jasmy's voice confirmed.

We shuffled along; our feet scuffed the dirt floor. The odd expletive echoed as someone tripped. Large and ominous shadows followed on the walls and ceiling caused by the beams of two flashlights behind us.

246

"How long is this?" Khelden said from somewhere in the middle of the group.

Noah stopped. My feet came to an abrupt halt, and I braced myself for the jostling that would follow. The three flashlights lit up the shaft well enough, but bounced around a lot as the holders investigated their surroundings.

"Why'd we stop?" Caleb said.

"Look!" Noah shined his light ahead.

The mound of dirt and rocks didn't quite block the tunnel, but it made for an interesting if difficult obstacle to get around.

"Shit!" Beth cried out. The rest of the group chuckled.

I held my hand out for Noah's light. "Let me see that." I shined the beam on the walls and ceiling, noting the debris did not appear to come from inside the tunnel. With the visual inspection over, I approached the mound.

"What do you think?" Noah's voice said behind me as I bent to pick something up. "What did you find?" Beth called from behind Noah.

I held up the dirty and torn paper. "The missing page of information I'd given Archie." I tore the paper into pieces and sprinkled them on the ground. "I think we can climb over this part here. These rocks aren't going anywhere." I said to Noah and pushed against a large one that stuck out from the heap.

"Okay, me first," Noah said.

"No, my idea, me first. Hold this and shine it through here," I said, handing him the flashlight.

"What are we doing?" Hester called out.

"Climbing over," Noah answered.

A small rock from the bottom rolled a little under my foot as I clambered the hill of rocks and dirt and crawled down the other side. A few abrasions and bumps later, we'd navigated the rocky obstacle. Twenty minutes after that, we found ourselves at the end of the tunnel, staring at a wooden door.

The three beams of light converged on the exit; a door that led into an old garden shed that disguised the entrance to the tunnel. Shimmering dust particles undulated in the beams, disturbed by our presence. The tiny bits rose and fell, swirled, and scattered, their movement like a murmuration of black birds playing in the air.

I stretched my hand forward towards the handle. In my mind the door transformed into the large cabinet standing sentry in the attic room of the old house, its macabre secrets locked inside. I squeezed my eyes shut, erased the memory, and refocused my attention on the present. The metal knob turned in my grasp, and I pushed the door open. My ears expected a squeak, but the hinges operated with little effort and rewarded me with silence.

Daylight weaved its way between the gaps of the wood-cladded shed. Flashlights clicked off behind me as I stepped towards the door and opened it into the yard.

Long blades of grass tickled my bare shins. Pine scent from the surrounding trees filled my nose. Birds sang and insects buzzed. My tongue poked out between my lips and tasted salt. I wiped my hand over my damp face.

The old house loomed in front of us. The back door was wide open, inviting us to enter. A gust of wind blew through the timbers; needles and leaves hushed in the disturbance. The door banged shut, bounced, and opened again.

"Looks like we're being invited in." Khelden moved toward the house, and the others followed.

I looked at Beth and Caleb, the only ones who hesitated along with me. Beth shrugged. She pulled her shoulders back and her chin led her forward, Caleb on her heels.

Alone, I took a deep breath, held it for a second and let it escape as slowly as I could. Another gust caught my hair and blew a piece between my parted lips. I swept it away, crossed the yard, and went into the house for what I hoped would be the last time.

Once I'd entered, my feet kept going. They carried me all the way through the house and out the front door, which was no longer nailed shut. Everyone else scattered. The old place wasn't huge; it wasn't necessary for me to investigate, and it wouldn't be long before the others joined me. Though I hoped it would be soon, I couldn't way to head to Kearney. I sat on the step of the porch and dug the toe of my shoe into the dirt.

I jumped as the front door behind me banged closed and interrupted my attempt to comprehend the voice whispering inside my head and my niggling thoughts.

"Move over," Beth said. I shuffled over to the right and she sat beside me.

"Anything?" I said. Though I didn't have to ask; I already guessed they wouldn't find anything, wouldn't find him. My suspicion that he waited for us in Kearney grew. Gus was crazy, but he was far from stupid. A brilliant psychopath made him a dangerous man.

"Nope. Just some old camping gear in the living room." Beth leaned forward and picked a white pebble out from the hole I'd dug with my foot. She placed it in her palm and stared at it. The stone levitated and then flew out of her hand, bouncing twice on the ground before disappearing into a patch of weeds.

The door banged again, but it did not startle me this time. "Any room?" Caleb said.

Beth and I shifted to opposite sides of the steps and our baby brother squeezed his tall, lean body between us. He stretched his long and hairy legs out in front.

"How the hell did you get so tall?" Beth said what I thought.

Caleb placed his hands behind him and supported his weight as he leaned back, giving us a little more room on the step. "Looks like I got the good genes, sis."

"Pfft! More like a mutation," Beth quipped.

I stifled a laugh. "The rest still looking for stuff?" I slapped at a mosquito and flicked its dead body off my arm.

"Searching, exploring, rummaging. No one's been in there since the day we found you." Caleb crossed and uncrossed his ankles.

I reached down and picked a small yellow flower growing close to the front step. "Wish we hadn't told mom we'd only be gone a few days." I twirled the stem between my fingers and watched it spin.

"WE didn't. I did," Beth said.

I shrugged. "But we didn't let on any different." I dropped the flower to the ground. Part of me regretted having picked it.

"A few days." I shook my head at the impossibility; it was more likely a week.

"Guess we shouldn't have said anything," Caleb spoke.

"Again, not WE. Me." Neither Caleb nor I argued Beth's point.

I stood up and stretched my arms above my head. "She will have a fit if we're not back early."

"Who?" Noah appeared on the porch.

I sighed. "We told our mom we'd be gone for few days at the most."

"Again, *I* told Mom." Beth lay back on the porch and drew up her knees.

"Don't worry about it." Noah walked over to the railing and gave it a shake before he leaned up against it. He folded his arms; the sleeves of his t-shirt tightened over his biceps.

"Oh?" My eyebrows rose. "Why not?"

Noah cocked his head. "How hard did she try to stop you?"

Beth sat. "What do you mean?" Her icy gaze narrowed as she fixed on Noah.

"When you told her you were leaving for a few days, how hard did she try to convince you to stay?"

I conjured up the apartment, the conversation, and Mom's worried expressions. She hadn't been too keen on us leaving. "At first she said we couldn't go. But when I told her she couldn't stop me, she didn't argue. She also didn't persuade Beth that much either. She was a little more adamant with Caleb, but it didn't take long to convince her to let him go too. Especially when she couldn't refute the fact that he'd survived for weeks on his own."

Noah smiled. "So . . . "

"Mom was testing us, wasn't she, making sure we understood what we were getting into? Though if we'd agreed to not leave, she'd been happy to keep us there. Mom knew all along," I said.

"What?" Beth jumped to her feet and Caleb hauled his long and lanky body up from the steps.

"I thought it seemed too easy," Caleb said.

"I'd approached her, after your rescue, about searching for Gus here at the house, and a couple of other places, camps Marcus knew about. She shot it down, told me to drop it, said she'd lock Marcus and me in our rooms to keep us safe. But then he took that girl, Ingrid, and she changed her mind," Noah said.

"The day he abducted her, that exchange between the two of you in the cafeteria." Mom's speech replayed in my head. After, she looked at Noah and he nodded back. "That was when she changed her mind. She wanted you to put your plan into action and deal with the threat."

Noah nodded. "I met with her afterward."

"She knows everything then, the entire plan?" I rubbed my forehead.

Marcus stepped through the door, followed by the rest. "No, we didn't tell her everything, not the new strategy or about Kearny, just the original idea we'd come up with to search here, maybe a camp or two." The nine of us crowded the small front porch. "Maggie wanted something done, but she wanted the three of you to stay out of it."

"So, you were in on it too?" Beth glared at Marcus and folded her arms. "Who else met with her?"

"Just Marcus and me, we worked on the strategy, tightened it up," Noah said.

"Okay, wait." I held up my hand. "Noah, you approached our mom first, then despite her telling you to drop it, arranged middle-of-the-night meetings with us to work on this plan of yours, anyway?"

Noah nodded.

"Well ours, actually," Marcus said. "We had to get things worked out, just in case. That's why we met with all of you. You know, brainstorming."

Noah continued. "But we also figured if we ever got the go ahead, or even if we didn't, we needed more bodies, so we asked Aya and Khelden to join us."

I glanced at Marcus before I continued straightening out the chronology of this crazy idea. "Then when Gus took Ingrid, you and Marcus met with Mom again?"

"Yes," Noah said.

"But we agreed with Maggie not to include the three of you when the plan came into action. Sorry, babe." Marcus looked at Beth.

"That's when I approached Hester," Noah said. "The five of us wouldn't be enough."

"You mean the four of you," I said sweeping my eyes over Aya, Khelden, Marcus and then back to Noah.

Jasmy stepped forward. "No, he is right. I was, am, number five. Hester evened the group out. And before you get all protective," Jasmy turned her attention to Caleb, "I volunteered myself."

Marcus nodded. "That is true."

Caleb looked at Marcus and then back at Jasmy; his mouth partly opened.

"Not a good look." Beth reached a hand towards Caleb's chin, which he promptly swatted away.

"I overheard them talking," Jasmy pointed to Noah and Marcus. "When I told them about my ability, they had me talk to your mom. She did not want to agree at first, but then she saw it was the only way."

"Yet you continued to include us in your meetings." Beth's eyes darted between Marcus and Noah.

"We included you because we wanted you to be in on what was going on, to an extent. But we didn't want you involved in the actual execution. You've been through too much already." Noah's gaze softened as he studied me.

"And how were you going to stop us from going with you?" I said, blood flooding my cheeks. The sense of betrayal grew as Noah and Marcus unveiled their plan.

Marcus scratched his chin. "There were a lot of ideas, you know."

"Some were okay," Noah said.

"Most were bad," Jasmy whispered, and her gaze fixed on a quiet Caleb.

"And then we decided we couldn't come up with any decent or believable excuse," Noah said. "Not to mention the teddy bear, that changed everything. And having a definite search area made a difference. But I have to tell you, we didn't tell Maggie what you told us about the teddy bear. And she still thinks we're just searching this house and the surrounding property. Like Marcus said, Maggie doesn't know everything."

"What you're saying is the only reason the three of us are here is because you couldn't come up with a decent excuse?" I glared at Noah.

Noah leaned against a porch column. "Well, not exactly. There was no way you could stay behind once you made us aware the teddy was a message. The plan changed to convince Maggie to let you come along."

Marcus held his hand out to Beth. She looked at it for a second, then grabbed it, and he pulled her into an embrace. I didn't think I would be as forgiving.

"So, after agreeing with our mother to leave us behind, you switched gears and ended up convincing her we needed to come along," I said.

Noah ran a hand over the top of his head. "Mmm, I wouldn't say convinced. But this is a new era, and your mom recognizes that. And it's not like there are many residents at the compound to choose from for such a task. Everyone else there either has an essential job or isn't capable. She didn't have a choice but to let you go. And like you said, if you'd agreed with her not to leave, she'd been happy with that."

I folded my arms. Noah and I would discuss this again, but right now there were too many eyes on us. "Well, we're all here now. So, what's next?"

"We put this plan into action," Noah said. "We take the road out of here and then to Kearny. It'll be a long walk, but we should make it to the edge of town by late this afternoon. Once we get close, we'll separate and sneak into town as we planned." Noah pulled out a rough sketch of the area where we believed we'd find Gus.

Caleb folded his arms. "And what about Jasmy?"

"That part hasn't changed," Noah said, "she has to take the road into town on her own. Gus might hope April will understand his message, but his predatory nature can't resist a lone girl wandering into town."

"And if we find him? We've never discussed what we will do," I said.

Noah and Marcus exchanged looks. Hester, who stood behind Aya and Khelden, stepped forward.

"We bring him back. Or kill him," she said.

Thirty-Nine

The Cat Came Back

Welcome to Kearney - Population ~~953~~ 1. The blue and white sign greeted us in the late afternoon after nearly an eight-hour walk. A bold, black mark crossed out the population number and someone used the same coloured ink to write the single digit. The sign was an eerie reminder of the ghost town it announced.

"Did you do that?" I said to Noah. Kearney was his hometown. When our parents and others fled the compound the night of the fire, they came to the small community and found him. He was the only survivor.

Noah stepped toward the sign, reached up, and traced his finger across the number one. He shook his head. "No, that's new."

"What is?" Marcus said, towing Beth alongside him and joining us. A few seconds later, the rest of our group came to a halt.

"Someone crossed out the population number, and it wasn't Noah."

"Sooo, you're thinking..." Marcus dropped Beth's hand and wiped his forearm across his brow.

My pulse raced, and stomach knotted. "Gus." I swallowed the tightness in my throat.

"But you can't be sure," Aya said.

"What's that?" Beth stepped away from Marcus and approached the sign. She reached up and pulled a small, blue velvet bag off a nail sticking out from the back of the post. Beth looked up at me as she held the pouch by the yellow cord that sealed it.

I took the bag from her hand, untied the bow, and dumped the contents into my hand. A gold bracelet with a solid heart lay in my palm. "Yes, I'm sure it was him. He kept this on him, carried it in his pocket." I stared down the road leading into town.

Beth twisted a piece of her wavy hair around her finger. "Now what?"

Sunlight reflected off the bracelet as I returned it to its velvet home. I tied the cord and hung the bag back on the signpost.

Jasmy dropped to the ground, crossed her legs, and rested an elbow on her knee. In her palm, she cradled her chin. "Sorry, I cannot stand any longer."

"Me neither." Caleb joined Jasmy.

Noah pointed. "Do you think you can walk as far as the first house?" Mumbled affirmatives and head nods from the group answered his question. "Then we'll spend the night there, rest and eat. Tomorrow we'll find The Collector."

Caleb rose to his feet and wiped away bits of dried grass stuck to the back of his pants. Jasmy followed his lead and stood beside him.

Chickadees called their name, blue jays screeched, and crows cawed. In the distance, the faint song of a cardinal echoed through the trees as we trudged the paved road.

"What about wild animals," Jasmy said, "or pets?"

"Well, we saw some in the forest last year, squirrels, wolves, a moose and signs of other creatures. The virus killed some too, but not like humans. I think animals fared better. Noah?" I said, prompting him to add more.

We stopped at the entrance to a long driveway; a red brick home stood at the end. After a few seconds, Noah spoke.

"Pets?" he said. Jasmy nodded. Noah stared at the house. "The hospitals were full, clinics too. People stayed at home. There was nothing anyone could do. Families buried their own, and neighbours buried the last members of families. Friends buried friends—buried strangers. And then there were three of us left, and then two. One day, there was just me." Noah pulled his gaze away from the house and looked at Jasmy. "Some pets got sick and died. I searched every house in town and left the back door open to each. Dogs and cats came and went, I released rodents and rabbits, and dumped fish in the lake. The dogs and cats stuck close to their homes at first. But once their food stores depleted, hunger forced them away. There could be some, I guess, still roaming around. But I imagine they'd be wild now."

"Great," Beth rolled her eyes. "A pack of wild dogs is all we need."

Marcus wrapped his arm around Beth's shoulders. "Doubt we have anything to worry about. Wild dogs will not hang where there's no food. This town's been picked clean of that. Now, let's get to that house. Looks like rain." Marcus tipped his head back. Dark clouds replaced the bright sun, and the light breeze turned stronger, rattling leaves and branches.

As we approached the abandoned house, a drop of rain splashed on my cheek.

"Pee-yew, something didn't make it." Khelden pinched his nose.

The smell hit me the second he spoke, and the sight of the offending odour a second after that. A headless and large rodent lay on the walkway leading to the front entrance of the house.

"Let's go around back," Noah said.

The long grass brushed against our pant legs as we neared the gate between a free-standing garage and the back corner of the house. Khelden stepped forward and with his long reach, unlatched the barrier on the other side. The hinges protested as he pushed the gate back, and one by one, we filed through.

"Thought you said you left all the back doors open?" Hester questioned Noah.

"Yup, every place but this one. This was my house." Noah looked toward the back of the large yard. Three makeshift crosses rose from the long grass. "Come on." He reached under an empty flowerpot, produced a key, and unlocked the back door.

Every cupboard and drawer in the kitchen lay open. Noah stepped forward and closed each one while the rest of us watched.

"So, you had no pets, that is why the door was closed?" Jasmy pulled out a stool from under the kitchen island and sat on the dust-covered seat.

"No, I have... had a cat, a calico. Lilly got out the night everyone from the compound rolled into town. Haven't seen her since."

I reached over and touched Noah's arm. "Noah, you never said."

Noah shrugged. "Lilly'd been gone for weeks by the time you came here. There was no point in saying anything."

Hester pulled out a stool beside Jasmy and wiped the dirt off with her sleeve before sitting. "Why wouldn't you leave the door open anyway, in case she came back?"

"There's a cat door in the garage, and she can get inside there for shelter. I kept the back door to the house locked in case I came back. Now, let's go upstairs. I have something to show you."

Driving rain lashed at the window at the top of the stairs on the second floor. Noah opened the door to the master bedroom at the end of the hallway and we followed him inside the large room.

Despite the dark sky outside, enough light streamed in through the two large windows. A layer of dust coated everything in the room, including the hardwood floor. The only thing protected from the dust was the bed as a green plastic tarp covered it.

Noah pulled open a door inside the room leading into a large walk-in closet. "Wait there," he instructed to the rest of us pulling a flashlight from his knapsack.

Noah disappeared inside the closet, following the beam of light. Rustling and other loud noises emanated from the small room before he emerged with a large, plastic container in his hands. "Here, take this." He handed the container to Aya and returned to the closet for another round of noise making. A minute later and he brought out another large and seemingly heavier bin that he handed to Marcus. "Be right back." Noah smiled at me and vanished again.

When Noah appeared for a third time, he cradled another container in his hands and pushed the closet door closed with his foot. "So, I have a confession," Noah said, placing the bin on the floor beside the other two. "Before we left this town, I hid these in a hole in the wall at the back of the closet behind a dresser. This was my contingency plan; in case I didn't want to stay at the compound. There's food and water in the heavy one. With what we brought, should be enough to last us a few days. Also, first aid supplies and–"

Before Noah could finish describing the contents, Hester, Marcus, and Caleb opened the containers.

"And this." Hester's eyebrows rose as she lifted a handgun from the bin in front of her.

"And that," Noah said.

Later I woke to moonlight shining through the window, the rain a distant memory. Apart from the snoring coming from one of the other three bedrooms, the house was quiet. I rolled over to cozy up to Noah and found myself alone in the double bed in his old bedroom. "Noah?" I whispered and listened for his reply. When it didn't come, I rose from the bed, put on my shoes, and tiptoed out the bedroom door.

A soft light spilled in through a window in the hallway. Shadows of the trees outside played on the walls. My ears strained for any sound that might lead me in Noah's direction. A muffled noise came from the lower level, and I carefully made my way down the stairs.

Noah stood on the deck with the back door wide open. He leaned against the railing and looked out at the dark yard. "Lilly!" he called just above a whisper and made kissing noises into the air. He held a flashlight in his hand and shined the beam of light over the yard.

"Hey," I whispered and wrapped my arm around Noah's waist as I came to stand beside him. Noah's arm draped over my shoulder and pulled me close. "Did you see her?"

"Nah, I was just hoping... When I saw that dead mouse this afternoon, I thought maybe–" A loud clang from inside the garage interrupted him.

"What was that?" I whispered.

Noah pulled his arm away from me and took my hand. "Come on," he said, and we stepped off the deck and onto the wild lawn.

We leaned against the garage and listened, Noah's hand on the doorknob of the side entrance. I reached over and covered his hand as he turned the knob. "Wait! What if it's him?" My heart thudded.

"Who? Gus?"

I nodded.

"Here, take this." Noah handed me the flashlight. From his pocket he pulled out a large pocketknife and flipped out the blade. He leaned over and whispered in my ear. "When I open the door shine the light inside, eye level. Blind him with the light, I'll take care of the rest."

My heart pounded. "Are you going to stab him?"

Noah nodded. "If I have to. Ready?"

Every part of me wanted to run back into the house, but my feet wouldn't move. Adrenaline pumped through my veins; my hands shook. And without thinking, I nodded.

Noah's hand turned the knob, slow and steady. When he flung the door open, I shined the light over his shoulder. The beam reflected off the window of a mid-size car. Dust floated in the beam.

Another clang from the other side of the car near the front had me concentrate the beam of light on the large garage door. Noah motioned for me to shine the light along the opposite wall on the other side of the car. He dropped to his belly and looked underneath the vehicle, then popped back up to his feet. His quick movement reminded me of a burpee, only he lay flat on the cement floor with his legs sticking out the side entrance. "There's something on the other side of the car," he whispered in my ear.

We tiptoed toward the front of the vehicle. A large cobweb brushed against my face, and my hands frantically wiped it away. The flashlight beam moved erratically. "So much for stealth," Noah whispered.

"What stealth? We gave ourselves away when we came in here with this light."

Noah held up his knife. The blade glinted. "At least we have protection."

A low growl came from the opposite side of the garage as we approached the front of the car. "Stay there," Noah said, but he didn't have to caution me. My feet had no intention of moving.

The closer Noah got, the more intense the growl. "Noah, come back. Let's go. Whatever that is, it doesn't sound happy."

"Sh! It's okay." Noah's voice rose in pitch, and he ducked from my view.

"Noah?" The growling returned to a low rumble. "What's going on? I'm coming over," I said as bravery returned.

"No, stay. You'll scare her."

"Who?"

"Lilly."

Forty

Fatal Mistake

Dreams and unrelenting thoughts interrupted my sleep through most of the night. With each rise toward consciousness, I sensed Noah's own unrest. It was only when dawn came that rest found us. When we woke, it was to the sound of our companions rising and we soon realized we'd slept the morning away.

After a quick and meager breakfast with little conversation, we scattered. Noah headed for the garage, hoping to reacquaint more with his cat. Beth and Marcus plodded upstairs, while Caleb and Jasmy went to sit on the front porch. With Hester, Aya and Khelden exploring the rest of the house, I found a secluded spot at the back of the yard and meditated. It seemed no matter how much we'd discussed Noah and Marcus' campaign; it did nothing to ease the apprehension we now felt. Gus was a threat, but were we up for vigilantism? Could we be judge, jury, and hangman?

It was late afternoon; twenty-four hours had passed since arriving in Kearney. Procrastination over, we set out to complete the mission we put upon ourselves.

"We must split up soon," Noah said, taking my hand. My eyes caught sight of the pistol grip sticking out of the back of his pants.

"Then what?" Caleb stopped and forced the rest of us to come to a halt.

"Then we go on with the plan."

"Seriously? We already have it figured Gus will be at the brick house we stayed in months ago. Why don't we just storm in? He can't take us all on."

"Think about it, Caleb." Noah dropped my hand and stepped toward my brother. "Do you really believe he'll be there? Sure, he led us to this town, but The Collector won't be at that house. Hell, he can't even be sure anyone will come looking for him here, let alone April. We have to split up but stay hidden. Jasmy can walk down Main Street. Once she senses him, she'll draw him out."

"No!" I said. "Gus knows I'm coming after him, and he'll be at that house. He planned it this way." All eyes fell on me. "He was in my head, like Cecil. Only, he planted this seed to search for him." Everyone stared. "For days, weeks maybe, I've heard whispers, a subliminal message of some sort. I thought they belonged to Cecil, but it's Gus. He wanted me to come and find him, no matter what."

Noah nodded in Marcus' direction. "But looking for him was our idea."

"That might be true, but I would have gone on my own as soon as I had the chance. I think your idea gave me the opening my subconscious needed."

Hester twisted her long red hair and held the bun on top of her head. "So, he's sure you're coming to find him."

I nodded. "He might not know when, but sometime. Gus has all the time in the world to wait for me to show up. What he didn't account for was my being here with others."

"And when the fuck did he get into your head and plant all this shit?" Beth waved her hand in the air.

"The only chance he could, when he was getting me to remember Cecil's information."

The plan had to change, and Jasmy could no longer be the one to draw him out. Gus expected to see me alone, and if he watched from somewhere, my solitary stroll down the middle of the street is what he'd get. As for everyone else, they paired off and moved furtively through town.

Caleb and Jasmy disappeared behind a row of trees lining the left side of the road, with Khelden and Noah following several minutes later. Marcus and Beth did the same along the right side, with Hester and Aya flanking them. Jasmy had taught everyone how to clear their thoughts, concentrate on their breath, and nothing else.

I filled my lungs and counted to one hundred. Taking tentative steps forward, I cleared my mind of everything but searching for Gus. He could not get inside my head and learn there were others with me. If he did, it would be dangerous for everyone. As an opportunistic predator, if he could satisfy his urge to kill, he would. He'd gone a long while without killing until Ingrid and that would not have satisfied his need but only drive him to kill again. But Gus was also arrogant, and somehow, I had to make that work in our favour.

Insects buzzed around my head, attracted to the sweat covering my face. An occasional breeze rustled the leaves of nearby trees and shrubs, bringing a moment of relief from the sticky heat. My clothes pasted against my skin.

A large brick house caught my attention, and I stared at its windows, imagining the people who once lived inside the dwelling. The grass in the front yard was no longer what I imagined was once a neat and manicured lawn. Instead, shrubs and all varieties of vegetation grew wild. A blue Fiat

Toro sat in the drive. The driver side door wide open as though the driver had forgotten something and ran back inside the house to get it.

Another breeze offered a moment of relief. A gate across the road squeaked in displeasure from the disruption, and the screen door on the house slammed shut, then bounced open again.

Sweat trickled down the small of my back, and I licked my dry and sunburned lips. I stopped and took a sip from my water bottle. The liquid inside was no cooler than the air, but it eased the dryness in my mouth and throat. My heart picked up speed as I noticed the stop sign at the corner and the narrow south end of Hassard Lake across the road. A right on Main Street, across the bridge, and I would close in on my destination.

My pace slowed as I hugged the right side of the road, passed the last house, and red mini-van parked on the shoulder. On the corner stood the old liquor store, likely still full of its contents. While the occasional bottle of wine found its way to the storage room shelves, alcohol was at the bottom of the list of essential food supplies. Although, the infirmary at the compound had its fair share for medicinal purposes.

I kept close to the side of the liquor store and was about to turn the corner when Gus stumbled up the front step and yanked open the door. The unexpected sight caused me to cover my mouth with my hand and stifle the gasp that tried to escape. My heart thrummed in my ears as I pressed against the wall.

"Shit!" I whispered. My eyes scanned the deserted street, hoping to glimpse someone from the group who'd gone ahead of me. But by now they'd be surveying the house on Main Street, taking cover, and waiting for me to arrive.

I took a deep breath and crouched low. With my focus on controlling my breathing, I crawled around the corner and up the accessible walkway. I stopped and sat against the wall under the first window of the liquor store; the sound of bottles crashing to the floor made me hold my breath. My hands balled into tight fists and as I exhaled, I slowly uncurled my fingers. A Crow cawed. The unexpected noise started another round of heavy thumping just as my heart settled back into a somewhat normal rhythm. Silence once again fell on the desolate street and in my head.

Heat from the concrete radiated through my jeans as I rested against the pale-yellow siding of the liquor store. The lake across the road shimmered in the late afternoon sun. Small ripples disturbed the surface of the water, distorting the reflected clouds. I rolled onto my hands and knees. Tiny pieces of grit pushed into my palms. With another deep inhale, I slowly rose and peeked through the window.

Gus sat on the floor in front of the first shelving unit, with his eyelids closed, in a puddle of red wine and surrounded by broken glass. A bottle, loosely clasped in his hands, dribbled onto his lap. The liquid stained his pants and seeped out from under him like blood. The sight caused a flash of Caia lying in Marcus' arms, her blood pooling beneath her. I closed my eyes and erased the image. When I gazed upon the scene again, Gus stared toward the window, a drunken grin on his face. My thoughts roused him from his stupor. I ducked.

By now, my friends would be at the house where we believed we'd find Gus. Jasmy would try to sense him there and they'd be taking up positions soon, finding hiding spots, and waiting for my arrival. But the confrontation would not happen the way we planned, and the sudden opportunity bore a new stratagem. An idea that I could not form completely in my head as Gus was sure to invade my thoughts. So, with each piece of new strategy that came to mind, I cloaked it in images of white and jumbled memories.

Exhaling a steadying breath, I reached for the handle and pulled the door open, executing the first stage of my plan. The smell of alcohol permeated the stale air.

"S'a nice surprise!" Gus slurred.

Glass crunched under my feet as I stepped further into the store and passed the checkout near the door. Puddles of wine and other libations covered the grey tile. It seemed the mess Gus sat in wasn't the first made. Bits of multi-coloured glass glinted in the sunlight streaming in through the front window.

My heart raced faster than ever, and I feared it would burst. "Cut the crap! What do you want?"

Gus chuckled. "Well, if you muss'know, you dead." He lifted a hand from his lap and let it flop back down with a slap.

"Why?"

"Cuz you... know too... much." He tried to get his feet underneath him but slipped in the wine and fell, banging into the shelves behind him. Bottles rattled.

The drunken display in front of me gave me courage, and instead of leaving, I stepped closer. Gus couldn't know anyone else was with me, so I kept thoughts of my friends out of my head. "That's your fault, you made me remember. And it's too late now, everyone knows everything."

Gus moved to his hands and knees. Grabbing a rack for support, he pulled himself to an unstable stand. "Pfft! You would have remembered, isss what you do. Nah, April's gotta go." He took a shaky step forward, and I stepped back. "Come on, don't make this sssso hard. Promise it'll be over quick." He drew his finger in a slicing motion across his neck. A smile stretched over his face in stark contrast to the evil held in his eyes. I had no weapon, but the exit was not far behind me. Should Gus lunge forward, I felt confident his drunkenness would allow me to make my getaway.

A large piece of glass on the floor about halfway between us caught my attention. The veil protecting my thoughts dropped.

Gus snickered. "Oh, April, you'll cut yourself." He took another wobbly step.

Every muscle in my body tensed, and my pulse raced. I turned on my heel and ran toward the exit. Gus laughed. I reached for the handle and as I pulled, another force grabbed me from behind and yanked me away.

"Aren't I just the best actor," Gus whispered in my ear as he wrapped his arms around my waist and hauled me from the door. The smell of wine on his breath made my stomach turn.

I wriggled in his grasp, kicking out my legs. Bottles that met my struggle smashed to the floor. "Let me go!" I screamed.

Gus tightened his grip and dragged me further from the exit. I tried to reach for a bottle, but he swung me away from the shelf, and my feet connected with more unfortunate bottles. "See," he breathed hard, "I'm not as inebriated as you think. Imagine... my surprise–" I gripped the edge of a shelf as he pulled me past and held on, but my fingers slipped. He readjusted his hold and continued talking. "When I yanked open the door to this... establishment and saw your reflection in the glass. And that... stumble I took at the door, I tripped on the step." My hand seized a bottle, and as I brought it up, he swiped it from my grasp. Clear alcohol streamed from the rack like a mini-waterfall. But my struggling and interruptions didn't stop Gus from bragging. "When I saw you, I used the trip... to my advantage. Pretend you're drunk... I thought. So, I broke a few bottles, took two swigs. That red wine is god-awful and—well, I don't know what's worse, drinking it or sitting in the stuff."

The rear of the store was darker. High shelving units blocked the sunlight streaming in through the front windows. Boxes of wine bottles stacked up against the back wall, waiting for someone to empty their contents. Four bottles perched precariously on the top of one crate.

My breaths came in heavy pants. The booze-filled air burned my nostrils. Thoughts of my family and friends fought for attention. Hot tears blurred my vision as my muscles relaxed from fatigue. "Please," I begged as I saw the closed pocket knife carried in his hand for the first time.

Gus pulled me back toward the wall and bumped into a stack of boxes. Two bottles fell and crashed to the floor. He moved his arm from around my waist and up to my neck. I closed my chin down on his forearm, preventing it from pressing against my throat. "This will be quick," he whispered.

I took a deep breath, allowed my mind to go blank, and grasped the arm around my neck. In the same fluid motion, I stepped to my right and swung my left fist back towards my attacker. His gasp, the loosening of his arm, and the sense he'd crumpled behind me, let me know I'd hit my mark. The pocket knife clattered as it struck the floor in front of me, splashing in a puddle of red wine. As his body slumped forward, I pulled my left elbow upward and connected with his face. Free from his grasp, I dove for the knife. With a flick, the blade released.

"Impressive. Bitch!" Gus pulled me up from the floor and spun me around. A crazed glare replaced the evil I'd seen. I screamed.

Furrowed brow, pressed lips, narrowed eyes, and a hollow gaze dissolved in front of me. The lines in Gus's forehead slackened, his lips softened and parted, eyelids opened wide, and shock registered in his eyes. I wondered if my scream had reached him, broken through his psychopathy, and made him feel something.

His hands slid from my arms. I looked down. The thumb of my right fist rested against my chest, and my pinky pressed up against his. Blood seeped between my knuckles. I pulled my hands away, exposing the hilt of the knife. I stepped backward. A dark stain on Gus's pale blue shirt ringed the knife.

Gus fell back against the wall then slid down, landing in a puddle of red wine. His legs straight out in front of him and his head against the blocks reminded me of how he sat when I first spied him in the store. A remaining bottle sat next to him atop a box, undisturbed by the bloodshed. "What better way," he gasped, "to make my memory live on, but inside the head of someone... who can never... forget." Gus pulled the knife from his chest. The stain expanded. Blood mixed with the wine. And he breathed his last breath.

My sobs turned to gasps as my lungs struggled to inhale a proper breath. My legs too weak to hold my body, I crumpled to the floor and crawled toward the entrance. Glass pricked my hands and booze stained my pants.

Like a cat basking in the sun, I curled into a ball when I reached the exit. Voices from the dead echoed in my head, Cecil, Gus, Jasper—my father. I covered my ears, but it did not help. Images of my life played inside my mind. Finally, I managed a deep breath. When I let it escape, it was through pursed lips. Another exhale and then another until my heart slowed and my mind went blank. Exhaustion replaced the dissipating adrenaline. I closed my eyes and cried.

Forty-One

The Question

Not much time had passed when Noah's urgent voice interrupted my sobs. "April! Oh God, are you okay?" His hand rested on my shoulder, and my eyelids fluttered open.

I sat up, staring at him through tear rimmed eyes, and nodded.

"Are you sure? You're covered in blood?"

Red, wine-soaked jeans stuck to my legs; a spot of blood stained the front of my purple t-shirt. Fine scratches traced up my arms and weaved between the bruises. Abrasions marked my knuckles and palms. A fragment of green glass poked out from a superficial cut at the base of my thumb. The air reeked of alcohol. "Mostly wine. Some blood." I grasped the shard between my fingers and removed it, sucking in through my teeth as it stung more than I thought. "Where's everyone?"

"Looking for you. Jasmy couldn't sense Gus at the house, so she and Caleb headed up the road, hoping to get a better idea of where he might be. We waited, and when you didn't show, we split up. I saw you through the window. What the hell happened?"

My stomach lurched. "Gus."

Noah pulled the gun from the waist of his pants. "Where," he whispered.

"Don't worry. He's... dead," I choked on the last word. Visions of the horrific event replayed in my head.

Noah's eyes narrowed. "For sure?"

I nodded and pointed to the rear of the store. "Over there."

The front door of the shop opened, and the rest of our group rushed inside.

"What happened?" Marcus said, he focused on the gun in Noah's hand. Beth kneeled beside me and dropped her pack on the floor. "Don't move," she commanded and dug through the first-aid supplies.

"Beth, I'm fine."

She stopped searching for bandages and glared. "Fine! You're drenched in blood."

"Wine," I corrected. "Only some blood. And it's not all mine." All eyes rested on me.

Noah tucked the gun into the waistband of his jeans. "Gus." He pointed toward the back of the store and led Marcus, Khelden, Hester and Caleb through the debris.

"Looks like a damn war zone," Hester said as they disappeared behind the shelving.

Aya sat beside me while Beth cleaned the cuts on my hand. "Are you really okay," she said.

In what way? Physically? Mentally? Emotionally? Physically, I would be. The bruises would disappear, the lacerations would heal. But I couldn't be sure of anything else. "Yes," I said, deciding to focus on the physical pain.

Jasmy kneeled on the floor. "Oh, April, forgive me."

"For what?" I said as Beth finished wrapping my hand with gauze.

"For not sensing Gus was here."

"Jasmy, you and Caleb headed in a different direction, too far to pick up on any of our emotions."

She picked at her fingernails. "Yes, I know, but I still feel guilty."

"Well, don't. I will be okay."

Jasmy sighed. "Let me help you practice meditation then. I can help you control these fresh memories."

"Don't worry, you will." My lips formed a weak smile.

"Av, I am sorry," Caleb said as he and the others rejoined us.

"For what?"

"For not being here. What you suffered through... " he looked around the store, "all this. You are brave."

Marcus and Khelden nodded.

"No, I'm not." I rubbed the burning away from my eyes. "Help me up." I reached toward Noah. He took my arm and helped me to my feet. My legs wobbled for a second. "Where are you going?" I said to Beth as she sidestepped a large puddle of wine.

She stopped and spun to face me. "To see for myself."

"Not a good idea."

"I wasn't here when you needed me. I will not let you carry the burden of remembering this awful day by yourself." She turned on her heel.

"Wait for me," Ayanna called.

"Me too," said Jasmy.

Minutes later, we left the liquor store behind and plodded back to Noah's house. The sun was low when we arrived, and Lilly welcomed us at the backdoor, a nice surprise for all. The calico happily went inside when Noah opened the door. I still had told no one what had happened, and no one pressed for the information. For now, they could draw their own conclusions.

* * *

The next morning soft purrs greeted me when I opened my eyes to Lilly's yellow ones as she stared and blinked. Her paws kneaded the blanket covering my chest. I pulled my hand out from under the bedding and stroked the orange and black fur between her ears. The spot was the only scab-free place on the poor thing's body. Whatever battles Lilly had gone through, she'd survived. She was scarred but alive.

Lilly rose; her weight seemed to double as each paw sunk into me. She yawned and arched her back. Then, with a flick of her scrawny tail, she jumped from the bed and raced out the bedroom door.

"Don't let the cat out." Noah's voice called from the hall-way; he stood in the doorway and leaned against the door-jamb. "Did you get any sleep?"

I nodded. Despite yesterday's events, I managed to rest a little. "Is everyone else up?"

Noah walked toward the bed and sat. "Yup, but only just. Listen," he took my hand, "whenever you want to talk about what happened, I'm here."

I smiled. "Yes, I know."

"Okay, good. So, ready to leave this place?" Lilly jumped up between us and rubbed against Noah's arm.

I nodded and scratched the cat's head. "I think Lilly is too."

* * *

Chickadees zipped from tree to tree along the road, es-corting us from town. A gust of wind tickled the hairs on my arm, a soothing touch from Mother Nature. Noah read-justed the cat backpack, and Lilly stared out the bubble window.

Hester walked alone a little ahead of us. Wisps of red hair floated behind her as another breeze lifted them from her shoulders. I hurried to catch up to her.

"Hey," she said, keeping her gaze fixed to the road. The sun exposure from the last couple of days had pinkened her long straight nose and caused a dusting of freckles to appear on her cheeks.

"Thank you," I said.

"For what?"

"For saving my life."

Hester stopped for a second. "What?" I kept walking and this time Hester had to catch up. "What do you mean?"

"The self-defence stuff. I wouldn't be here if you hadn't shown me what to do."

"Well, you asked me to show you, and I did. Without that initiative... So, really, you saved your own life."

"Maybe, but I wouldn't have known what to do, so thank you."

"What... what did he do?"

My stomach knotted. "Choke hold," was all I said. When I told the story, it would only be one time. And once told, I would never speak of it again. Hester and everyone else would have to wait until I was ready.

"Oh! Well, I'm glad everything worked out. I mean..." Hester's voice trailed, and I continued to walk beside her for a few more awkward seconds.

Ayanna's laugh floated to my ears and gave me the excuse to hurry on ahead. "Ahh anyway, I have to ask Aya something so we'll talk later?"

Hester bobbed her head and smiled. "Sure, later."

"Great!" I said, then quickened my pace to catch up to Aya as she walked with Khelden, Jasmy and Caleb.

"Hey!" I said to the small group. Sympathetic smiles crossed everyone's face and Caleb dropped Jasmy's hand to put an arm around my shoulder for a brief hug. Since learning of Aya's abilities, I'd wanted to talk to her but did not know how to broach the subject. In the silent and awkward moment, I spent with Hester, I made up mind to approach her before losing my nerve. "Can I ask you something, Aya?"

"Ah, sure."

"Um, alone?"

Khelden flipped his cowlick. "Guess I'll keep Noah and his cat company." He turned and walked back.

"Come on." Caleb grabbed Jasmy's hand, and they jogged ahead. Jasmy turned to wave.

Several versions of the question I wanted to ask rolled through my thoughts. A monarch butterfly fluttered across our path, and I automatically rubbed the back of my neck. There was a loud hush as a gust of wind rattled leaves and stirred up dust on the side of the road. I caught a whiff of something sweet travelling through the air. Each tiny distraction pulled me away from my intent.

"So, you wanted to ask something?" Aya's voice made the wheel spinning in my head stop and land on one question.

"Can you talk to my dad?" I blurted with no further thought.

"Now?"

I took a moment to think and sighed. "No. When we get back to the compound."

"Sure, I'll try."

I stopped. "Try?"

Aya linked her arm through mine and lead me forward. "April, it's not like calling someone on the phone and waiting for them to answer. I can't promise you, but I'll try. Okay?"

"Okay."

"Can I ask why? I mean, other than the obvious reason of missing your dad, it seems like there's something else."

I nodded. "There is. I barely remember when he died. Yes, I get it. Strange for someone who never forgets. But I was still recovering from the dose of hypno-drug I'd given myself. Those few weeks back at the compound are a blur. My mom said Dad talked to me while he was sick. I just want to remember what he said."

"And you want me to ask him, right?"

My throat tightened and eyes burned. I nodded.

Aya took a deep breath and squeezed my arm. "Okay, but I make no promises."

Forty-Two

Hesitation

I would have preferred to take the road leading to the compound, but as they'd locked the front door, the tunnel was easier access. And so, we journeyed back to the old house, a trek that seemed longer with every step forward. Maybe it was the thought of seeing it again that caused me to drag my feet. What ever the reason, I was thankful everyone else walked ahead and gave me the solitude I requested after my brief conversations. Occasional bits of chitchat floated to my ears on the breeze, but I cared little about the words uttered. My mind focused on the views, sounds and smells of the present, resisting any urge to replay yesterday's events or any moment from the past.

There was at least another hour of daylight by the time my eyes caught sight of the rusty red roof through the trees. And while we could have taken the tunnel that evening, the trip to the house left us exhausted. Everyone agreed to stay the night. But despite my hesitation, I was in no hurry to return to the compound either.

Goosebumps erupted on my forearms in the hot air.

"Are you cold?" Noah said and wiped a hand over his sweat covered brow. I hadn't even noticed he'd joined me as we drew closer to our rest area.

I stopped rubbing my bare arms. "No, just not thrilled to be here again."

The others walked ahead toward the abandoned house. Dust from their scuffing feet scattered and shimmered in the early evening sun.

From our position, I watched as some plunked themselves on the front porch when they arrived. But Beth and Caleb stood further away. Beth tipped her head backward and looked at the window. The action was instinctual, habitual for us. Even now my eyes travelled away from Beth to the window and back.

"We don't have to stay inside." Noah's voice pulled me from the distraction.

"No, I'd rather not."

"Wait here." He took the backpack off of his shoulder and handed it to me. Through the plastic bubble I saw Lilly in the bottom sound asleep. She stretched and curled into a tighter ball. Before I asked what he planned, Noah left my side and headed to the house.

A tree stump, standing in the grass, caught my attention, and I waded toward it through the leafy vegetation. An iridescent green beetle crawled cross the remains of the tree. Its hard forewings opened and exposed a pair of translucent hindwings. They fluttered and then carried the insect away.

The rough bark snagged on the gauze covering my palm as I brushed off loose pieces of wood before sitting. I placed the cat carrier on the ground. Wispy blades of grass surrounding me swayed in the breeze. A yellow butterfly landed on the tip of a swaying blade and rested. Delicate, powdered wings fluttered as it balanced. After a brief rest, the butterfly lifted and flew away. Shielding my eyes, I followed its flight toward the sun dipping behind the tallest trees.

I rubbed my hand across the back of my neck and over my butterfly tattoo. I longed for the day when I too could drift to places unknown. "Fly free," I whispered.

My name floated to my ears. Noah waved to me from the front porch.

I stared at him, reluctant to move from my safe spot. But remaining seated on the tree stump all night was not a choice. The slow trod down the dirt road disturbed small pebbles, and they bounced off my shoes and flew into the grass. Lilly meowed. It seemed my movement disturbed her as well as the stones.

Noah smiled as I approached. "How about a tent? The label says it sleeps ten. Might be a bit close, but we should all fit." He stepped up onto the porch and retrieved a large, oblong-shaped bag from behind the porch's railing. The black and orange nylon bag was torn at one end and one of the canvas handles hung by only a few threads. Fortunately for Noah, the other handle was intact, and he carried it down the steps.

I pointed back toward the stump. "Let's set that up over there? I don't want this place to loom over us." While I had no intention of sleeping inside the tent, the idea seemed confining, I wanted the others nearby.

"Sure," he said, "but we might need to flatten the grass a little. Are you joining us?" Noah turned and said to the others. No one hesitated as they grabbed their packs and walked away from the house.

I pulled Lilly from her carrier and attached a long lead to her red harness. She bounded through the weeds and perched on the stump where she groomed herself between sessions of bug hunting. After tramping the grass, Noah and Hester set up the ten-person tent over the flattened spot. While the grass was high along the road and near the stump, there was an area further away where the grass and weeds hadn't grown as wild. The patch being much closer to the forest edge made a perfect spot for a small campfire.

We gathered branches and other larger bits of wood. By the time our campsite was ready, the sun's rays no longer shone through the trees. The red sky morphed into purple as the first evening stars twinkled.

Flames licked at the branches; wisps of perfumed smoke rose toward the dark sky. A loud snap and tiny sparks shot out into the night. Quiet voices and tired yawns mingled with the sounds of the fire and chirping crickets. An owl cried its ghostly song. I inhaled and focused on separating out each individual scent that made up the air. It was a painstaking process, but a necessary distraction that kept the memories at bay. That and stroking Lilly's fur while she curled up on my lap. While I had learned to refocus my thoughts when awake, I could not stop them when I rested. As exhausted as I was, I did not want to sleep.

"April, try to get some sleep," Noah whispered in my ear.

"But I can't rest in that tent, Noah."

Noah chuckled. "If you haven't noticed," he motioned with a nod of his head, "the tent is now full. So, guess it's more an eight-person tent."

My eyes focused beyond the campfire to the empty spaces where others had sat earlier. "When did that happen?"

Noah's arm wrapped around me and pulled me close. "Marcus and Beth were the last to climb in about twenty-minutes ago."

Stars dotted the black sky, but on a moonless night their light wasn't bright enough to show more than a dark shape of the tent behind me. "Well, I'm sure they're comfortable in there." I rested my head against Noah's shoulder and closed my eyes.

"Huh, I doubt it. The air hasn't cooled that much." Noah tossed one of a few logs found buried in the long grass near the stump onto the dying fire. In seconds, the piece of wood burst into flames.

The fire mesmerized us, and we fell into the silence.

"Noah," I said after a long while. "I'm sorry." The fire snapped and sparks shot into the night sky.

"For what?" he said.

"For being angry with you."

"When were you angry with me?"

"When you told me of your plan with Marcus and my mother. I didn't like that you kept a secret from me, but I understand now why you did. And it was unfair of me, I kept one from you about my hypnosis sessions. So, I guess we're even now."

Noah chuckled. "I didn't keep you out of it to get even, it was to protect you."

"Yes, I know. But let's not keep secrets from each other anymore. I've had enough to last me a lifetime."

"Sounds good to me."

"Okay." I snuggled closer to Noah and allowed the crackling fire to lull me into relaxation.

"April?"

"Hmm," I murmured. The fight to stay awake no longer a priority.

"Sit up a moment." Noah spoke from what seemed like a tremendous distance.

My body did as he said, and I righted myself with eyes still shut. The dying flames of the fire flickered through my closed lids. My lap grew cold as Noah lifted a sleeping cat and settled her back in her carrier for the night. Then he placed his hands on my shoulders, lowered me, and I lay on my side. The soft fuzz of a blanket rubbed against my cheek. Noah's warm body curled behind me. His arm encircled my waist as he pulled me close. His lips brushed the top of my head. I smiled and drifted away.

Forty-Three

Contact

Noah rubbed my back. "Did you get any sleep?"

For the last hour, I watched dawn arrive while focusing on every sound my ears picked out in the early morning hours. Anything that diverted my attention from the nightmares in my head was a blessing. "Some."

"Liar."

"Did you?" Even in the dim light, I saw the red in Noah's eyes.

He turned away and stirred the coals from last night's fire and added tinder. The dry grass ignited and Noah threw on several broken branches. "A little."

"Liar." I lifted a sleepy cat from her carrier and attached the wire cord to her harness. Lilly arched her back, yawned, and then sauntered off into the long grass. I pulled my knees up to my chest and watched the small flames devour the grass and twigs. Noah placed a few more sticks on the bur- geoning fire. "Sorry," I said, knowing my tossing and turning was partly to blame for his lack of sleep.

"Want to talk about it?"

"Yes." I shook my head, contradicting my mouth. "But not now." The dreams and memories that had haunted me during the night faded, but I suspected it wouldn't take much to revive them. I needed peace and if it wasn't when I slept, it would have to happen when I was awake. "Anyone else up yet?" I rested my chin on my knees.

The sound of a zipper behind us made us turn and look toward the tent. Marcus climbed out and stretched his arms above his head. He gave a small wave, then turned and zipped the tent up before sitting by the campfire.

"Sleep well?" I said with a half-smile.

Marcus looked at me. "Pfft! What do you think?"

"Should have stayed out here with us," Noah smiled and returned to stirring his fire.

"Well, someone thought it'd be more comfortable. Good thing she's cute." Marcus plopped his lean body on the ground beside me. "How long have you been awake? The sun's barely risen." He looked up at the sky.

"Not long," I said.

"All night," Noah said at the same time. I glared at him. "Not all night. Just didn't sleep so well."

"Didn't you just say I shoulda slept outside the tent? Doesn't sound like it was much better out here."

Noah shrugged. "You would have slept fine out here."

Approaching footsteps made us turn. Beth's wild bed-head brought a fleeting smile to my face. She instinctively put her hand to her head. "What a shitty sleep," she grumbled as she tried to comb her fingers through her knotted hair. "It was hot and someone snored way too loud." She plunked herself beside Marcus. "Where's the cat," she said as an afterthought.

I pointed to a clump of tall, swaying grass. Seconds later, the rest of our group joined us by the fire, yawning and grumbling. By the look of everyone, no one got much sleep.

We dined on a meagre breakfast of canned peaches. When we finished, Marcus and Caleb headed for the tent while Noah rescued Lilly. She'd wound herself around a small stand of saplings at the edge of the forest. Moments later, my brother and Marcus returned, their arms laden with sleeping bags and blankets and Noah with his cat. Everyone curled around the small, crackling fire and drifted off to sleep as song birds sang lullabies. Even I slept, wrapped in Noah's arms. And when my eyes opened a short time later, I dared not move. Instead, I focused on Noah's rhythmic breath and stared at the remaining flames and glowing embers.

The sun was above the treetops by the time the rest woke in much better humour and a little more rested. We took no time taking down the pitiful camp and tossed the borrowed items inside the front door of the old house. There was nothing left to do than to head back to the compound. We returned to the tunnel; our scuffing feet and the odd whispered words the only sound to disturb the trip.

Cheers of joy and jubilation drifted up the hallway and greeted our ears as Caleb pushed open the tunnel door. Yet as we stepped over the threshold and into the compound, there was no one there to receive us.

"What's going on?" Caleb spoke as excited voices came from the communications room. Our group moved as one to investigate.

"Mom?" I said as my mother stepped out from the comms room and headed in the opposite direction, having not seen us.

She spun around. "You're back!" A huge smile spread across her face; her blue eyes sparkled. She hurried towards us and gave each of us a brief hug. She turned her attention to me and held my arms. "What happened?" Her gaze drifted to my bandaged hands.

"Later, Okay?"

Mom's eyes narrowed as she nodded her head. "Well, I see you brought a friend." She touched the plastic window on the cat backpack.

"What's going on, Mom?" Beth said.

"Well, it seems we aren't alone anymore," she said. "We finally made contact."

* * *

I stared up at the ceiling above my bed. My head spun with thoughts of the most recent events.

While we'd been out ridding ourselves of the threat Gus posed, the communications team established contact with The National Microbiology Lab in Winnipeg. My mother was familiar with the Containment Level 4 facility, having worked there during her early years of infectious diseases research. It was there where she met my father. Even Cecil had once been a part of that community.

Staff and their families had shut themselves inside the facility. The scientists worked tirelessly, and like us, thought they'd found a vaccine several times over only to have each one fail. Several mobile labs set up in various locations throughout the globe also had had no success. Unlike us, they did not have the exact blueprint for Cecil's complicated, man-made virus. While they'd come close something was lacking.

The winter months brought them a reprieve, and they restocked supplies on recon missions. They learned many areas around the world suffered significant loss of human life and had been in touch with the Centre for Disease Control in Atlanta, Georgia. Unfortunately, they'd lost contact with the BSL 4 facility in the early spring, just as their mosquito season began. Despite trying daily, they had as yet been able to regain communication.

Once we learned of the latest events, it was time for our debriefing. We gathered in the cafeteria with my mom and a few others. And I explained what had happened between Gus and me. I didn't leave out a single detail; the retelling was as vivid and complete as if those listening had been there. There was no need for questions. When I finished, I excused myself and went to my room to meditate and settle the terrifying images and unsettling emotions my story evoked.

An hour later, when I finished meditating and calming my mind, I took a deep breath and exhaled a loud sigh. In the few hours since we'd returned, our lives changed. The seventy-two plus hours that had passed while we were away were no longer significant. There was a more important excursion to plan for, and we only had days to prepare.

It was urgent we take the knowledge we had and most of the remaining vials of vaccine to a larger lab where they could produce more vaccine. We'd had to decide which facility to go to, the one out west in Winnipeg or south in Atlanta, Georgia. Both were about the same distance from our compound, but given that NML no longer had communication with the CDC, it was a simple decision. The responsibility was ours, to make sure we delivered the information safely. Our team of scientists and the contact at NML decided that further discussions over the radio was unwise. There was no telling who may hear our broadcast, if anyone, and we could not fathom what dangers lay beyond the areas we'd explored. Five years of panic and the steady decline of humans would make survivors desperate.

The journey west would be a long one. Since GPS was not an option, a recon team headed to the closest town to search for old maps or atlases in every establishment and home. In the meantime, my mother wrote out the directions to the Trans Canadian Highway and then on to Winnipeg from there. Two of the solar cars would make the drive, leaving the other half of the fleet behind. We couldn't be sure who should go and how many were necessary for the trip. But one thing was for certain, I would go. Whether anyone else knew it, I would make the trip before I lost my mind completely.

Forty-Four

Remembered Words

A cacophony of disjointed voices echoed in my ears and faces swam behind my closed eyelids. I opened my eyes, forcing the images to retreat. For the second time during the night, a nightmare interrupted my sleep.

As my eyes adjusted to the dark, and my pulse slowed, the whispered words from my dream came to mind —*secret, rot, merciful, awry,* and *free.* Cecil, Gus, Jasper and my father had said much more, but those words stuck in my brain, heart, and soul. Words spoken by four men who'd affected my life, for the best and for the worst. And while those four men would live in my head, only two had a place in my heart. And it was my heart I would listen to. I let the dream be, deciding it was not worth attention, and neither were Cecil and Gus.

I flipped back the sheet pulled up to my waist and sat up in bed. The thoughts and ideas rolling through my head would not let me sleep, and there was no use fighting them. When insomnia had struck before, I'd spend time painting murals, but I no longer needed to do that. The white and sterile walls of the compound were now alive with colour. Not just from my hand, but from others who'd contributed.

The reason behind their paintings was unknown, but my murals were a way of keeping the world we once knew alive.

The floor was cold beneath my feet as I strode toward the door. When I reached it, I turned and walked the few steps back toward the bed. Thoughts of leaving the compound both excited and depressed me, but I would not stay behind—could not. My mother had to let me go, even if she didn't want to, and I would not take no for an answer.

Adrenaline fueled my pacing, and my stomach knotted. Tears threatened as a smile pulled at the corner of my lips. My emotions bounced from excitement to fear, sorrow to happiness.

When dawn arrived, I sighed with relief, though reluctant to tell my mother of my intentions.

The walk to Mom's apartment was not short enough. Even if she lived in the room next door, the journey would have been agonizing.

Each rap on the door grew with intensity as I waited for her to answer. Finally, after the fourth bout of knocking, my mother opened the door.

"April! What's wrong?" She tightened the belt of her lilac terry robe.

"Can I come in?" I squeezed past her and made my way to the couch.

Mom yawned. "Sure. You look worried, is something wrong?"

"No, not really. Please sit." I patted the cushion.

"What's going on?" Mom said, sitting in the seat beside me.

"Mom, I have to go." The words spilled from my mouth before my brain could organize what I had rehearsed.

Mom narrowed her eyes. "Go?"

I sighed. "To NML. Please, you have to let me go."

Mom reached over and touched my hand. "Yes, I know."

"What?" I thought she'd at least ask why.

"April, you must go."

"Why?" If Mom didn't need to know my reasons for leaving, I at least wanted to know hers.

"April, I've known for a long time, that if someone had to leave to find help, it would have to be you. Though who should join you. . . " Mom stood, "that choice wasn't as easy. Before any of this was an actuality, when it was just a 'what if', who would go, who would stay. But you answered that question yesterday, and the decision became clear."

My eyes narrowed and brow furrowed. "What do you mean?"

She sat again and reached for my hand. "Honey, I've never doubted your inner strength and ability to handle any challenge."

I took a deep breath and exhaled away my racing heart. "Anxiety issues and all?"

Mom cocked her head. "That doesn't define you. Av, you are strong and brave. The anxiety, while a hurdle, is far less significant than your willingness to persevere and survive. You're the one who said you had to go. Are you doubting this now?"

"No, I should go, and I need to. I'm just trying to understand why you want me to go."

"Honey, I don't want you to leave. If anyone else could take your place. . . But the fact is, you are more than capable. And if that's not enough, how about that you have the answers to the questions the people at NML might ask stored in your head? There will be questions, and you are the only one who can answer them without fault. You read Cecil's manifesto and Jasper's journal. Making you as efficient as the information in those books."

"And the others?" I had a good idea who, but I wanted her to say.

"There's no doubt in my mind, now, that all of you have to go."

"No doubt?"

Mom shook her head, then took me in her arms. "No doubt. But it would be a lie if I told you there wasn't fear in my heart." Mom had needed no convincing. Part of me was relieved, another part scared, and another much smaller piece, a little hurt that she'd agreed to let me go without complaint.

* * *

I was a bit early for the medium session with Aya. She had suggested meeting in the centre hallway, away from any potential interruption, and I was glad. The door to the deserted corridor made me uneasy. When I had it open, I stepped into the dark. The beam from the flashlight bounced off the walls as my feet echoed down the hall. The light illuminated the butterfly mural and emphasized the individual portraits that made up the spots on the colourful wings. It would be the last time I stepped into that vacant part of the compound. The last time I set eyes on the tribute to those who had since moved on to another world. I sat across from the mural, rested my head against the wall, closed my eyes and waited.

Moments later, light filtered through my eyelids as echoing footsteps touched my ears.

"Hey," Aya said, sitting on the floor beside me.

"Hey."

"That is such a great mural."

"Thanks." My eyelids fluttered open.

"The others are nice too, but this one... is so moving." Aya's voice cracked with emotion.

"Are you crying?"

Aya cleared her throat. "No."

"Good, because... well anyway, I can't deal with that right now. Sorry."

"No problem." She sniffed, and we fell silent. "Do you want to get started?" she whispered after a little while.

Goosebumps rose on the back of my neck. "Okay, how?"

"Ask a question."

"Any?"

"Sure."

"What if my dad doesn't answer?"

"Don't worry, he will, he's waiting." In the dim light, I saw the grin on her face.

"Where does this come from?" I plucked the necklace from under my t-shirt, having asked for my locket from my mother. The heart with the engraved butterfly dangled from the gold chain.

Aya closed her eyes and spoke. "The necklace was a gift from your Mom and I."

"What for?" Anyone could have guessed that, but I wanted more proof. Despite believing in her ability, a small part of me remained skeptical.

Ayanna took a second to respond. "For your thirteenth birthday."

I nodded. "What did you joke about on my birthday?" That morning's conversation replayed in my head, and I felt the bedsheets against my skin and the weight of Mom's hand on my leg. The night before, my father found me asleep in his desk chair with my head on his desk, an old notebook pressed to my cheek. The coil rings had left a temporary mark.

I stared at Aya and waited for her to answer. She laughed and spoke my father's words. "An old notebook and the worry the coil rings left a lasting impression on your cheek."

My heart skipped, and I blinked away the burning in my eyes and swallowed the ache in my throat. "Daddy, of all the things I remember, every beautiful moment and every horrible detail, there is one piece, one most precious moment that I cannot reach. What did we talk about before you... left?" I laced my fingers and put my palms together.

Aya smiled. "He did most of the talking, though he was weak, as you had only started becoming lucid. But you did speak a little."

The news that I had spoken surprised me. "Please tell me everything, no matter how insignificant. I have no memories from that time."

Aya closed her eyes again. "I told you I was so happy they had found you. That I never gave up hope, that you are strong. I told you how proud I was to be your father, to be Beth's and Caleb's too, and how lucky I was to have married your mother." Aya reached for my hand. "April, you never disappointed me," Aya continued speaking my father's words.

I closed my eyes and envisioned the quarantine room where he spent his last days.

"April, your dad wants you to know how incredible he thinks you are—all of you."

"Dad, you said I spoke a little, what did I say?" I waited in the silence for Aya to speak, to tell me the words I did not remember saying.

Ayanna opened her mouth, paused, and closed her lips again.

I squeezed my hand into a fist; my nails dug into my palm.

Her lips moved again. "Quiet down your thoughts, close your eyes and breathe. Listen to your heart, Keep your mind at ease."

I gasped, and my hands shook. Without thought, I recited the rest of the verse, like I had that day. "Look for the cloud's silver lining, the joy inside the pain. Like laughing when you're feeling sad and playing in the rain." I swallowed. There was more to the poem, but I stopped there. Those were the words I spoke—said with him. "Love you, Dad," I said. I had told him that too.

Aya's eyes glistened as she spoke the last words my father said. "I love you too, Av, and always will."

The brief conversation between my father and I had not been seamless. He'd coughed and struggled for breath between words. And it was only when he recited the poem, he'd written years ago, that I'd found my voice. I swallowed the emotion building in my throat. "Thank you, Aya," I managed and turned away.

* * *

The grass tickled my ankles as I sat cross-legged by my father's cross. Fresh wildflowers lay at its base and filled a glass vase leaning against the wood marker. Somewhere an osprey screeched, disturbing the somber scene. A monarch butterfly flitted around the cross, hovered over the flowers, then landed on my knee. Its wings slowly opened and closed. Tiny black feet tickled my skin. As I moved my finger toward the beautiful insect, a sudden gust kicked up a patch of loose dirt from my father's grave. The butterfly lifted from its perch, and I watched it fly away. "Thanks, Dad," I said and blew a kiss to the disappearing speck of orange. As if to confirm his presence a mysterious and faint scent of hickory smoke floated on the breeze. The smell of campfires was one of Dad's favourites.

I turned my attention back to the cross. "I remember everything now," I said. The memories of our last day together as clear in my mind as if it had happened yesterday. My heart ached, but I smiled through the pain, recalling memory after memory, each one happier than the last. When the time came for me to leave, I kissed my fingers and pressed them to the cross. A single tear tracked down my cheek as I walked away.

The cross in the ground was only a reminder of where my father laid to rest. I carried all the love and memories for the both of us. And no matter where his body lay, I took his spirit with me.

Forty-Five

Free

There was much to carry out over the coming days. As the recon team found few useful maps, we had to combine what we had with the directions my mother remembered from working at NML. There were supplies to gather, and goodbyes to say. While I planned on saying my goodbyes when we left, there was one I had to make before that day came.

The grey sky threatened. Warm winds stirred up dust and blew through the pines; branches rattled and needles hushed. The smell of ozone caused my nose to crinkle. Vibrant greens of the forest stood out despite the clouds. And I was glad I'd chosen to walk the road and not the tunnel.

I'd refused company. This was a trek I had to make alone, of my free will, and one I planned never to repeat.

The house appeared smaller. Dwarfed by the trees. The ominous presence and foreboding atmosphere diminished. The weathered old building faded into the backdrop in contrast to a week ago when it loomed over us. One day soon the abandoned shelter would become a pile of rubbish. The thought caused a smile as I walked past the front porch and paid no mind to the round window.

After crossing the small overgrown field beside the old house, I entered the stand of pines. Wood crosses poked out from the long grass and wildflowers. The cemetery surrounded by sky-scraping evergreens was almost invisible. I stopped at each cross and offered a silent prayer before moving to the last grave.

I stomped and flattened a small patch of grass beside the cross and sat on the ground, closing my eyes. Shadows of swaying trees flickered behind my eyelids. Buzzing insects and singing birds eased my mind. The sun warmed the top of my head. Aromatic scents of pine and wildflowers wafted in the air. A warm breeze fluttered my hair. For several minutes I focused on my breath and absorbed the surroundings. Nothing entered my mind as I dissolved into nature. The peace and relaxation of deep meditation was like a warm and cozy blanket. When I opened my eyes, I placed my hand on the grass-covered mound of Jasper's grave.

"Hope you don't mind, but I gave Jasmy your journal. Jasper, you would be proud of your little sister; she has your brave heart. Anyway, I don't need it anymore; everything is in here." I tapped the top of my head and smiled. "And I promise, I will tell your story. Everyone will hear how you saved us. How you began Cecil's end." A bright red cardinal landed on the low branch of a tree in front of me, and his song echoed through the pines.

I patted the ground under my hand. "Jasper, I won't be back." My voice cracked. "But I'll never forget you." I rose to my feet, brushed the grass from my legs, and wiped a hand over my eyes. "Goodbye, Jasper, and thank you," I said and blew a kiss into the wind.

The exact location of the isolated grave was difficult to pinpoint as I moved further into the pines and away from the small cemetery. But I sensed what I searched for was somewhere nearby.

I stopped walking and addressed my surroundings. "Unfortunately, I won't ever forget you either. But I can guarantee, you will get nothing more than a fleeting thought. You left us in a room to rot. Funny how things changed. May you rot in hell—Cecil." I turned and marched out of the thick bracken where they buried his body in an unmarked grave.

My steps were light and free as I made my way back to the compound. The weight of darkness and pain lifted from my heart. The memories would always be there, but they no longer limited me, and I was the one in control.

* * *

Like the night before the first day of school, I tossed and turned. Too excited to sleep, too sad to rest, too worried to doze as I prepared for freedom.

Not a single member of the compound missed the farewell breakfast. Even those who had never regained awareness were there. The room filled with the sounds of clanking cutlery, scraping chairs, and enthusiastic voices. Mom sat beside Caleb, across from Beth and me. Her blue eyes shone with a mixture of excitement, pride, and sadness. We kept the mood light, reminiscing of happier family times. Beth and Caleb recanted memories of family adventures, and I did not correct any inconsistencies but smiled with fondness. Noah rubbed my back and laughed at the stories. While I enjoyed the moment a part of me couldn't wait to escape, though I hated leaving my mother. But she was a strong and brave woman, and it was a comfort she'd have Lilly to cuddle while we were away.

When breakfast ended, my mother rose from the table along with a few others. She kept her left hand on Caleb's shoulder, her fingers flexed as she squeezed. The skin had thinned; blue veins and tendons showed beneath the almost translucent covering. "Today is a day," she cleared her throat, "for a glorious celebration." Her grip tightened on Caleb. White knuckles, their edges trimmed in light pink, showed through her skin. "Today we mark the beginning of freedom." Her eyes locked on mine for a moment before returning her gaze on the tables of people behind me. "In two weeks, this brave team," she indicated with a wave at the members at our table, "will reach the NML in Winnipeg. Once there, they will share the knowledge we have gained."

Excited voices rose in the cafeteria. Mom gave them a moment, and they dimmed much like the volume control on a radio.

"It is with hope, that soon when implementation of a vaccine program becomes widespread, we will rebuild what we lost. Our health, our homes, our lives, and our freedom." She raised her fist above her head.

The cafeteria erupted into cheers and once again our mother waited for the room to quiet. "Today," she said in a much more subdued voice, "today, we begin anew." She looked upon us with eyes brimming.

* * *

While the others packed the two vehicles we were taking, Caleb, Beth, and I followed our mother to her apartment. The four of us walked in silence; only our footfalls echoed in the hall. Mom opened the door, and we filed in ahead of her. The click of the door closing behind me made me jump.

"Well, this is it," Mom said as we sat on the couch.

Beth picked up the sleeping calico and placed Lilly on her lap, and Caleb took a spot on the armrest. "But it's not forever." Beth said, her free arm around Mom's shoulders.

"Yes, I know," Mom said, "though it feels like it." She looked at me. We'd discussed earlier that I had no intention of returning to the compound. But I could not speak for the others, and even at this moment did not know their plans.

"Mom, I'll come home as soon as possible," Caleb announced his goal. My little brother had suddenly turned from a young teenager into a man.

Mom shook her head. "Only if you're sure it's safe, and not alone."

Caleb rolled his eyes; the teen was back. "Okay, Mom."

"Promise me," she placed her hand on Caleb's leg.

He smiled. "Okay, I promise."

"Sorry, Mom, I don't know when I'll be back. Maybe you can join us once we set everything up." Beth leaned forward and kissed Lilly between her ears.

"Beth, I can't leave here, not right away, if ever," she said to Beth, but her eyes fell on me.

I pulled my shoulders back. "Sorry, I won't return here, not to this place. Never."

"Av, it's okay." Mom's eyes softened as she reached across Beth's full lap and grabbed my hand. "And I will never ask you to. We'll meet someplace else." Mom squeezed my hand. "Don't worry." She dropped my hand and stood. "Don't forget this." She reached for the silver box on the bookshelf and held it out to me. "Winnipeg will need these."

I narrowed my eyes. "Cecil gambled, didn't he? He suspected you and dad discovered the glitch in the virus and had hidden it from him, but he couldn't be sure. If something happened to him and his suspicions were correct, our combined knowledge would lead to an effective vaccine and treatment, saving the rest of the world. Providing, I remembered the information he implanted in my head."

Mom nodded. "And if he was wrong, the virus would continue its destruction, and since he was dead, it wouldn't matter. Maybe with proper lab equipment and time, we would eventually find an effective treatment, but not before more loss."

"But what if he'd survived?" Caleb said.

"Then he'd have everything and all the power."

Beth scratched Lilly under her white chin. "Lucky for us that bastard's dead then."

I unclasped the chain around my neck, opened the silver box and placed my butterfly locket next to Beth's and the special key. "But why these?" I looked up at my mother.

She sighed and sat back on the couch.

"Well?" Beth said.

"Remember when we gave the locket to you?"

I nodded. "Dad said they were meant for secrets."

Mom laughed. "Well, I can assure you, not the kind that ended up being placed inside them. These were just lockets, and we intended to take family photos and put them inside, but things were busy and we didn't get around to it. Anyway, once we realized something was going on, we knew we needed to keep important information safe. These lockets seemed the perfect and least likely place to keep the SD cards. Your Dad was handy."

I nodded as a conversation from the past played in my head.

"And the box? The keys? The way the hearts open? Lockets don't require mechanical intervention to open them." I look at my parents for the answer.

Dad winks. "No, they don't, but I may know a thing or two about mechanics, operating a soldering gun, stuff like that. The compound had a lot of useful equipment at my disposal. It was just a matter of redesigning and crafting objects we already had."

"But Dad didn't make the box, right?" Caleb said.

I turned the sliver box around, admiring the intricate detail of the engraved butterflies.

"No, I've had this trinket for a long time. This was just a perfect container, that's all."

"And the engravings?" Beth touched the butterfly on the side. "Looks like the ones on each locket."

Mom nodded. "A complete coincidence, and one thing that had drawn me to those lockets. The butterflies reminded me of the box."

The small apartment filled with an uneasy and heavy silence.

"Well," Mom said after a few moments, "we should get going. I'm sure the others are waiting for you." She stood with open arms. The three of us rose in unison and entered her embrace. "I love you so much." The group hug lasted a few minutes, and then she hugged us individually. Tears she'd held back so many times tracked down her cheeks.

The walk to the front entrance was quiet, and several people waited to say their goodbyes.

Mom touched my arm and held me back for a moment. "You have the manifesto, right?"

I nodded. "Yes, it's packed away and already loaded into the car."

"Tell me you'll come back. Not here, but somewhere." Her eyes pleaded.

"Oh, Mom!" I took her into my arms. "Of course, I will. This isn't goodbye forever, not between us, just between me and this place."

"Yes, I know, I'm just being silly."

"No, you're being a mom." I kissed her wet cheek.

"When did you become such an amazing adult?"

I shrugged. "I've lived a lot this past year."

"Yes, you have." Mom squeezed my hand. "You better go." She took a deep breath, settled herself, and wiped a hand over her eyes.

"Okay, I love you. And we'll keep in radio contact."

She nodded. "Go."

I walked through the vestibule and out the front door. Several people had gathered on the lawn. It was still early and hard to tell what the weather would be like, for the moment, there was an overcast sky. A warm breeze blew through my hair, and I closed my eyes.

"Hey, you okay?" Noah's voice interrupted my thoughtless mind, and he laced his fingers with mine.

I tilted my head up to the sky. "Never been better."

"Just finishing packing the last few items and then we'll be on our way," he said.

I opened my eyes and faced the cars. Most of the well-wishers had gone back inside, a few scattered here and there, some helped load the last remaining things. My mom stood at the entrance, leaning against a pillar that supported the small roof overhead. The grey brick above the door no longer showed traces of the sign that once announced the name of the compound. She gave a weak smile and waved, and I returned both of her actions.

Marcus and Beth leaned against a vehicle, supervising and giving out orders to Caleb and Jasmy, who stuffed a few things into the back of the SUV. While Hester, Aya, and Khelden finished packing up the second vehicle.

"Can you give me a head start?" I said to Noah.

His eyes narrowed. "What do you mean?"

I shrugged. "I want to walk out of here by myself."

"Okay, we'll pick you up at the gates?"

I shook my head. "No. The crossroads."

"That's a bit of a walk," he said. "Looks like it could rain." He tilted his head back for a second.

I smiled. "Noah, it's not like I haven't made the trek before." I thought of the most recent when I visited the small cemetery on my own. "And I'm not afraid of a little rain; I'm not made of sugar." *Are you made of sugar? You won't melt!* Dad's voice whispered in my ear.

"Sure, we can hang back. I'll tell everyone I forgot something. Are you positive you don't want me to walk with you?"

I shook my head, unable to speak. He must have known that doing so would reduce me into a sobbing mess.

"Okay." Noah leaned over and kissed my forehead. "Meet you at the crossroads."

My lips pulled into a weak smile, and I waved one last time to my mother, before walking out the drive.

Pebbles bounced off the toes of my shoes as I stepped through the gates of the compound. The trees lining the road hushed when the wind blew and rattled their leaves. The branches swayed and bowed as though saying farewell. My steps grew lighter the further ahead I walked, and it felt like I was weightless.

A small drop of rain landed on the bridge of my nose. I gazed upward at the swirling grey sky, and the drop trickled.

A large bird soared high above the trees, sailing on the wind—free. I spread my arms, closed my eyes, tilted my head, and turned a slow circle. A smile stretched across my face, and my heart beat a peaceful rhythm. I was finally free, and my father's voice once again whispered in my ears.

Quiet down your thoughts,
Close your eyes and breathe.
Listen to your heart,
Keep your mind at ease.

Look for the cloud's silver lining,
The joy inside the pain.
Like laughing when you're feeling sad
And playing in the rain.

Let your imagination soar,
Keep your eyes on the prize.
Don't give up on chasing dreams
Or catching butterflies.

Spread your wings and fly,
Don't be chagrinned.
Float way like the leaves,
Dancing in the Wind.

Epilogue
June 10, 2031

I killed my first mosquito of the season today. Manitoba has a terrible mosquito season, so I'm told, and with the heavy snow melt and rainfall this spring, it will be nasty. What better place than here to prove to everyone the vaccine works? People at NML are nervous. Not the scientists, or my friends and me, we know it works. But the others living here, well, I guess I can't blame them.

Anyway, before I get too far ahead of myself, let me go back a little. It's been a while since I've written anything in a journal. It's not as though I'm going to forget what's happened. That's impossible. I'll remember everything forever unless I suffer from a traumatic brain injury or dementia. But Jasmy suggested I write my thoughts and feelings out more often. She said it would help me gain control of my emotions. I know she's right, but every time I think about picking up a pen, I find a reason to put it down. The thing is, just writing out my feelings doesn't seem to make sense, at least not without context. I mean, my thoughts and feelings are in relation to events that affected my life. Anyway, this morning I promised myself to record everything that happened after we left the compound and arrived at NML nearly ten months ago. Maybe it's not a great idea, I mean

I've told this story so many times. And whether it helps, I guess I'll find out. In any case, it's for posterity.

This won't be a moment by moment telling of everything as it occurred. For the sake of time (and paper) this is the shortened version, or as my dad would say—in a nut shell. And so, let me begin.

It thrilled me to finally be free. To leave the compound behind and start a new life away from confinement. But I missed my mom and still do. We were all excited and a little scared, wondering what we would find. It took us almost two weeks to arrive at NML as we limited driving between four to six hours a day. Every time we pulled off the road, we made sure it was near some town. It was a bit nerve wracking heading into the communities and exploring. We saw dogs, cats, and other wild animals, but no humans. We left notes behind in pharmacies or grocery stores, announcing our visit, explaining our mission, and perhaps giving hope to survivors too afraid to make their presence known. Larger cities we left unexplored, but we left behind evidence of our passing through. We picked up a few small cans of black paint and brushes from an abandoned hardware store in the first town we'd stopped and painted large messages on highway signs. While we'd wanted to leave directions to the compound's location, we opted instead for messages of hope. We wouldn't risk the lives of the others by leading anyone with nefarious intentions to their home.

By the fourth day of the journey, our moods grew low. And it was more peaceful to keep to ourselves, choosing only to speak a few careful words to each other. We were all on edge. The stress of finding ourselves alone in such a vast area was more than we could bear. Even now when I think about those first days, the despair returns. But then something amazing happened.

At the end of the fourth day, we drove into a small community, and Jasmy sensed something she hadn't in a long time. We parked the vehicles in the lot of a high school, and the second we climbed out and stretched our legs, Jasmy blurted, "someone's here." I can hear her voice in my head as clear as if she were sitting beside me as I write. Anyway, goosebumps erupted on my arms, just like they are now.

Caleb asked her if she'd seen someone to which Jasmy responded, no. But she explained that she sensed them. There was something about the school, and I remember having that being-watched sensation. It reminded me of the cameras at C.E.C.I.L. At once our attention turned to the school. Caleb called out then and pointed to a window.

We all saw her peeking out from behind a curtain. The little girl smiled and waved. Her unruly black curls bounced as she jumped up and down. My heart skipped at the sight of the young child, both with excitement and dread. I wanted to run to her and ask how had she survived on her own. But after a few seconds my question was answered when I glimpsed a woman with long, greying hair ushering the child away from the window. Our gazes met before the curtain closed.

Moments later the same woman appeared at the door, a shotgun in her hands. She asked us what we wanted and then in the same breath told us to move on. The woman (we found out later her name was Lena and the little girl, Opal) said there was nothing for us there. From the corner of my eye, I saw Noah reach his hand behind him toward the weapon he hid in the back of his pants. At that moment my stomach knotted, and I told him to stop. Thankfully, he listened to me and folded his arms over his chest instead. Just then, the little girl peeked out from behind the woman and waved, an impish grin on her dirty face. For a moment, the woman took one hand off her gun and guided the small child behind her. That simple action gave me the courage to step forward and speak. I couldn't stand the thought of that poor girl living behind closed doors, and I wanted to give them hope.

I held up my hands and told them we meant no harm, that we were travelling through on our way to Winnipeg. The Woman appeared surprised and asked what we thought we'd find in Winnipeg. Without going into a lot of specifics, I told her we were heading to the National Microbiology Lab. That soon they would have nothing to fear and everything would be over. She didn't understand. So, I explained further how we'd come from another lab where scientists discovered a treatment and vaccine for the virus. When she lowered her gun, I told her we had room for two more it they wanted to come with us. But Beth didn't like my invitation, and she let me know with a harsh whisper of my name.

The woman scarcely believed what I told her, but I assured her it was all true. That soon, no one had to die from the virus anymore. Once again, I invited them to come with us, but the woman chuckled instead. With a smile on her face, she explained that she and the little girl were not alone.

Marcus was the first to question just how many lived at the school. We gasped in unison as she told us thirty-three inhabitants stayed at the school. As she spoke, curtains on the windows facing the parking lot pulled back. Men, woman, and children stared at us from behind the glass. The unexpected yet pleasant surprise caused a smile to stretch across my face.

Just then, Noah wanted to move the conversation inside. But as he stepped forward, the woman held up her hand. She apologized and explained that they had no disease within the walls of their school and wanted it kept that way. They stayed inside, away from mosquitoes, especially during their active times. As it was early evening, the doors to the school would be closed for the night. As the inhabitants allowed the curtains on the windows to fall, the woman stepped back inside and pulled the doors closed.

I called to her before she'd shut the door and asked if there was anything they needed. She told me they were fine, and we were welcome to spend the night anywhere in the town. That's when Aya spoke and told the woman we'd send help as soon as possible.

The excitement of finding so many people alive made it difficult for sleeping that night. But the discovery improved our moods and raised our spirits as we travelled to Winnipeg.

When we finally arrived at the doors of NML, Drs. Leila Yen and Nigel Strauss (both of whom knew my parents well) greeted us. The doctors escorted us down a long corridor that opened into a large area. One hundred and sixty-four people lived within the walls of the research facility, and everyone greeted us. The excitement was palpable.

Once fed and rested, our hosts gave us a tour of the facility. We learned of their failures and successes, and their restored communications with the Center for Disease Control in Georgia. Then a small team of scientists led us into a boardroom where they debriefed us.

We told them of Cecil and his manifesto. I told them verbatim what he'd written. How he'd planned on keeping any success with vaccines and treatments confined to C.E.C.I.L. He'd had no intention of sharing his discoveries. Eventually, the residents at the compound would be the only survivors. Despite people like Marcus and Noah living through the first onslaught of the virus, mutated versions would ultimately cause their demise. When it came to the part about our talents, mine was obvious. The others demonstrated their abilities or spoke of them. Then I told Jasper's story, sharing with NML that his action to start a fire at the compound was Cecil's undoing.

Hours later we emerged from the room exhausted but satisfied we'd divulged everything. Dr. Yen escorted me and my siblings to their communications room, and we contacted our mother. The connection was the first we'd had since after leaving our compound. Radio comms had reached their limit on the second day of our trek, and though we kept trying, we could not make contact. Hearing her voice had brought tears to all of our eyes.

The following morning, Dr. Strauss informed us over breakfast that the team would begin working on the new research to create vaccines and treatments with the information we'd provided. At the moment he spoke, it was as if the surrounding air grew lighter. And for the first time, I truly believed the nightmare was over.

Both the NML and the CDC, having received the information for the Butterfly Flu by Dr. Strauss, waived the normal protocol for vaccine production. There was no time for that. Fortunately, RNA vaccines are safer so they forwent animal testing, all phases of vaccine trials, and any regulatory controls (though I'm not sure that would have been an option anyway). Like Cecil had told me, producing RNA vaccines was quick and did not require large manufacturers, so they could make it here at the lab.

I should also make mention that the CDC recently contacted the Spiez Laboratory in Switzerland, and they shared the research with them.

As far as understanding the sheer devastation, it remains unclear. But by the reports coming from the locations we are in contact with, it seems the worldwide death toll could be in the billions. With pockets of survivors spread out around the globe. Until the production and distribution of vaccine and treatment becomes widespread, more will die.

Before the snow hit, Caleb directed a small team of doctors back to the community of survivors we'd encountered. They piled into two vehicles and brought supplies and a communication radio, which they left at the school. Finding everyone in good health and spirits, they left the group with the promise to return with vaccine as soon as they could.

Even with the harsh winter, everyone living at the school survived. Last month the team returned and vaccinated the group with the second batch of vaccine, the first distributed to everyone living at NML a month earlier. Caleb, Khelden, Jasmy, and Hester continued on their own back to Mom and the others after journeying to the school last month. The rest of the team returned to NML along with six members from the school group.

When spring arrived, the doors to the facility opened for the first time since lockdown, thanks to the new vaccine. And unlike the last two years, teams search for survivors daily. Apparently, when the virus was at its worse and hospitals crowded over with the sick and dying, people gathered in other large facilities throughout the city and sealed their doors. These are the buildings that they explore and so far, small pockets of survivors emerge almost every week. It is hoped that as the searches become widespread, more survivors will come forward. People are working hard to establish communications, broaden solar and electrical power and other utilities. Life is returning to the city, but it is far from normal. There are reminders everywhere of what humanity has endured. Discarded masks and rubber gloves litter the streets. Signage forewarning the end of days or telling residents to stay safe still hang in windows, from light poles, and on sides of buildings.

As for more recent events, Beth, Marcus, and Aya leave for the compound tomorrow. Both Caleb and Beth promised to come back here in a few months, but I'm not sure they will. I feel as though something is pulling them back to the compound, and it's not just Mom. As for Noah and I, we are happy here at NML for now, but I'm not sure how long that will last. At least for me. I feel this tug sometimes and it scares me. Like there's a giant magnet somewhere, and it's trying to draw me closer to it and further away from everyone else. But it has abated—for now.

I spoke to Mom tonight as I do every Friday. She is happy that soon she will have two of her children by her side. As usual, the conversation turned to when she would see me. And as usual, I said, soon. As much as I miss my mother, I can't go back there. I can't go to the compound, Kearney, Algonquin Park, even our family home. Cecil ruined all of those places for me. So, until my mother feels she can leave for several days and can meet me elsewhere, I don't know when I will see her again. And when the tug returns for me to escape and free myself from this place, I may be further away.

Father's voice never leaves my ears, even now I hear him telling me not to burn the midnight oil. I keep him alive, listen to his idioms, silly dad jokes, and if nothing else, he helps drown out the always present whispers of Cecil. And when his expressions aren't enough, I recite his poem out loud, dreaming of the day the wind carries me away.

Until next time (if ever there is).
April

Dear reader,

We hope you enjoyed reading *Dancing in the Wind*. Please take a moment to leave a review, even if it's a short one. Your opinion is important to us.

Discover more books by Sandra J. Jackson at https://www.nextchapter.pub/authors/author-sandra-jackson

Want to know when one of our books is free or discounted? Join the newsletter at http://eepurl.com/bqqB3H

Best regards,
Sandra J. Jackson and the Next Chapter Team

About the Author

"Only my characters truly know what's happening—I just hold the pen."

Sandra J. Jackson works as a finance assistant when she's not creating characters and building worlds. And when she isn't writing down the stories from her imagination, you can find her tending to her Victorian style garden. Sandra loves spending time with her husband, young adult children, her two cats and dog. She also enjoys hiking, kayaking, photography, and travel.

Believing anything is possible, you will always find a little bit of that belief in her writing. Other novels by Sandra are:

Promised Soul – Next Chapter Publishing (Creativia) 2018
Playing in the Rain Book 1 Escape Series – Next Chapter Publishing (Creativia) 2018
Catching Butterflies Book 2 Escape Series – Next Chapter Publishing (Creativia) 2019

You can connect with Sandra through her website at
www.sandrajjackson.com
or on Facebook at
facebook.com/SandraJJackson.author.

CPSIA information can be obtained
at www.ICGtesting.com
Printed in the USA
LVHW051019231220
674967LV00008B/208

9 781034 078593